"Chung-Cha belongs to Christ," Fath(
me, God will still watch over my dau

The agent chuckled.

"And what if I destroy her?"

Praise for *The Beloved Daughter* by Alana Terry

Grace Awards, First Place

IndieFab Finalist, Religious Fiction

Women of Faith Writing Contest, Second Place

Book Club Network Book of the Month, First Place

Reader's Favorite Gold Medal, Christian Fiction

*"...an engaging plot that reads **like a story out of today's headlines**..."*
~ Women of Faith Writing Contest

*"In this meticulously researched novel, Terry gives readers **everything a good novel should have** — a **gripping story**, an uplifting theme, encouragement in their own faith, and **exquisite writing**."* ~ Grace Awards Judges' Panel

*"The Beloved Daughter is a **beautifully written story**."* ~ Sarah Palmer, Liberty in North Korea

There was silence for such a long time Kennedy wondered if there was a problem with Carl's antique cell phone. Finally, Rose asked, "And so what happens if you get pregnant, and you're too young to actually have a baby?"

Defying all laws of inertia, the acceleration of Kennedy's heart rate crashed to a halt like a car plowing into a brick wall. "What do you mean?"

"Like, what if you're too young but you still get pregnant?"

"How young?" Kennedy spoke both words clearly and slowly, as if rushing might drive the timid voice away for good.

"Like thirteen."

Praise for *Unplanned*
by Alana Terry

"Deals with **one of the most difficult situations a pregnancy center could ever face**. The message is **powerful** and the story-telling **compelling**." ~ William Donovan, *Executive Director Anchorage Community Pregnancy Center*

"Alana Terry does an amazing job tackling a very **sensitive subject from the mother's perspective**." ~ Pamela McDonald, *Director Okanogan CareNet Pregnancy Center*

"**Thought-provoking** and intense ... Shows **different sides of the abortion argument**." ~ Sharee Stover, *Wordy Nerdy*

"Alana has a way of sharing the gospel **without being preachy**." ~ Phyllis Sather, *Purposeful Planning*

Simon exhaled as he stretched his arms. "I wish we didn't have to say good-bye." His voice was distant.

Hannah stared at the moon. She would never sit here beside him again in this garden. "There are no good-byes in the kingdom of heaven," she whispered, hoping her words carried the conviction her soul lacked.

Praise for *Torn Asunder* by Alana Terry

*"Filled with suffering, yet ultimately has a **resounding message of hope**."* ~ Sarah Palmer, Liberty in North Korea

*"Alana has a **great heart for the persecuted church** that comes out in her writing."* ~ Jeff King, President of International Christian Concern

*"Faith and love are tested beyond comprehension in this **beautifully written Christian novel**."* ~ Kathryn Chastain Treat, Allergic to Life: My Battle for Survival, Courage, and Hope

*"**Not your average love story** - wrapped in suspense, this story of faith will stop your heart as you hope and weep right along with the characters."* ~ Nat Davis, Our Faith Renewed

*"Torn Asunder is an **enthralling, heart-aching novel** that calls your heart to action."* ~ Katie Edgar, KTs Life of Books

Note: The views of the characters in this novel do not necessarily reflect the views of the author, nor is their behavior necessarily being condoned.

Beauty from Ashes
Copyright © 2017 Alana Terry
978-1-941735-37-4
July, 2017

Cover design by Victoria Cooper.

www.alanaterry.com

Beauty from Ashes

a novel by Alana Terry

"... to comfort all who mourn,

and provide for those who grieve in Zion—

to bestow on them a crown of beauty

instead of ashes,

the oil of joy

instead of mourning,

and a garment of praise

instead of a spirit of despair."

Isaiah 61:2-3

CHAPTER 1

I'd rather be just about anywhere else, but Jake wanted to come this morning, and I'm sick of arguing with him. Don't have the energy to fight. I hardly do these days. It's a blessing, I'm sure, or else I would have said some nasty things by now. Not the kind of things you apologize for in the morning when you wake up and your mascara's caked onto your face and your eye sockets are so puffy and black you'd frighten a raccoon. I'm talking about the really bad things. The things that destroy couples, even ones who haven't gone through half of what we have.

Four hundred and fifteen points. I added it up once. I found this quiz online, and it's supposed to tell how much stress you've gone through in the past twelve months. Getting married, that's a hundred points right there. Pregnancy racks up another sixty, which is half of what you get when you add a roommate, and in the past year I went from living by myself to sharing a trailer with two adults and a newborn. Fifty points for moving? Yeah, does living in a hospital room count?

There was even a category for *serious illness in the family*, which added on another eighty tallies. As if getting married is more stressful. Of course, *serious illness* could mean anything from measles to cancer. Whatever psychologist or clickbait-hungry web designer invented the quiz, what would they know? But at least one of the categories made me laugh. *Problems with the in-laws.* Yup, I earned each and every one of those twenty-five points, thank you very much. Maybe I shouldn't complain. Jake's mom is with Natalie right now, or else there's no way he and I would be out anywhere. I didn't want to come here, but at least now I don't have to deal with Patricia. She's the kind of mother-in-law who would intimidate the bride of Frankenstein. She means well. Have you ever noticed how many horrible people there are in this world who go around *meaning well*? And she's a nurse, or at least she used to be, so Natalie's safe. Physically, I mean. Still, nice as it is to get a break from Jake's mom, I'll feel guilty and jittery until we head back.

I still don't know why Jake dragged us here. Neither of us thought to dress up or anything. That's the first thing I noticed. Small country church in Orchard Grove Middle-of-Nowhere, Washington, and I'm sitting here in maternity pants. Jake's not looking much better in that old Seahawks jersey. I look around and count two other men without ties on.

Just two.

Oh, well. If people want to stare, that's their problem. I can only imagine what they're thinking about us, like that pinched-nose woman in the front row sitting straight as a rail. Reminds me of one of my foster moms, a single woman in her sixties, never married. Which was a good thing, at least. There wasn't a single ounce of kindness in those sharp-as-tack bones of hers. Out of all my foster moms, I seem to recall liking the plump ones best. Not the really fat ones like that Trudy lady or whatever her name was who sat on the couch stuffing her face with junk food all day. Man, I hated those soaps she used to watch. I was so glad to be out of that house. Was she the one right before Sandy, or was that earlier? I couldn't keep them all straight even if I wanted to.

I wonder why I'm thinking of them now, these foster families that creep into my memory like a squid with all those disgusting, grasping tentacles. Sandy's the only one I still talk to. The only one who was ever like a mom to me. She'd be all puppy-dog excited to know that Jake forced us both to church today. She's like that. So preachy all the time. No, *preachy*'s not the right word for it. Preachers like that Bishop Cameron Hopewell or whatever his name is on TV who bangs his fist on platforms and shouts about hell, money, and sex, most often in that order. Men like him always wear toupees, too. Did you ever notice that? Like Donald Trump all gung-ho for the Lord.

Sandy's not like them. She's a Jesus freak, for sure. She'll get preaching on the resurrection or salvation or the Holy Ghost like nothing else. But there's something kind about the way she does it. Like she doesn't want your money and isn't about to hand you an immediate ticket to hell if you sneak a boy through the upstairs window and mess around a little bit because he says *Don't you want to?* so many times you have to give in every once in a while or else he'll find it somewhere else. Sandy was upset when it happened, but not in the angry way like those TV guys would have been. I didn't get the sense she was mad, more like she felt sorry for me.

I hate it when people feel sorry for me. Maybe that's why these past few months have been my own personal Hades. It's like walking into what you think is an empty apartment only to find everyone you know has shown up for a surprise pity party, and you're the star attraction.

I hear it all the time online. *I can't believe you're going through this. You must be so strong. Hugs and kisses, XOXO*, all that junk online that nobody really means. I hate it, but the funny thing is that if enough time goes by and I don't get at least a message or a comment asking how I'm doing, I start to wonder if everyone in cyberland's forgotten about me, and I throw up a picture of Natalie in all her medical gear because I know that's bound to get a response.

The incubator picture from the first day, it went totally viral. Got something like a hundred and fifty shares. Now, the most I can hope for is maybe five or ten likes. I guess after four months of the same type of sick-baby photos, you get a little bored. God knows I would.

Jake is squirming next to me, and I feel somewhat smug since he was the one who made such a big deal about us coming to church in the first place. I think he's trying to make a deal with God, which sounds funny when you think about it, but we do it all the time.

God, if you make him notice me, I'll tell the world how grateful I am. Hashtag blessed.

God, if you get that anesthesiologist to give me my epidural before the next contraction, I swear I'll never use your name in vain again.

God, if you keep my baby girl from dying, I'll be a better person, invite you into my heart a dozen times over, just name your price.

Yeah, I know all about making bargains with heaven. And I know Jake feels guilty. We both do. Like maybe if we hadn't hooked up, if we'd *kept ourselves pure* like those youth pastors and TV folks told us to, God wouldn't be punishing us right now. That's what some idiot said to me online at least. It wasn't the first day, but pretty shortly after that, not even the end of the first week. Can you believe it? He's not someone I know well. Went to Sandy's church out in Boston. Man, I'm so glad to be away from the East Coast, away from people like Tom McMahon.

So picture this. Natalie was on a ventilator, and my foster mom posted a picture asking everybody to pray, and "Elder Tom" shoved in. He's not an elder anymore, by the way. Doesn't even go to St. Margaret's. He and Sandy's husband got into a major fight a few years back and parted ways. Last I heard, "Elder Tom" has started up a new church of his own. God only knows what sadist would go there. I mean, what kind of human being, let alone a pastor, would make a reference to David and Bathsheba under a picture of a dying baby with tubes shoved down her throat?

Sandy deleted the comment right away, probably hopes I never saw it in the first place, but I did. I'll never tell her, because she's done so much for me, like coming up to sit with me during Natalie's surgery, but I wish she had told Elder Tom to take his smug, judgmental attitude and rot in the underworld. I mean, deleting that post is one thing, but it doesn't really get to the heart of the issue. Which is that Tom McMahon thinks my baby deserves to die.

That's what the David and Bathsheba reference meant. I had to look it up. I don't have all those Bible stories memorized anymore, but all it took was a quick Google search. David committed adultery. Nobody says if Bathsheba was willing or not, because let's face it, all those men who wrote the Bible wouldn't have thought to ask about a little detail like that, would they? Anyway, the goodie-two-shoes king sinned, and God punished him by killing their child.

For God so loved the world, right?

Can I get an amen?

CHAPTER 2

I know I'm probably breaking two or three of the Ten Commandments right now, but I can't help checking the time on my phone every thirty seconds. It's not that I hate church. I'm not that kind of person. I know some people believe that Christians are all self-righteous hypocrites, but I could never say that. Not after living with Sandy. I sometimes go months without thinking about my past, about the anonymous foster parents that gel together in my memory like giant, faceless blobs. But it's different with her. It's hard to say where I'd be if Sandy hadn't taken me in. Probably so strung out on drugs my teeth would have fallen out and my hair gone frizzy like in those posters warning kids against meth. I'm proud to say I haven't touched the stuff. In fact, I could count on one hand all the times I've taken anything harder than speed. I'm sure that if it weren't for Sandy, I'd be way more more screwed up than I already am, and that's saying a lot.

The funny thing is, Sandy and I went years without talking. She didn't even know I was pregnant. We never had a falling out or anything. It's just that after I finished high school, I packed up and left the East Coast faster than a hooker at a truck stop.

I never looked back. Which is a good thing. I remember before I got pregnant with Natalie, I was at an interview trying to land a job at this assisted living home. After I left the convenience store, I really needed the money. I'd already been out of work for three weeks, and my bank account was overdrawn by day five. My landlord told me to apply for unemployment, but I knew if I did, I'd have to explain what happened at the convenience store, which I wasn't ready to do. Not yet. Maybe not ever. So I was at the assisted living place, Winter Grove, and I was talking to this shaggy-bearded director, and he asked about my greatest strength. Just to keep me on my toes, I'm sure. All the blog posts I read in preparation told me he'd want to know about my weaknesses.

So I couldn't figure out what answer he was looking for. In school, I was always pretty good at English and grammar. I have a vague memory of winning a spelling bee back in second or third grade. But seriously? If all I've got to do is take old people to the toilet and back, why would this Tom-Hanks-in-*Castaway* lookalike care how well I did in English class?

I thought about telling him something sappy about relationships or whatnot, how I'm just full of compassion and love helping people, especially the frail and infirm who can't even raise their spoons to their mouths without dribbling applesauce down their chins. But I wasn't sure I could get through an answer like that without gagging. I couldn't tell him the truth, though. Couldn't tell him that my biggest strength was making sure I never got stepped on. Ever. A childhood in foster care teaches you like nothing else to fend for yourself. But I knew this director wasn't looking for an employee like that. He was staring at me, his brows knit together like he knew as well as I did this interview was a waste of our time, and I was about to stand up and leave when it hit me.

"I'm really good at moving forward," I told him. He still looked kind of bored, so I tried to explain. "I never look back."

And I still feel that way, for the most part at least. That's why I went so long without thinking about Sandy. Why I never tracked her down online or sent her a pregnancy announcement. As good as she was to me, she belonged to my past, the past that I walked away from as soon as I finished high school. I didn't even wait for the ceremony. Sandy mailed me my diploma a week or two after graduation. She called me a couple times once I moved, but then I stopped making payments on my cell phone, and a few years went by where we didn't talk at all.

Natalie changed all that, of course. Just like she changed everything else. I hope I don't sound like an ingrate or anything. I never said all the changes were bad. Like marrying Jake. A hundred stress points right there, and the online quiz doesn't know if we have a happy marriage or not. A hundred points whether you're married to a hen-pecked mama's boy or an abusive drunk who cracks two of your ribs then dumps you off at the ER before he goes out to party with his bar-hopping buddies.

The pastor's droning on, it's something about King David, and I remember enough from the Bible to know that he wasn't really the poster-boy for righteous living. I pull out my phone, swipe the screen, and check the time again, wondering when the sermon is ever going to end.

CHAPTER 3

The pastor's young. Not fresh-out-of-college young, but pretty close to it. Mid-twenties is my best guess. He's got darker skin. Maybe Hispanic. Or Native American. It's hard to tell. I wonder if he has kids. I know he's got a wife. I spotted her less than two minutes after I sat down. I didn't see her talk to him or anything, so I couldn't tell you how I knew who she was. Maybe the way no one else is sitting next to her except for that white-haired granny lady in the atrocious blouse. Or the way she kind of leaned forward when the pastor stepped up to the podium, or whatever that tall thing up front is called. And he just seems like the kind of man a mouse like her would go for. Strong. Confident, maybe even a little cocky if pastors are allowed a hint of arrogance. And she's this shy little thing sitting in the third row. I hate it when women slouch, by the way. It makes them look so weak. She's got these frail shoulders with this thin lilac sweater wrapped around them. Christmas is in a week and a half, and she's dressed for spring.

Part of me feels sorry for her, truth be told. She's not even my age, hardly out of her teens by the looks of her. I'm pretty sure she doesn't have kids. I can't be positive, though. She might have a baby she drops off in the nursery or something, but she seems like the type of mom that would keep her brood close by. One on the hip, one in a front pack, and a third in the oven.

That kind of mom.

Which means she doesn't have kids. Not yet. I'm sure she will soon. Those razor-straight hips will broaden out, and that flat chest will miraculously fill with milk. She could afford to gain a good ten pounds, pregnant or not. I wonder what the pastor thinks of her. Skinny's all the rage, but that doesn't mean men have stopped appreciating curves.

I stare down at the front panel of my maternity pants. I don't have to wear them anymore. I could fit into a few of my pre-pregnancy clothes by now. God knows I've been trying hard to lose that last fifteen pounds. With Jake's mom moving in and taking over the cooking, it's a wonder I'm not anorexic-skinny. That woman cooks the same way she doles out affection — sparingly. I thought hospitality was a big stinking deal in Asian cultures. But every night when I reach for a second helping of whatever stew or casserole she's constructed, I feel her iron gaze of disapproval. I should be used to it by now. I've seen it every day since she barged into our home.

I think deep down she's probably like "Elder" Tom McMahon, probably secretly convinced that what happened to Natalie is my fault. Of course, Patricia isn't religious, so she doesn't have misogynistic Bible stories to back her up, but she's spent the past year telling her son he could do better than me.

Every once in a while, I wonder what would happen if I just

leave. Patricia is so stoked at the chance to play house in my kitchen. Change the bandages on my baby. I can't even pump breast milk anymore without giving Natalie colic, so she's on a totally synthetic diet. Straight up amino acids poured directly into her feeding pump.

The family would be just as well off without me. Maybe even better. Patricia's the one with all the medical experience, and she and Jake never fight.

Ever.

Maybe I sound like a martyr, but isn't church the place to be honest with yourself? Jake doesn't need me. He's got Mama there to do all the cooking, all the cleaning, and to do it better than I ever would. Patricia made that clear the day she pulled fuzzy leftovers out of the fridge, narrowed her almond eyes. I swear that woman's fifty-five if she's a day, but her complexion is nicer than mine will ever be. But she gave me such a snotty look when she tossed the moldy Tupperwares into the trash, so disapproving. As if she'd forgotten I'd been in the hospital for months. As if she thought I had nothing better to do once we brought Natalie home than clean out the grody food left in my fridge.

I know Patricia wants me gone. She never says so, but those glares make it perfectly clear. I don't even have to be looking at her to sense the hot disapproval boring into me, right between my shoulder blades.

And she's always there. I mean always. I'm already four months postpartum. It's high time Jake and I had the chance to enjoy a little alone time in the bedroom, but we can't because that woman never leaves. Man, I wish she were the religious one so she'd go to church once a week and at least give us a few hours' privacy.

I should be grateful for Patricia and everything she's done. Jake reminds me of that all the time. Patricia does too, come to think of it. Of course, she never comes right out and says so. That woman has mastered the art of the haiku insult. So understated but with that bitter twist at the end.

Kind of like her cooking, now that I mention it.

"Tiff," she'll say, "were you sick often as a child?" As if Natalie's problems could get passed down from your genes. Because nothing like this has *ever* happened on the Matsumoto side of the family, she points out every few days. Then she wants to know if my mom had any issues delivering any of her babies. As if she's forgotten that I'm a foster brat. As if Jake hadn't already told her that my mother was a crackhead and hooker who abandoned me in a high-school bathroom stall and who I'm sure is rotting away right now. Whether in jail or the grave is anybody's guess.

Patricia knows all this, and she still asks. It's always when she's doing something with Natalie, too. Those physical therapy stretches that are supposedly going to keep my daughter's muscles from decaying from lack of use. Rubbing her cheeks in a vain attempt to wake up damaged nerves in hopes that she might one day learn to smile. Changing the bandages around her G-tube site, still tender from surgery. I can tell Natalie hurts, because she scrunches her face up in such a gut-wrenching way that even someone as cold as Patricia should feel sorry for her. But Patricia had training as a nurse, as she tells me at least a dozen times a day, and she's used to this kind of work, which means she doesn't have an ounce of empathy left for my little girl. A whirlwind of efficiency. That's what Patricia is. Or maybe a monsoon.

Natalie's making some progress, though. The pastor's talking about thanking God during hard times, and I know I've got plenty of reasons to be grateful. I mean, she wasn't supposed to make it out of the NICU at all. The hospital social worker even scheduled a meeting for us to talk with this lanky man in a drab suit about funeral arrangements *when the time comes.*

That's why I don't need a pastor to remind me to count my blessings. Because in spite of all we've gone through, Natalie is a blessing. *She's a blessing*, I would remind myself back in Seattle when I woke up at five in the morning to pump a couple ounces of breastmilk and make it to the NICU by the time the night nurses went off duty. *She's a blessing*, I told myself when the neurologist showed us the hemorrhages on the scans. Who would have thought there's an actual difference between brain-dead and vegetative? You learn something new every day, right?

I'm staring at my fingernails, trying to remember the last time I had them done. I wasn't in the third trimester yet. Funny, isn't it, that when the doctors put me on bed rest, all they worried about was whether or not Natalie's lungs were developed enough to breathe outside of the womb. They gave me tons of fluids and set up nurses who looked like Olympic rugby players to guarantee I never got out of bed. Everyone was shocked that I didn't go into labor until thirty-six and a half weeks. I was so sick of hospitals by then. Which is ironic if you think about it now. I was so ready for Natalie to come out, ready to take her home.

Man, what a fool I was.

I glance from my grubby fingernails to Jake. It's still so hard to think of him as my husband. We haven't even bought rings yet. He's fidgeting more than usual. I can tell he's bored with the sermon. Which I guess is a good thing, since it means he probably won't haul us here next week, trying to appease God just by showing up. As if we could trick him into thinking of us as devoted believers.

I'm staring at the pastor now, distracted by the way the purple stripes on his tie clash against the maroon base of his shirt. But he finally invites the congregation to bow their heads in prayer, the sign that it's almost over. I should get home, go check on Natalie. This is the longest I've been away from her since we came home from Seattle. But part of me wants to ask Jake to stop somewhere for lunch. Of course, he'll be thinking about his mother, who by now has a dish of something or other browning in the oven.

I ask him all the time how long Patricia will stick around, but he never gives a definite answer. I swear that woman treats us like we're a couple of twelve-year-olds. I'm sure she's convinced that if she were to leave now, Natalie would starve to death by sunset.

As if Patricia is the only one in the family who knows how to dump a bottle of formula into a feeding bag.

The pastor says amen, and I realize I forgot to bow my head. It's just as well. There's no fooling God. He already knows how pathetic of a Christian I really am.

CHAPTER 4

"Greet one another on the way out," the pastor calls to us, and I'm glad Jake and I are in the back row. No time for overzealous church ladies to make meaningless chitchat or impose their uninvited hugs on either of us. I clutch my phone, wondering if we should call Patricia to let her know we're on our way. If we don't, she'll politely complain that she had no way to know when lunch should be ready. If we do, she'll pitch a very understated fit about how we shouldn't expect her to rearrange her schedule to cook for us, because don't we know she has a sick grandchild to look after?

Trust me, Patricia. We know.

I'm ready to leave, but Jake hasn't moved. Neither has anyone else, I realize. Nobody except that old lady sitting next to the pastor's wife. She's standing up now, leaning forward, asking the preacher something. What does she think this is? A question and answer session? Who ever heard of a church service going past noon? We've got places to go. Diapers to change. Casseroles to choke down.

I'm about to nudge Jake, but the pastor's holding out the wireless mic. Not a good sign. "Real quick before we dismiss," he begins. I know better than to trust a preacher who begins any sentence with *real quick.* "Grandma Lucy has asked for the opportunity to close us in prayer today. Grandma Lucy." He hands her the mic, and I roll my eyes. This lady is way too white to be the pastor's grandma, which means she must be related to his wife. What kind of sap calls an in-law *Grandma?* There's no way you'd catch me acting that familiar with Patricia. I can barely claim her as my mother-in-law without wanting to puke.

Grandma Lucy is a petite little thing, not quite as wispy as the pastor's wife, but now that she's standing I can detect a hint of similarity. She's wearing this gaudy blouse, salmon-colored, the kind of nylon that's got that old-school sheen to it. The collar alone is the same size as some of the cuter tees I used to wear before I got pregnant. There's something familiar about her, but I can't place exactly what.

All right, I think to myself. Let the old lady pray, and then we're out of here. I've already decided it would be stupid to ask Jake out for lunch. Not only would it start World War III with Patricia, I don't even want to be with him. I mean, I know he's trying to be a better person and everything. We both are after what we went through. But come on. Church was two hours if you count the drive. We could have gone to the movies. We could have walked the mall. We could have thrown in some Christmas shopping, at least if we had any money to spend. It's our first time alone together in months, and he wastes it all on a boring sermon.

Sometimes I wonder if this is the same man I met at the

19

convenience store. Could he have changed that much in a year? Things were so carefree back then. Carefree if you don't count everything that led up to me quitting my job, at least. But good came from that too, I suppose, just like the pastor was talking about. It was when I was dead broke and unemployed and had no chance to make rent that Jake showed up.

We'd hung around each other a couple times before. Every so often it worked out where I relieved him at shift change, and he'd stick around for a little while afterward. Especially at night. Cracked a few jokes about making sure I didn't let any creeps into the store. It was kind of touching really, the way he wanted to keep me safe.

Too bad it didn't work. But that's another irony for you. If I hadn't been working alone that night, I wouldn't have been forced to quit my job. And that's what got me so broke I had to move in with Jake when he asked. I didn't have any other options. It makes me sound desperate when I put it that way, but that's not how it was. Jake was fun. Cute. Sort of quiet in an endearing way. I liked him.

If it weren't for the attack, I might have never ended up with Jake. Or maybe we'd still be a couple, but we would have taken things slower. Wouldn't have so much baggage now.

You can never know for sure, can you?

I find myself wondering what the pastor would think, what he'd say if he knew the half of it. *Why did you let someone in after closing?* I can almost hear the disapproval in his voice. He'd probably want to know what I was wearing that night too. Well, it was summer. I was hot. The store didn't have any AC, and the air from the fan never reached behind the register.

Did you drink with him? That's the million-dollar question, isn't it? Because obviously, if I drank with a dimpled stranger in the store that I was supposed to have locked up fifteen minutes earlier, that automatically means I was asking for it. Right? I couldn't work there afterward. I didn't even give my two weeks. Didn't try to go back. Sent Roberto a text, and that was it. I didn't think I'd see Jake again. But then he popped up, right when I needed him.

He doesn't even know about the attack. I mean, he knows, but we've never talked about it. When he asked me why I quit, I just told him some guy had been bothering me and Roberto wouldn't let me switch my shift to days. Jake didn't press for any more information than that, and I didn't offer it. I honestly didn't expect the two of us to get serious at all. I wasn't looking for anything long-term. From everything I understood, he wasn't either.

And then Natalie came. Man, I was so sick at the beginning. Even before I missed my period, I knew it either had to be pregnancy or the flu. I lost so much weight. I wish I could go back to that size now. Fit into that little backless tee.

Just a fling. A few weeks, a month or two at most. That's all either of us expected. But Natalie changed all that, just like she changed everything else. Some pee on a stick, a teary-eyed conversation at two o'clock in the morning, his promise that I

21

could do whatever I wanted and he'd support me all the way.

It's funny. I thought he'd want to get rid of her. That's what I would do if I were him. Even with the positive test, neither of us expected to stay a couple for the long haul. Jake was young. Working a nine-dollar-an-hour job. But there he was, telling me I could do whatever I thought was best. We didn't talk about money, not early on, but I knew I'd get child support out of him if I asked.

And then it came out that I couldn't make rent, so he suggested I move in with him. I was sick from the beginning, puking all the time. And Jake was there to make me some peppermint tea, pass me the paper towels so I could clean up after myself.

Man, he's changed so much. Now I can't even get him to clean up after himself when he leaks all over the toilet seat.

Good thing Mama's there to do it for him.

CHAPTER 5

So Grandma Lucy's done praying, but she's still got the mic, and now she's droning on about the day of salvation. I can tell she's super spiritual because she's using all the right phrases, the kinds of things Sandy and her women's Bible study ladies used to gab about. Redemption and sanctification and *glorify this* and *magnify that*. Some people really need to get over themselves, know what I mean? I've been staring at the time on my phone now for seven minutes straight, and Jake hasn't made an attempt to move. Seven stinking minutes, but it feels like an eternity. And after an eighty-six-hour long labor, I know what an eternity feels like.

I'd already been in the hospital on bed rest for four weeks. I was so stoked when I finally went into labor. I couldn't get her out fast enough. Deliver the baby, wrap her up in a blanket or two, and finally go home. Home, where you can watch whatever shows you want instead of giving yourself carpal tunnel clicking the hospital's stupid remote looking for something decent. To binge-watch a whole season of CSI in one sitting, no commercial breaks. No interruptions from well-meaning nurses jabbing their fingers inside to check your cervix and see if you're dilated.

I knew it wouldn't be easy with a newborn. I wasn't that naïve. But Jake and I had been getting along ok. It helps that I wasn't so hormonal toward the end of the pregnancy. I was actually looking forward to being a mom. I mean, you already know about the woman who brought me into the world. It's not like the bar was set uber high.

So I was going to push out my baby, and I was finally going to leave that stinking hospital. Breathe the fresh air again. Urinate without having to measure it down to the cc. Man, I was ready to go home. Jake was too. I mean, he stopped by the hospital every day, but there's just not that much to do there. I mean, what do you even talk about?

"How was your day?"

What would I have to say? "I peed out 400 cc's this morning."

Looking back, I can see that our relationship was getting a little strained during that time. Whose wouldn't be? I just figured we'd get home, we'd have our daughter to take care of together, and life would go back to normal. Or maybe even better than normal, because all that extra time on bed rest got me thinking. Imagining. Planning. I was never much of a reader, but the hospital had this crazy huge stack of pregnancy magazines to flip through. I swear there must have been a whole decade's worth or more, a long enough span that the newer ones started contradicting the older. The *Baby's First Step* cover might have an article that tells you to nurse your baby right before bed so she'll sleep through the night and won't wake up hungry, but then when you get to the *Taking Time for Mama* issue, it's all about training her to go to sleep on a slightly empty stomach so she doesn't have to feel full to get rest.

I wasn't looking forward to breastfeeding if we're going to be totally honest. I'd read enough about sore nipples and mastitis to realize it would be uncomfortable at best. I figured I'd try it out for a few weeks, see how it went. But it's not like I had this romanticized notion of smashing my baby against my boob and falling in love and nursing her until she started kindergarten. I guess I was curious, though. Wondered what it would feel like.

Natalie's sixteen weeks old, and I still don't know what it feels like to nurse a baby. I'm positive it's more comfortable than a breast pump or else the human race would have died out before we ever evolved past living in caves. I hated pumping, but at least it was something I could do. Something that only I could do is a better way to say it. I swear her grandmother jinxed her or something, because the whole time Natalie was in the hospital, she handled my breast milk just fine. Then we took her home, and within twenty-four hours, Patricia showed up on our doorstep, suitcases in hand. Four days later, Natalie was so uncomfortable the pediatrician told us to take her off breast milk completely. Natalie takes this predigested formula now, nothing but nutrients and amino acids with this sickening sweet vanilla scent. You know what it smells like? Those disgusting diet drinks I used to take in junior high. The thing about formula is that anyone can prepare it.

You don't even have to mix in water. Just open the bottle, measure out the right amount, and dump it into the feeding pump.

Jake couldn't understand why I was so upset after that appointment with Dr. Bell. He knew how sick I was of pumping. Who wants to feel like a dairy cow five times a day? So in his mind, getting premade formula and having Medicaid pay for all of it was great news.

Only it wasn't. I don't think it would have been half as bad if it weren't for his mom and her smug smile. "Maybe something you're taking doesn't agree with her," she'd suggest, and that's just how she'd say it too. *Something you're taking.* Which I'm sure in Patricia's lingo meant drugs. Which I wasn't on, by the way, not during the pregnancy or now.

I think Patricia was secretly thrilled about it all, really. Because now there isn't a single thing I can do for my child that she can't do better. She has her nurse's training to thank, even though that woman hasn't worked an actual nursing job since Bush was president. The first Bush, I mean, not the second.

That's what makes me think about leaving sometimes. I know it's the deadbeat thing to do, but given my family history, would you have expected me to stick around this long? If Natalie needed me, that would be different. Can you believe I waited sixteen days in the NICU just to see her open her eyes? And you know what? She didn't even notice me. I was no different to her than any of the nurses in their colorful scrubs. When Jake holds her, I swear something clicks in that injured little brain of hers. She seems

26

comfortable. Even tried to scratch his chin once. When I hold her, she's completely oblivious. Even Patricia claims Natalie smiled at her. I'm sure she's lying, because my child doesn't smile. At anyone. But that doesn't change the fact that my baby doesn't even know I'm alive. I hate to say it because it sounds so stinking cruel, but I'm not sure she knows much of anything. Sometimes when Patricia's busy in the kitchen, I hold Natalie while she's getting her tube feeding, and I watch. Waiting for something to happen. Even when she's got her eyes open, she never looks at me. Never. Looks. At. Me. And then she gets fussy, so I put her back on her little wedge, and she finishes her feeding in peace and quiet. What kind of baby doesn't even want to be held?

I had such high hopes for myself as a mom. I had it all figured out. I was going to stay at home for the first year or so. Maybe take in an extra kid or two for babysitting. I was going to give Natalie everything I never got at that age — a home, a sense of belonging, affection.

I remember laying around on bed rest, flipping through those mommy magazines and daydreaming about story time. That's the one thing the articles always agreed about, even the older ones. Read to your kids from the day they're born. I had the picture squared away in my brain. Me on the couch, with Natalie nestled up against me. In my imagination, we always read Dr. Seuss because honestly, I didn't know any other kids books, but I was going to learn. I'd get a library card. Check out books there. And we'd cuddle and read, and it would do wonders for her development. Wonders for our relationship. That was the plan.

And now look what I've got. A kid who doesn't even recognize me. A kid who can't make eye contact. A kid who won't even live to see her first birthday.

CHAPTER 6

Natalie came home from Seattle and got put on an apnea monitor. Makes this horrible, piercing siren noise whenever it can't detect her breathing. Usually it's false alarms. It hardly wakes me up anymore, especially now that Patricia has moved the air mattress into the nursery. She says it's because I need to catch up on my sleep, but by the tone in her voice, I know what she means is I'm a lazy, no good baby mommy that her son had the unfortunate opportunity to knock up.

I'm going to talk to Dr. Bell about it this week, actually. Not Patricia, of course — the apnea monitor. Jake and I already signed one of those DNR forms that says we don't want heroic measures, you know, when the kid needs CPR or something. The neurologist and the pulmonary specialist were all for it, the lung guy in particular. Since Natalie can't even swallow her saliva, it's only a matter of time before all the germs in her mouth make their way into her lungs. So if she doesn't die from choking, it'll be the pneumonia that does her in. Jake and I both agreed. We didn't even fight about it. The way the doctor put it, we knew we were doing the right thing. For Natalie, I mean. That was before we left Seattle, before Patricia moved in. She doesn't know about the

DNR, and frankly it's none of her business. I shouldn't feel guilty for signing it, shouldn't feel like I'm just abandoning Natalie because she's too hard to take care of. That's not the kind of mom I am. The kind of mom who ditches an unwanted baby in a bathroom trash can.

It's for the best. I know it is. And whenever I start to doubt myself, I remember what that neurologist said, that even if we prolong her life, the chance of Natalie being anything more than a vegetable is ridiculously low. I appreciate the way he didn't mince words. Didn't feed us false hope. Just sat us down and gave it to us straight.

Dr. Bell, the pediatrician here in Orchard Grove, she's the only one who thinks we should wait, give Natalie more time to develop before making up our minds about the DNR. She's the one who gave us the apnea monitor, and that's what I need to talk to her about when we go in to see her Wednesday. Because it's completely unnecessary if you think about it. Let's say the monitor goes off, and let's say it's a real event, not a false alarm. Then what? We don't start CPR. That's the whole point of those forms we signed. We could call the ambulance, but what are they going to do? Stand around singing *Kumbaya* while they watch her turn blue and then that horrid shade of gray? Think about it for a minute. If your kid's going to die in the middle of the night, do you want the bells and whistles going off just so you'll be awake for it? Wouldn't you rather just get up in the morning after a long night's rest and find out that …

Never mind. I wonder how long that granny lady's going to keep up her Holy Spirit babble. She's quoting Scripture now, at least I assume it's Scripture. I don't know. Maybe she's just ad-libbing. The pastor's standing off to the side with this awkward look on his face that makes me want to chuckle. You can tell he doesn't know quite what to do. If Grandma Lucy weren't a relative, I'm sure he would have found a way to seize control of the mic by now. That's just the kind of man he seems to be, the kind who takes charge. Doesn't waffle.

Not like Jake. I swear, that boy can never make up his mind about anything, especially now that Mama's around to do all his thinking for him. Even in the NICU, Jake's whole *doctor knows best* attitude drove me batty. I mean, picture this. Our baby was only three weeks old and just a few hours out of surgery where they put a tube right into her stomach so they didn't have to feed her through her nose anymore. And my old foster mom Sandy was there for moral support, flew all the way from Boston to Seattle to be with me. So she and I were having lunch together in the cafeteria while Jake stayed with the baby. And right in the middle of our coffee, he texted and said something like, *I think she's in pain.* I mean, he was right there, probably all of two feet away from the nurse, and he was texting me about it.

So I told him to tell somebody Natalie needed pain meds. I didn't think anything else about it until later in the evening when I went over to see her myself. She didn't cry (still doesn't, actually), but she was obviously uncomfortable. Wouldn't you be if someone sliced a four-inch hole in your abdomen and stitched a tube to the inside of your stomach?

I told the nurse, "I thought you guys gave her more pain meds," and she said no, the morphine was giving her problems. Natalie couldn't keep her oxygen levels up, so she could only have Tylenol.

Tylenol? I got stronger stuff when I got a tooth pulled.

"Ok," I said, "how long has it been since her last dose?" And the nurse looked at her chart and told me five hours. I freaked out. After getting Natalie what she needed, I stormed to Jake and demanded to know why in the world he hadn't gotten our daughter the pain meds like I told him to. He shrugged and said, "The nurse said she could only have it every six hours."

You know what gets me totally insane with anger? Not the fact that the doctors were so stupid they put a tiny baby on nothing but Tylenol immediately after a major surgery like that. Doctors are imbeciles. They have no idea how to tell if a baby's in real pain or not, especially with kids like Natalie who don't cry.

No, what gets me the most — I'm fuming now just thinking about it — is the way Jake let them do their thing, didn't ask a single question. When I called him out on it, he got this annoying whine in his voice and asked, "Well, what did you expect me to do?"

So I told him exactly what I expected him to do. March to the charge nurse like I did, ask for more effective pain management, and when she didn't take me seriously, demand to speak to the doctor. Wham bam, fifteen minutes later our baby's back on morphine. And guess what? Her oxygen levels held just fine.

Six hours my butt. I wonder how Jake would feel if he ever gets himself fixed down there and all he can take afterwards is a single dose of Tylenol every six hours.

The really pathetic part is when we had that big argument, it was exactly a year from our very first date.

Happy anniversary, darling.

CHAPTER 7

"I hear a voice of one crying in the wilderness," Grandma Lucy's saying. I can't tell now if she's preaching or praying or quoting Bible verses from memory or what. She's got one hand raised up toward the sky like she's the stinking Statue of Liberty. I still haven't figured out why she looks familiar to me. "Weeping and great mourning," she continues, and I surprise myself by actually recognizing the reference. You wouldn't know it to look at me now, but for a few years in Massachusetts, I was really into youth group and church junk like that.

It's kind of funny in a way, and also kind of sad, how into that lifestyle I got during those few years I spent with Sandy. I mean, I wasn't just the sullen foster kid the pastor's wife dragged to church on Sundays. I couldn't wait to go. All my friends were at church, not at that preppy white-kid charter school where nobody like me would even dream of trying to fit in. And it wasn't like Sundays were the only church days. Youth group on Tuesdays. Bible quiz Thursdays. I still remember that youth pastor with his crazy dreadlocks and corny T-shirts. But you know what? He knew about my past and didn't judge me. Not once. And he made sure I fit in. I think he must have planned it behind my back,

34

because the very first night I showed up at youth group, three different girls asked for my phone number, and two of them texted me a day or two later.

It seems so long ago, that time at Sandy's church. But I loved everything about it. I was so naïve back then, so stinking starved for love. I would do anything to feel like I belonged. Even stand up at that youth retreat and walk up to the front of the aisle, knees shaking, head dizzy like I'd just downed a can of beer on an empty stomach. And I didn't just stand there at the altar and pray for forgiveness. I actually knelt. Clasped my hands in front of me and sobbed my heart out to the God who promised to wash away all the mistakes of my past.

Nobody warned me back then about religion, about how you might escape your guilt, but you can't throw off your DNA no matter how hard you try. And that's how it worked. I did it all, the spiritual retreats, the abstinence pledges, everything the people at Sandy's church said I should. I'd forgotten about it until just now, but I even woke up an hour early once a week my whole junior year to attend this before-school Bible study. I was completely sold out. I read this book once, this collection of stories of Christian martyrs, and I remember thinking, *I'm going to be just like them when I grow up.* I even told Sandy I thought God wanted me to become a missionary.

It's hard to say what happened. Halfway through my junior year I started sleeping with Lincoln Grant. (I know what you're thinking, and yes, that was his real name.) He wasn't my first but the only one I'd been with since I moved in with Sandy, the only one I'd been with since I walked down that aisle in tears, desperate to sell my soul to God like some affection-starved hooker on her knees begging for acceptance.

So I was giving into temptation with Lincoln every so often, but I always felt bad afterward. Always asked God to forgive me. Told him I'd try to be stronger next time. I was still reading the Word nearly every day and working hard on the Bible quiz team, and maybe you'd think that makes me a hypocrite, but I just think it makes me a human. I mean, nobody's perfect, right? And who's to say the kid who sneaks someone like Lincoln Grant into her foster family's bedroom window is any worse than the so-called Christian girls who were so eager to spread the juicy gossip once they found out what we were doing?

Grandma Lucy's going on and on, and it's the same basic verse — I remember it from Bible quizzing, remember it because it was so morbid and I never got why they made us memorize it — except she's saying it differently. I wonder if she's been reading from the augmented Bible, or whatever that version is where they add so much extra stuff. I wouldn't know. But it's a little off from what I recall.

"The voice of a mother weeping for her child."

My hands are clammy, and my heart feels like it did that day at the youth retreat before I walked down the aisle. Jittery, like I've had caffeine dumped into my veins. How did she know? She's never met Natalie. Nobody in this room has except me and Jake.

"Weeping tears that fall like angel dust before the throne of God."

Angel dust? Sounds like something you'd stick under your tongue at a rave. But just when I think that Grandma Lucy's gone completely off script, there it is again. That feeling in my chest, that flutter. Like this stranger is some kind of psychic who can read my thoughts. Knows exactly what I've gone through.

"Refusing to be comforted," she says, and all of a sudden, her raised palm is leveled straight at me, like she's Iron Man aiming her shooting beam or whatever it's called right at my forehead. "Refusing to be comforted because her children are no more."

So there it is. I hate to admit it, but for half a minute there, she almost had me going. Almost had me believing that she was talking directly to me. I'm not superstitious, but when you think about all the things she was saying, that could have been me. Almost. I let out my breath, realizing now how long I've been holding it in, and stare at that awful salmon blouse she's wearing.

I shut my eyes for a minute. Stupid of me to let her get under my skin like that. Stupid of me to believe that some ancient grandmother who probably hasn't upgraded her wardrobe since the seventies could actually be talking to me. She's nothing. Just a batty old woman rambling on because the pastor was stupid enough to hand her the mic.

A batty old woman who needs to shut up so I can get out of this church and get home to my little girl.

CHAPTER 8

But Grandma Lucy doesn't shut up, much as I want her to. Much as I need her to. She's going on now about this person in mourning, this person in such need of comfort. I don't think she means me, but I'm not sure anymore. It wouldn't make any sense. I've never met this woman before. Never talked to her. At least I don't think I have. But why does it feel like I should recognize her? She was sitting ten rows ahead of me in church all morning, so it's not like she even had that entire hour and a half to study my body language and come up with clues about me.

About my family.

She's moved on. She's carrying on about the disciples now. But I'm not paying attention to that. I'm still fixating on the part about *refusing to be comforted.* Because I've been there. I was there four months ago in that delivery room.

Refusing to be comforted. Back when I memorized that verse in Bible quizzing, it sounded like such a horrible thing this woman did. Like she lost her faith in God and went into hysterics and couldn't get over herself. That's what I thought when I was a teenager. I know better now. Not only about the devastation and loss but àlso the joy of holding a perfect newborn who's more precious than your own breath. Stroking that skin. That skin! You could spend a hundred grand on coconut oils and still never come close to matching that silky feel.

Jake and I sometimes joked about our daughter before she was born. What would she look like? I mean, he's half-Japanese, half-white, and I'm black, at least partially. So what would that make our kid? When I was pregnant, I fantasized about this beautiful baby with chocolate skin and almond eyes, which sounds really romantic if you think about it. And when she came out she was even more perfect than I could have imagined. So stinking perfect. Dark, even darker than me, which was a surprise. She was tired, but so was I. What do you expect after an eighty-six-hour-long labor? The nurse had just finished weighing her and cleaning her off, and she was all bundled up like she was a little baby-wrap sandwich.

She wasn't more than few minutes old, twenty's the max. And Jake was there. I was surprised he made it through the entire delivery. I honestly didn't expect him to stick around past the first couple hours. I asked if he wanted to hold her, but he was too nervous, and I laughed at him. Right in his face. Said something awful like, "What do you think's gonna happen? She's just gonna stop breathing?"

And a plump lady in scrubs came in and said we should try to breastfeed, but Natalie was so tired she wouldn't open her mouth. So Jake leaned forward, and his eyes got all scared, and he asked, "Is she ok? Is something wrong?" And the nurse laughed at him too and made a joke about first-time dads.

So she said she'd check back a little later and that we could all get some sleep, and I was all for that. But Jake was worried and didn't want me to nap with Natalie in bed. He was afraid she'd roll off and get hurt or something, so I finally said, "Here. Either you hold her or just leave me alone because I haven't slept in three days," and I hadn't. Not even after the epidural.

So I passed out right away. I was groggy from the meds, and I didn't wake up until that plump nurse came in the room again. "Did you need something?" she asked me, and I was still a little spacey and couldn't figure out what she was doing there. "Did you ring the button?"

"No, I did," Jake said, and I immediately wanted to go back to sleep and not even think about him. I mean, he could be immature at times, but I seriously expected him be a little less pathetic about the whole new-baby thing. I couldn't have been asleep for more than half an hour judging by the time. And he got so worried he had to call in the nurse?

"It just seems like something's wrong," he told her, and she gave me this look. You know what I mean. The *wow, you can tell he's a newbie* kind of look and she rolled her eyes at me. Not in a rude way, more like teasing. Like the two of us were there making fun of Jake and he didn't even know it.

Except the joke ended as soon as she took one look at my

daughter. "How long's she been like this?" she asked me, as if I'd know anything about it. And Jake was as useless as an empty deodorant container and said he didn't know, except the nurse wasn't waiting for his response. She picked Natalie up and ran out of the room calling — no, screaming — for the doctor. And she called my OB by her first name. I should have known something was wrong then, but I was still so doped up on pain killers that it didn't fully register until about three seconds later. That's when the intercom sounded.

Code blue. Maternity ward.

And it was so weird hearing a code blue come from the maternity ward. Like you'd expect it in the ER or operating room or something. Not the baby area.

And Jake was shouting after the nurse, and he ran out the door. I wanted to ask him what was happening, but I couldn't because the moment I opened my mouth, this wail came out of me. Except it wasn't from my throat and it wasn't even from my gut. It was deeper than that. Like a demonic creature that gets uncovered from somewhere in the earth's core and it's never supposed to make it to the surface except it does, and then nobody can figure out what to do.

And all I knew was *my baby girl is dead.* And Jake didn't shut the door when he ran out, and if my legs worked I would have run right after him except I couldn't because I'd just delivered our daughter not an hour earlier.

And my ears were ringing, bursting with the sound of my own

hideous howl, and I hated myself for being so useless. So helpless. *My baby girl is dead.*

That's why I can't get past the part where Grandma Lucy says *refusing to be comforted.* Because I've been there. And it's the worst kind of hell I'd ever wish on anybody.

CHAPTER 9

Jake asked me just a few nights ago why I haven't cried. I mean, I cried the first day in the labor and delivery room, and he was there for that. There were two nurses, a doctor, and one other — I think she might have been a chaplain or social worker or something like that — and they were all leaning over me like I was the patient. Leaning over me, their faces literally six inches away. So close I could probably guess what they'd each eaten for breakfast by their breath. Leaning down, holding my hands, rubbing my shoulders. Only four people, but I swear there were eight hands touching me right then as they told me what happened.

My baby had stopped breathing, but she still had a faint pulse. There were flight nurses on the way, straight from the Seattle NICU where they'd gotten special training for events like this. That's always what they call what happened to Natalie, her *event*, like it's a stinking wedding reception or Halloween party that you hire a planner to coordinate. I hated the way they kept on crowding in on me, but at least I knew my baby was alive. As soon as I heard that code blue, I'd just assumed she was dead.

It took an hour for the flight crew to land, and another few hours before they got Natalie stable enough for the medevac. My OB discharged me early. Gave me a prescription for iron pills, recommended witch hazel for the tearing, and stuffed a few oversized pads into a plastic bag along with the cheery samples of free formula and brand-name diapers they give out to all the moms post-delivery.

Congratulations on your new baby.

I was going to ride with Natalie on the medevac jet. They could only transport one parent, and there wasn't any question it would be me. They wheeled Natalie out in this self-contained incubator into the hall to say goodbye to Jake. The glass was thick enough it looked bullet proof. Who knows? Maybe it was. Jake walked up to her, but she was just lying there totally knocked out, like she was in a coma or something. And I remember wondering what kind of goodbye he would give. There wasn't a way for him to touch her or anything. I almost expected him to put his hand up to the glass, but he didn't.

"Can I get you anything before you go?" he asked me, and I don't even remember how I responded. What kind of help can a twenty-two-year-old convenience store salesclerk offer a woman who's only an hour off her epidural but is getting ready to fly halfway across the state because her baby stopped breathing for no apparent reason?

And I wondered if he felt guilty, if he thought what happened was his fault because he was the one who was supposed to be watching her. Then I wondered if he thought it was my fault because I was the one who took a nap. Or maybe he assumed I did drugs or something and that's what this was about.

Maybe it was my fault. I don't know. But I'm not a substance abuser. There was a night last spring where I was finally over my first-trimester pukiness, but I still didn't have an appetite and it had been a horrible day at Winter Grove, the assisted living home, and I just needed a glass of wine. That's it. A single glass of wine. Not even full, more like three-quarters. Just a hair more than half, really. Jake was working late so I knew he wouldn't fuss about it, so I poured myself a glass, plopped on the couch, and turned on the TV. I was going to clean up after myself before he came home. I just needed to get off my feet. He was never going to know about the wine except I fell asleep. So he came home, and there I was, completely crashed out on the couch. He saw the wine glass and assumed the worst. He was raving mad. It was the first time I'd ever seen him that ticked off. He threw the glass at me. There's still a huge red stain on the back of the couch.

I was hardly awake, but I started yelling at him because who does that to anybody, let alone a pregnant woman who's sleeping after a back-breaking shift at the old fogies' home? But then I saw the wine bottle he had in his hand, the one I left on the counter because I was so tired after wiping leathery, wrinkled butts all day, and at least then I understood why he was going postal on me. I convinced him I wasn't drunk. I let him smell my breath, everything. I hadn't even finished all the wine in the glass before

I conked out, which is why there's such a big a stain today. So he calmed down and apologized, and then he took my hands and said, "I just want you to do everything you can to take good care of her" — *her* being Natalie because I'd found out it was a girl just a couple weeks earlier.

I'll blame it on the hormones until the day I die, but I started crying then. It wasn't just because I was exhausted and emotional and my quiet, shy boyfriend had just thrown a wine glass at my face. It was because I realized then that he really planned to stick around. That if I screwed up and something happened to our daughter, I wouldn't just be hurting her. I would be hurting him.

I suffered through the rest of the pregnancy stone-cold sober.

So that's what I was thinking about when the emergency crew got ready to fly Natalie away. That Jake probably assumed this was all my fault. They hadn't done the brain scans yet. I didn't even know hemorrhaging was a thing you had to worry about after a delivery that long. I was afraid I'd messed everything up, and that's why Natalie was dying, and Jake knew it was my fault.

So I told him I didn't need anything, but I'd call him when we landed in Seattle, and he didn't say a word. Didn't even look at me. Just stared at Natalie, and all I could think was *I'm never going to see him again.* Which made me a little sad, but it wasn't that big of a surprise. The real shocker was that he'd stuck around so long. Not quite twelve months since our first date, and now we didn't just have a baby. We had a dying baby. What kind of couple survives that?

I said goodbye to Jake, and I figured it was probably for the last time. Even if he did stick around a little while longer, I was certain things would never be the same between us.

And they never were.

CHAPTER 10

There's something funny about those six weeks we spent in the NICU, because it was summer when Natalie was born and early fall when we left, and to this day I can't keep track of the time of year. Just this week, I ran to Walmart to get some more diapers. I could have asked Jake to do it on his way home from work, but I needed an excuse to get out of the house. Away from his mom.

So I grabbed the cheap Walmart brand. Natalie's still in a size zero, but I think she'll be moving up in the next couple weeks. I can tell the ones she's got are getting a little tight. I was checking them out — I think I'd picked up some noodles too, something Patricia needed for that night's dinner — and the guy at the counter told me merry Christmas after I'd paid. And even though the whole store was flaunting those cheesy tinsel decorations and scrawny artificial trees (which I really shouldn't knock because Jake and I don't even have a tree set up, scrawny or not), I seriously was surprised that it was December. For some reason, my brain was still stuck in August. But that's the other thing. Even though I thought it was August or maybe September at the earliest, I couldn't have told you if that meant Christmas was coming up in a couple more months or if we'd just celebrated it a few weeks earlier. It's such a disorienting feeling. I get it all the time, like I was in the hospital so long that something in my biological clock went haywire and that's why I never know what day or month I'm in. Heck, I'd be happy if my brain could just keep me in the right season.

It doesn't help that I'm stuck inside so much. We've gotten some snow, so you'd think it'd be pretty clear in my head we're in winter, but even those visual cues don't help. And Orchard Grove's so ugly this time of year. The snow never sticks around long enough to look nice. I guess that's one thing the East Coast has going for it, enough snow to actually cover everything, litter and dead tree limbs and all. Here, it's just enough of a dusting to make things slushy for the week. You think of white when you think of Christmas weather, except out here it's really more brown than anything else. Brown with a hint of gray.

The most wonderful time of the year.

Of course, when Natalie was born, it was still August, and I'm sure that's why my brain's all screwed up. It's like I haven't moved on since then, like I'm trapped in this eternal in-between zone. What's that kids book where it's always winter but never Christmas? That's how I feel. Like even though we sang *The First Noel* before the pastor started preaching this morning, I'm still going to wake up on Christmas totally shocked to find myself in December. What happened to Labor Day? Halloween?

49

I remember Thanksgiving, but that's only because Patricia was here and barricaded herself in the kitchen for the whole day, so I had to take over Natalie duty. Stand guard over her crib with that suction machine so every time she started to choke on her spit I could shove a tube down her throat and yank it all out. Man, that thing's gross, how at the end of the day you've got to empty this canister that's like three hundred cc's of just drool and secretions. But without it, my baby can't breathe, so that's what we do.

Thanksgiving dinner turned out nice. Patricia's not a bad cook, really, just a persnickety one. You know who she reminds me of? Rabbit from *Winnie the Pooh*. I'm not joking. Because Rabbit always pretends to be helpful, but it's just his excuse to be bossy, and even when he is actually doing good, he does it in such a cross, mean-spirited way.

I sigh, trying not to be too obvious. I hate that I think about Patricia all the time. Hate that my husband's Mommy Fear has caught me, too. It's like we tiptoe around her, him and me both. I almost think that's why he hasn't initiated anything in the bedroom yet. Like he's afraid she'll ground him or something.

I'm just glad I didn't have to grow up in a home like that.

I'm staring now at the decorations around the church. You can tell someone took their time to make the sanctuary look nice. Not *homey* nice like you'd expect if you walked into a log cabin with a roaring fire and three or four generations plus all the aunts and uncles and cousins squished around the piano singing *Silent Night*. More like what you'd expect if you walked into a fancy Seattle department store. Like even out here in the middle of central Washington the church ladies paid someone to make the sanctuary look perfect. Even though you can appreciate the professionalism, you don't quite get the feeling like you're about to sit down and open presents with family.

Something about the pastor's wife catches my eye, and I wonder what she thinks about Granny's little microphone coup. Is she embarrassed? God knows I'd be. But maybe she's like her grandma. Maybe she's one of those holy rollers and doesn't mind as much. She's so young. Was I ever that little? I can't believe I'm already talking like that, like my better days are all behind me. Are they? I sometimes wonder.

But things won't always be this hard. Natalie's either going to improve or she isn't, and either way it's going to get easier.

It has to get easier.

It's funny. A lot of my friends, people my age, were surprised when I said I was keeping Jake's baby. They knew we hadn't been together that long. I was making ten dollars an hour changing Depends and soiled bed sheets, and he had his thirty-hour a week gig at the convenience store. Not the kind of income you'd expect for a family bringing a child into the world. It's actually a good thing we didn't make more money, though, because then we wouldn't qualify for state insurance, and we'd be bankrupt ten times over before the year's up.

As it is, we pay for Natalie's diapers, and we pay for gas to get her to and from her doctor appointments. Everything else the state covers, even our stay in Seattle. It's funny. I didn't expect Jake to come out there. But then one afternoon I went to the Ronald McDonald House to pump, or "express my milk" as the nurses called it, and there he was, checking in at the front desk. Or at least getting ready to. We ended up sharing a room, which had its ups and downs for sure. I was on "pelvic rest" for the first month — that's the actual medical term my OB used, so we couldn't get too romantic or anything — but we sometimes cuddled at night and that part was pretty nice.

Now that I think about it, we were probably closer to each other there in Seattle than we'd been before. Certainly closer than we are now, although a lot of that has to do with the fact that Patricia is like the Christmas fruitcake that you can never get rid of. I was surprised Jake bothered coming out. At first I thought it was just because he was worried about Natalie. I'd known from the beginning he would make a good dad. But he didn't even go to see her that first day. I think he was scared to, and I don't blame him.

Jake thinks it's weird I haven't cried much since that code blue, but he doesn't know about the first day. I'd started bleeding during the medevac flight to Seattle. I mean, of course I'd bleed, but this got sort of serious. Soaked right through a huge hospital-grade pad and the disposable undies the nurse had given me before I checked out. There were some pretty big clots, too, and the flight nurses were worried about me. So once we landed in Seattle, they whisked Natalie off to the NICU, and I had to get checked out by one of the OBs there. It was this drab-looking man, almost like that teacher guy from *Ferris Beuller*, you know, the guy with the monotone? He sort of talked like him too, and he was pretty upset that my OB back in Orchard Grove had discharged me so early. As if I would have let the flight crew take Natalie on that jet by herself. I guess there was a problem with my stitches, and I really wish the local doc had fixed that up before the epidural wore off, because *ow*.

But anyway, after that I had to go talk to all these people about paperwork and logistics, and I'd forgotten my bag at the Orchard Grove hospital. I mean, who would be thinking about that sort of thing? Well, it took a lot of phone calls to get all the numbers and stuff they needed to bill insurance, and by the time I was finally free to see Natalie it had been probably three or four hours.

So I walked to the NICU. I really needed a wheelchair or something, but I was too embarrassed to call that number they have on those courtesy phones. I mean, I'm young and healthy and don't need someone to push me around. Except I overdid it that first day and had to go back to that Ferris Beuller guy the next morning. Thankfully he didn't stitch me up again, just gave me better pain meds (which I took) and told me to take it easy (which was a pretty good laugh given my situation at the time).

Anyway, when I finally reached the NICU that first day, I felt like everything down there was about to fall right out. I mean, stitches or no stitches, I had just pushed a six-and-a-half-pound baby out a few hours earlier. I knew I was a mess from all that extra bleeding, but even though the nurse at the Seattle OB's gave me a whole bag full of pads, there was nothing she could do about my pants. But I already told you I'd left my bag at the hospital in Orchard Grove, so what choice did I have? There's a trick I learned growing up that if you feel out of place or intimidated, it's best to pretend you're the most arrogant brat the world has ever seen. That's the only way anyone is going to take you seriously. Let down your guard, and they'll trample you in a heartbeat. So I walked up to the NICU station, pretended that not only did I know my pants were a bloody mess but I actually planned it that way, thank you very much. I told the person there — she's called a HUC, such a strange word, isn't it? — that my daughter had just arrived from Orchard Grove and I wanted to see her.

"What's your daughter's name?" the HUC asked with her cute little manicured fingernails poised over her keyboard, and my stomach dropped even more forcefully than it had when the medevac jet landed in Seattle.

"Umm ..." What kind of mom doesn't even know what to call her own child?

The HUC blushed. I hate it when people get embarrassed on my behalf. "You know what?" Her voice was too chipper, like she was trying to sell me some of those health oils that are all the rage these days, particularly amongst perky secretary types. "If she just got in here, they probably haven't had time to enter her information into the system yet. It's probably under your name?"

She said the last part like it was a question, so I told her who I was and studied her face when she frowned into the screen. Why was she looking like that? Could something have happened to my child from the time we got off the jet until now? It was only a few hours. And we were at the best medical center in the state. I mean, I can understand a baby dying at the hospital in Orchard Grove. But here in Seattle ... There was no way anything could happen to her here.

The girl must have found whatever it was she was looking for, because suddenly she was all smiles again. Smiles and dimples, and she told me to follow her, but she walked so fast I remember nearly crying because I was in so much pain.

When I was sure I couldn't take another step without ripping every single one of those new stitches out, she stopped in this little room with an incubator. "Ok, wait right here, and I'll go find your nurse."

My nurse. As if I was the one who had stopped breathing. As if I was the one who needed a ventilator tube shoved down my throat just to stay alive.

Before I could ask her anything else, Miss Chipper was gone, and there was a split second where I found myself wondering why she'd left me here in this room with some random child.

You'd think I would have recognized my own baby, right? But I'd only held her for those couple of minutes right after she was born. I was so tired then. Maybe if that epidural had worked half as well as it should have, I could have gotten some sleep or at least some rest before the delivery. I wouldn't have needed that nap so bad. I would have been awake to notice something was wrong.

Maybe if I were a better person, a better mom, none of this would have happened.

It was my fault that I was here. It was my fault that Natalie had stopped breathing.

It was my fault that I didn't even realize the child lying in that incubator was my own.

CHAPTER 11

So Jake thinks I haven't cried, but he didn't see me that afternoon. You remember I told you about that scream after the delivery when I thought my baby was dead? This was different. This was completely silent. Natalie was in her own room, but there were glass windows all around, and the HUC hadn't shut us in or anything, and I didn't have the energy to close the door.

I didn't even know if I was allowed to close the door. I knew *my* nurse would be bustling in any minute (have you ever known a hospital nurse who doesn't bustle?), and I didn't want her to catch me in the middle of my hysterics.

So I cried, but it was totally soundless. I read this thing online, how some scientist once put tears under a microscope and found that there are like a dozen kinds. I mean, I guess we all know that there's happy tears and angry tears and squinting-at-the-sun-too-long tears, but this guy actually proved they're different on a microscopic level. And these tears in the NICU, all I can think to call them is hot tears. I mean, lots of tears are hot, but these were different. Almost burning, which sounds clichéd except it isn't because they literally did burn.

Well, almost.

That's the state I was in when the nurse bustled in (I told

you she'd be bustling), and she closed this cloth curtain so I had a little privacy and pulled up a chair so I could sit down. I'll probably bless her for it until the day that I die, but she didn't even say anything. Didn't touch me, didn't pat me on the shoulder and lie about how everything would be ok. She just gave me my space, showed me the button to press if I needed anything, and said she could see all the monitors from her station so I didn't have to worry about my daughter.

Then she left me alone. Bless her bustling little heart.

So Jake's wrong about me not crying, but he's right that I don't do it very much. What's the point? It's not like I felt any better when it was over. I knew there were a ton of things I had to do. Get a room at the Ronald McDonald house. Find a pharmacy to get those iron pills the doctor ordered because I'd lost so much blood on the flight over. Take myself someplace where I could buy underwear and new pants, although with my wallet still in Orchard Grove I had no idea how I was going to manage that one.

So that's why I called Sandy. And yes, in case you're wondering, I still had her number in my phone even though I hadn't talked to her in three years. Yes, I felt horribly guilty for ignoring her for so long only to ring her up when I was in so much trouble. But even though I felt like the biggest brat in the history of foster brats, I knew Sandy wouldn't see it that way.

And she didn't.

"Oh, sweetie," she gushed as soon as I told her who it was,

"you have no idea how glad I am to hear from you. God brought you to mind during my morning prayer time, and I just couldn't get you out of my head all day. I looked you up online. Saw that you're expecting a precious little baby, and I told Carl there's no way I'd be able to get a good night sleep until I found a way to get in touch with you. I've been praying for you all day. How are you, little darling?"

Sandy's the only person in the world who could call me *little darling* without getting a black eye or a whole mouthful of curses.

"I'm ok," I lied. I didn't expect it to be so hard to hear that worry in Sandy's voice. That love. Why hadn't I stayed in touch after high school?

"Now, I saw you post something about being in the hospital on bed rest. Is that where you're calling from?"

My throat hurt so bad it felt like I had swallowed a spoonful of glass. I promised myself not to cry and told Sandy, "Yeah, I'm calling from the hospital, except I'm in Seattle now." I had to stop there or I would have turned into a blubbering mess.

"Uh-oh." Sandy's the type of person who can't hide a single emotion. Maybe that's why I fell out of touch. I didn't want to let her down. Didn't want to hear the disappointment in her voice when she learned how much I was messing up my life. "Do they think the baby's coming too soon? Is that why they sent you there?"

I never knew until then how your heart could be torn in half like that until your lungs hardly have any room to expand at all. "Actually, she was born this morning. Everything was ok at first, and then something ..."

I couldn't finish the sentence. Not with my child right there with all those breathing tubes and an IV the flight nurses had to put in her forehead because the veins in her arms were so stinking small. And without asking any other questions, Sandy began to pray for me. Right there on the phone.

I wish I had it recorded or written out so I could remember exactly what she said. What I do remember is the peace, this big tidal wave of warmth that swelled over me. Of course, it vanished as soon as she said *amen*, but I wasn't surprised. I knew enough about church things by then to realize that's the way it always works. Like how I felt so alive, so loved and cherished and wanted at that youth retreat when I knelt in front of the entire St. Margaret's youth group like some kind of deranged martyr. That feeling stayed with me a day and a half. Exactly. I remember because that altar experience was on a Saturday night, and by Monday at lunch Lincoln Grant and I were making out in his dad's truck in the parking lot at school, and once fifth period started I realized the feeling was gone for good.

Gone. Gone. Gone.

Just like that song from *Top Gun*.

Woah, woah, woah.

Still, I was glad when Sandy prayed for me, and she called

me every day after that to keep in touch, except it wasn't the sort of smothering attention like Patricia gives. It was nice. Sometimes if I was busy, I'd let it go to voicemail, and she'd just say something sweet like, "Hey, honey. It's me, just calling to see how everything's going. I wanted you to know I'm praying for you. Call me any time."

That's the kind of person Sandy is, and if you don't have someone like her in your life — even if it's way in the past like mine — I truly hope you find someone like that soon.

CHAPTER 12

"So, this brain bleed thing, it happened while she was being born?"

I rolled my eyes. I'd been telling Jake the same thing for five days, but it wasn't until he got to Seattle that he started to process any of it. He wanted to come right away, he told me, but he had to wait until he got his paycheck, and then he needed to wait until his buddy Marcos was driving out that way because Jake didn't trust his beat-up lemon of a Pontiac to make it all the way over the North Cascades. I tried not to show how surprised I was just to see him at all. But I couldn't hide how annoyed I was at all his questions. "Go to the NICU and talk to the nurses. Or go in the morning so you can catch the doctors doing their rounds. Ask them all the questions you want."

But he wanted to hear it from me. Jake's sort of fragile that way. It makes sense when you think about how stinking sheltered he was his entire life. I mean, his mom didn't even let him watch *The Little Mermaid* growing up. I still don't know if it's because of the sea witch or because of that teeny seashell thing Ariel had going on, but seriously. I was watching slasher flicks with one of my foster dads when I was still missing my two front teeth. I'm the first to admit the system screwed me over at least a hundred times before I'd even started my period, but at least I'm not afraid of the truth. At least I don't need to drive two hundred and fifty miles to hear the bad news from my girlfriend because I can't pick up a stinking phone and ask to talk to some NICU docs.

Well, that's Jake for you. I don't want to complain. I sometimes wonder if I could have handled that time in Seattle if I were all by myself. I mean, Sandy came for a few days, stayed with me when Natalie was having her surgery, and that was huge. But it's not like Sandy could drop her entire life out there in Boston and live with me indefinitely. They're not doing foster care anymore, but she and Carl just adopted a little boy from South Korea. The kid's a handful from what I could gather. Sandy's not the kind of mom who would complain, so I'm sure I don't know the half of it, but it's not like I could have just expected her to live with me there in Seattle while I got things sorted.

So yeah, I guess I'm glad Jake showed up. I mean, we got married, right? That's got to tell you something.

A hundred stinking stress points in one ten-minute ceremony. Maybe that's why my back is aching in this hard pew. I glance over at his hand, wonder what kind of ring I'd get him if we had the money. Because of course, that's the down side of him coming out to Seattle. Five weeks off work. I never expected him to stay there with me the whole time. It's not like the Ronald McDonald House is the most sought-after honeymoon destination, know what I mean?

For a minute, I let my mind wander to another reality. A reality in which we sue the OB and get a huge settlement. Jake and I have all the money in the world and can go anywhere we want. I've never been out of the country, even to Canada. Not as if I'd know what to do once I got there. Eat maple syrup and watch a hockey game?

I think if I could choose anywhere to honeymoon, I'd pick something like Hawaii but out of the country, just so I can say I left the States. The Bahamas might be nice. I'm not sure. Do you need a passport to get there, or is it one of those things like Puerto Rico or whatever?

Man, I'm so stupid. Here I am thinking of a big fancy honeymoon, and Jake and I are so poor we couldn't even buy passport photos.

Guess we'll be staying local after all.

My daydream dies away like a cheap Fourth of July sparkler, and I realize that Grandma Lucy is still going at it. I wonder if that woman ever gets laryngitis.

"Jesus took the little child up in his lap," she's telling us, and I can see now that other people are fidgeting. Part of me wants to just tell Jake *come on, let's get out of here*, but part of me wants to hear more. Because even though I still think she's crazy, there's something deep inside that's telling me to listen. Or maybe that's wishful thinking. Maybe I'm just hoping for some kind of heavenly message in a bottle.

That would be nice. A direct word from God telling me Natalie's going to be just fine. Or the other way around, a message saying she's going to die and I don't need to feel guilty about that stupid DNR. A message that none of this was my fault, even though I might not even believe God himself on that point.

Grandma Lucy's got this Holy Spirit sway going on in her hips, which makes me wonder if she was a dancer when she was young. I'm surprised when I find she's still harping on those thick-skulled disciples, but she says, "And he told the twelve, 'The kingdom of heaven belongs to the children.'" As soon as she says the words, I can see it. You're going to think I'm the one who's batty now, but I couldn't make this up even if I wanted to.

Even if I needed to just to prove my own sanity.

I see him. God. Jesus. Whatever you want to call him. I know the real historical person didn't look like those illustrations in children's story-book Bibles, except now he does. In my mind. The glowing robe, the brown beard, everything. He's white as a singer in a boy band, too, but he's got her on his lap. Not some nameless child like Grandma Lucy seems to think.

No, her. My Natalie. My baby girl.

Except she's not a baby, she's ... I don't know. Five? Six? The age you'd be around the time you'd start losing your first tooth. Because she's missing her two front ones. I can tell because her entire face is lit up in a smile. And when I say *lit up*, I'm not using a figure of speech. I mean her face is literally glowing, but when I get a better look, I realize the light's actually coming from him. He's got his arms around her, and he's gazing at her. He's not even looking down at her. He's holding her there on his lap, but she's right at eye level with him. If I were to tell you about his eyes, you won't even believe me. I mean, I know there are movie stars or whatnot and everyone's like *man, they've got such gorgeous eyes*. Well this is totally different. Those eyes, his eyes — it's like they could gaze at her forever and never lose a single ounce of love. Admiration. Then it hits me.

He's proud of my daughter. God. Jesus, whoever this shiny guy I'm seeing is, he's actually proud of Natalie. I mean, I'm not surprised that he loves her so much, but that affection ... so tender.

And then she looks at me, those almond eyes. Her skin is dark like mine, but her black hair is soft and silky like her grandmother's. If any of this is real, if I remember any of this after I'm done wigging out, I know that my stomach is going to drop those few inches every single time I think about the way she looks at me.

I can't figure out why I'm crying, why the tears are streaming down my cheeks. They're hot, too. Like streams of lava. Except it doesn't hurt. Not physically. What gets me is the emotional pain. That fist-in-your-gut kind of *whoosh* that knocks the wind right out of you. I feel that now. I feel that when she looks at me. Because she loves me so much. I can see that. This little girl who's never once smiled at me, who's never once given any indication that she has a clue who I am, she's there on his lap just beaming at me. Like I'm her favorite person in the world.

And she's so gorgeous. So. Stinking. Gorgeous. Just beautiful, and I don't mean the kind of girl who would wear a five-hundred-dollar dress and twirl a baton in front of a panel of judges to get a trophy. This is far more real. Far more lasting. She's got joy and innocence and youthful energy just gushing out of her, and that's what makes her so perfect.

I adore her. It hits me like a wall of heat when you open up the oven to pull out your mother-in-law's golden-topped casserole. I adore this child. So much so that it's like the feeling is being squeezed out of my chest by someone's fist, like they're wringing my heart out and I'm pretty sure I'm going to die but that's ok because now I've seen who she really is.

Except that's not right either, because even though I'm spun out on Holy-Ghost hallucinogens, I'm still sober enough to know that I have a sick little baby at home who doesn't smile, doesn't acknowledge me, doesn't even like to be cuddled by anyone, deity or not. Then that wall of heat I just mentioned turns into something more akin to a steam roller, and I realize *she must be dead.*

That's what this vision means. Natalie died while we were wasting time at church, so now she's in heaven, where apparently she's destined to live out the rest of eternity as a perpetual kindergartner. That's what the verse Granny Lady quoted meant. *Refusing to be comforted because her children are no more.*

No more. My heart repeats the phrase with each beat. *No more. No more.*

My daughter is no more.

What other explanation could there be? Now it's a different kind of tear rolling down my cheeks. The grieving kind. I know because I feel one splash onto my forearm, and it's only the mourning tears that ever splash. So I go back to wishing I were dead. Except now it's because my heart is dripping with so much despair, not love, and there's nothing left for me here on earth but to go and join my daughter — now perfect — in heaven, if God will even accept me there after all that I've done.

CHAPTER 13

Jake's got his arm around me, and I'm sure he means well.
Sure that in his mind, it's the perfectly reasonable reaction when
your brand-new wife is sitting next to you bleeding tears out her
eye sockets. I'm not making any noise. Since we're in the back
pew, I doubt anyone notices me unless it's Grandma Lucy. I
wonder, does she know? Does she realize what she's just done to
me, or is she so Holy Spirit stoned she can't pay attention to
anything else?

Refusing to be comforted because her children are no more.
That's the depressing verse I had to memorize at Bible quizzing.
The one I could never get why a bunch of teenagers like us would
have to know by heart.

Refusing to be comforted ...

Except now all Grandma Lucy seems to be able to talk about
is comfort. She's used the phrase *balm in Gilead* — which I
remember from high school English class — twice already, and it
doesn't sound like she's going to let up anytime soon. I think she's
planning to shove comfort down all our throats before she'll ever
relinquish that mic.

"I will heal her," she's saying now, as if she's turned herself into God's direct mouthpiece. "I will guide her and restore comfort to her," and my clammy hands and hummingbird-wings heart make me realize that she still talking about me, except now I don't know what it means. What kind of comfort can I expect if Natalie's in heaven and I'm not?

"Then you will call, and the Lord will answer. You will cry for help and he will say, 'Here am I.'" Something about what she says — or maybe it's more the way she says it — makes me wonder if my interpretation wasn't entirely accurate. Because if my daughter's really dead like I thought, I know in the center my soul that I would be just like that woman in the Bible verse, refusing to be comforted. Except that's not how I feel right now as Grandma Lucy keeps one hand raised up like an eighty-year-old rock star. Like that old dude with the huge lips, the one who did that Super Bowl show a while ago. But her words bring me nothing but comfort. I know I once said it would be a good thing when my daughter dies, but that was before I saw her. The real her. So I start to think that maybe that vision I got wasn't a picture of Natalie in heaven. Maybe it was more like a picture of her soul, of the little girl she would have been if it hadn't been for that brain hemorrhage. Or maybe — do I dare hope? — maybe that's the picture of the little girl she's going to grow into one day. Not just in heaven when of course everyone's perfect. But right here on earth.

"Everlasting joy will crown your head. Sorrow and sighing will flee away. Then you will find your joy in the Lord, for he has endowed you with a crown of splendor. For his salvation will last forever, and his righteousness will never fail."

My tears have stopped, for now at least, and I realize that this stranger, this Grandma Lucy lady with her above-the-waist slacks and ridiculously oversized collar has given me something that no doctor or nurse or pediatric specialist ever could.

Hope.

"He will shelter you with his strong and mighty love. You don't need to be afraid. The valley of the shadow of death holds nothing to fear, for he is with you. He is there, pouring his love into your weary heart. So don't lose courage. Don't fear the shadows. Just when you think the darkness will consume you forever, he will make your night shine like the noonday sun. Let those who walk in the dark, those who are crouching in fear in the night of despair, let them trust in the name of the Lord who hides you in the shadow of his hands. Even in the midst of trial and storm, his unfailing love for you will never diminish."

And I realize then as Grandma Lucy pauses that I don't want her to be done. I need to know more. All this about comfort, it must mean Natalie's going to be ok. Right? Isn't that what you would take away from her whole batty speech? But what if my first idea was right? What if Natalie's already died? I glance over at Jake. His mom would have called by now, right?

So I don't quite know how I feel as Grandma Lucy sheepishly hands the microphone back to the pastor. I didn't notice earlier how short she was. If I were to stand next to her, she wouldn't come past my shoulder. I still can't place why it feels like I've met her before. Part of me wants to talk to her. Wants to ask her what it all meant, but what if I'm wrong? What if she doesn't even know who I am? What if she has no clue about Natalie or any of that?

Then why would she have said any of those things?

The pastor gives a brief dismissal, and I stand on shaky legs. I've got to hold on to the back of the pew to keep my balance. I don't look at Jake. He'll think I'm nuts. He puts his arm around me. Protective. He's ready to go. Probably afraid of keeping Mama waiting any longer. But I don't want to leave. Not yet. I glance at the front of the church. I just want to get one more look at Grandma Lucy. If she sees me, if she makes eye contact, I think I'll know. I'll understand what she was trying to tell me.

Except she's hugging the pastor's wife, and Jake's got the keys in his hand, and my stomach's growling in anticipation, but my skin's prickled with worry about Patricia and what she'll say if we're late for lunch.

I don't shake Jake's arm off me. I don't walk up the aisle. I don't talk to Grandma Lucy. But as Jake leads me out the church, there's one single question swirling around my brain.

What if that bat-crazy lady wasn't talking to me at all?

PART TWO:

Patricia

CHAPTER 14

"Tiffany, I didn't know you'd washed that hoodie already." That's the first thing Patricia says to me when I walk into my trailer, and she's staring at the formula stain I got on it yesterday.

I don't know why I'm surprised. Patricia says things like that all the time, and usually I don't let it get under my skin. But she's so good at them, those subtle jabs. I can't complain to Jake, because he doesn't see them. He grew up that way, grew up with a mom who expressed herself in haiku insults like, "Oh, good. Your skin's really cleared up." And she'd be referring to the big zit on his nose that was getting smaller but she'd be staring at the massive breakout on his chin, and it takes someone as naïve and docile as Jake not to see the bitterness infused into each little micro-observation.

I shrug and straighten out my milk-stained hoodie. "Yeah, well, I would have started a load of laundry earlier, but I thought you would need it this morning to dry out a few of those wrinkles."

Jake's not saying anything — he never does — and Patricia's smiling so sweetly, probably because she knows she's got perfect skin. She scrunches up her eyes, and I'm sure she's taking in my own complexion and that's why she purses her lips together so smugly. "I'm sorry lunch isn't ready yet, but I had to guess what time you'd be home."

She raises her eyebrow at Jake, still with that sucking-on-a-lemon pucker to her lips, and he just gives her a sheepish smile and says, "Sorry 'bout that."

The food is on the table by the time I've changed out of my dirty sweatshirt, and Natalie's asleep, so I know we'll eat in peace. It's nothing like they said it would be, this new-baby experience.

The mommy magazines talked about babies demanding all your attention, but unless it's her feeding time or she needs her airway suctioned out or her apnea monitor's beeping at us, Natalie's just there. Like a piece of furniture. A piece of furniture that's cost the state over a half million dollars in medical bills by now. I'm just glad no one expects us to handle that with Jake's thirty-hour-a-week job making change behind a grungy cash register.

Patricia's been here for two months now, and she still hasn't cooked the same meal twice. It sounds impressive, but she manages it so that everything tastes the same no matter what she makes. I'm serious. She's like a short-order cook at a ho-hum diner. Did I tell you she serves rice at every single meal? It's not even like you'd get at a Chinese restaurant where it's all sticky and gooey and kind of sweet. Nope. We're talking brown, long-grain, super healthy. She doesn't add salt or anything. And it doesn't matter what else she's cooked. Chicken and dumplings with a side of rice. Potato and veggie casserole with a side of rice. Rice with lasagna? Yeah, that's how we roll with Patricia in the kitchen.

So lunch today is sort of a sloppy joe casserole with pasta, and we've got our mandatory scoop of plain rice on the side. It's like she's afraid we're all starving. She makes enough for leftovers, and then she's got this whole system set up for who can eat what when. It's like breaking into a bank vault just to sneak anything out of the fridge. I gave up trying weeks ago.

"So? You went to church today?" Patricia's voice lilts upward in a little disapproving tone as she eyes her son.

Jake nods as he shoves another spoonful of rice into his face. It's one of his quirks. He eats just about everything with a spoon. Even his spaghetti, which is about as gross to watch as it sounds.

I force myself not to squirm in my chair. I'm not a junior-high kid getting interrogated for cutting class. But Patricia's scowling at us like we've been caught smoking weed in the school bathroom.

"And how did you like it?" She's smiling at me now. When I first met her, I thought that smile meant she accepted me, that she enjoyed my company and wanted to get to know me better. I almost laugh to think about that now.

"It was pretty good." The only reason I say this is because I know it will upset her more than if I whine or complain. Besides, I haven't had the chance yet to sort through how I feel about that whole Grandma Lucy business.

Natalie makes a little noise from her bassinette in the living room. She's not even fussy, but Patricia scoots back her chair with a melodramatic sigh, like she's the Queen of stinking England forced to endure a rock concert in her honor.

"I'll get her," I say, and I give an attempt at that sickening sweet smile. I'm not the expert at it that she is, but I'm a fast study.

Patricia waves me away and picks up my baby. "No, no. I wouldn't expect you to inconvenience yourself."

I'm getting just as good at this game as she is, and I reach out and take my child. "You worked so hard in the kitchen getting lunch ready. Why don't you let me have her for a while. It's no trouble at all."

She frowns at me, but I'm holding Natalie, so what's she going to do?

"I'm surprised you don't have more of an appetite," Patricia says, and that's how I know I've won this round. When Patricia makes a comment about my weight or eating habits, it's only because she's run out of anything else to say. And it doesn't bother me, not in the least. I read all about it in those mommy mags. By summer time, I'll be ready to wear those cute backless tees that would make Patricia look like an AARP streetwalker if she tried them on herself. That's why her comments about my extra baby fat mean nothing to me.

Absolutely nothing.

We chew and swallow in silence, and I only have to get up from the table three times to suction out Natalie's throat. If you haven't seen the kind of machine she needs, imagine a tiny vacuum cleaner connected to a long, skinny tube. The tube part's called a Yankauer, which I never know how to spell, but the way you pronounce is a perfect match for its job description. Just picture the Queen of England saying it in her stuck-up accent. *A Yankauer.* Because it yonks the saliva right out of your throat.

"So the baby's doctor appointment is this Wednesday?" Patricia asks. She never uses Natalie's name, which makes me happy, truth be told. Jake wanted to name our daughter after his mom, and I think he must have told Patricia that at some point because she gets the lemon face nearly every time she hears the word *Natalie*, and she refuses to say it herself.

Another point for me.

The funny thing is I didn't even settle on that name until Natalie was about to undergo her surgery. She spent the first two weeks of her life as *Baby Girl Franklin*. That's what the hospital HUC entered her in as on the computer system. And all of Natalie's paperwork and medicine and even that little tag she wore around her ankle called her that.

It's funny because I thought naming someone was some real official process, but we didn't get around to the birth certificate paperwork until a few days before Natalie was discharged from the NICU. They were supposed to do it way back at Orchard Grove, right there at County Hospital, but having me sign a piece of paper so my baby could get her own Social Security number wasn't high on anyone's priority list at that point. So as far as the government is concerned, she was *Baby Girl Franklin* for the first six weeks of her life, even though I settled on Natalie by week two.

It came about when Jake and I were having dinner in the cafeteria, and dinner was always worse than lunch. At lunch, they made it a point to cook well for all the nurses and doctors. By the evening, the only people left at the hospital were a few night workers and folks like us, which usually meant that we got some sort of reheated leftovers. I don't even remember what we were having that particular evening. It's a small wonder that I complain about Patricia's food being bland after I survived those six weeks in Seattle.

Jake and I were pretty tense that day. We'd just come out from this big meeting. When I say big, I mean just about anybody with a title was there: the NICU doctor, the charge nurse, Natalie's primary care nurse, the social worker, the occupational therapist, the intestinal specialist, and the lung guy all met with us in this big NICU conference room. I remember thinking the decorations there were atrocious, totally out of place. It was all those staged photographs of dressed-up babies. You know the ones I mean, like when there's a little girl with a sunflower hat sitting in a pot, or a newborn in a ladybug getup taking a nap in a pile of rose petals. The ones that really trip me out are when they dress up the babies like angels and take pictures of them sleeping on white puffy clouds. I mean, do these photographers think about what they're doing? Do they think angel-babies are cute? Have they ever seen an unconscious newborn who stopped breathing an hour after birth?

Anyway, all these specialists wanted to talk with me, and Jake came too. I already knew what the meeting would be about, so I was ready for it. The gut guy had been lecturing me about it for a couple days now. Mansplained to me how Natalie still wasn't able to suck on anything so it was time to put in a G-tube. It was the first I'd heard of the thing. Even at the assisted living place where I worked, by the time someone got too out of it to swallow, they were shipped off to a nursing home. In my opinion, Natalie didn't need something as drastic as surgery until we figured out if her swallowing would improve by itself. Maybe I was in denial, I don't know. Like you could blame me if I was. I told him I didn't want to do the procedure, and that's why he set up this special meeting in the board room with the creepy infant photos.

Everyone there started talking over each other, telling us what a good move it would be for Natalie to have the surgery. We could take her home sooner since otherwise they couldn't discharge her from the NICU until she could breastfeed or take a bottle. It would be more sanitary too instead of having the nurses thread that catheter into her nose and down her throat, which always makes me gag when I think about it.

The gut doctor expected it to be an open and shut case. He thought I'd sign off right away once I had that many people telling me what to do. He obviously had no idea who he was dealing with. We're talking about the girl whose drunk foster dad once staggered into her room in the middle of the night and tried to shove his hard, smelly self against her. But I rolled over and hammer-fisted him in the groin and swore I'd call 911 if he came within five feet of me again, and the next day I told the school counselor and was out of that house by dinnertime. So I think I can handle myself against a sixty-year-old doctor and his room full of cronies with fancy initials after their names, titles that don't mean their possessors have an ounce of street cred or know what's best for my baby.

Anyway, I left that meeting still convinced we didn't need to rush the surgery. I mean, it's not like Natalie was in danger of starving without the tube. I think it just would have made the nurses' job easier, and that's exactly what I told the gut doctor and everyone else he brought in to manipulate me. But Jake, well, that was another story. I mean, we're talking about the boy who probably hasn't disobeyed an authority figure since preschool. That's partly why I'm still surprised when I wake up and remember he's my husband. What did we see in each other? I'm still not sure I'll ever figure that one out.

Of course, he and I weren't married yet, not when we had that big interview with all those hot shots. It reminded me of that period in history you learn about in school. You know, the Interrogation or whatever they call it. No, the Inquisition, that's what it is. And that's what got me mad, how forceful they'd been. Like just because they were the doctors we had to do whatever they said. Only Jake wasn't upset, and that's why I was ticked off at him in that empty cafeteria.

"Doesn't it bother you they're pushing a procedure she doesn't even need?"

He stared at his plate and refused to meet my eyes. "I don't know. Maybe."

"Maybe what?" I hate it when he mumbles.

"Maybe it's a good idea after all."

"Oh, yeah. Cutting a hole in her gut's going to really improve her quality of life, I'm just sure of it." I didn't care who heard me. The only people nearby were a cafeteria worker wiping tables, another tired-looking couple with a whiny toddler, and a few single guys in scrubs.

Jake shrugged and shoveled something or other into his mouth. After growing up with Patricia's cooking, he probably felt right at home forcing down that cafeteria food every day. "The doctors all seem to think it's a good idea," he said.

"I don't care what they think."

Didn't he understand? Couldn't he see? This wasn't about what was or wasn't a good idea. This was about who was in control of our daughter's health. He might be ready to roll over and let someone else play God with her little six-pound body, but I wasn't about to give up that easily. The fact that he was made me sick.

Jake didn't say anything. That boy's like a deer in the headlights when anyone within a twenty-foot radius gets angry. I swear, if we go out somewhere and he hears a couple shouting at each other, he wants to curl up in a fetal position and wet himself.

That's why I had to try so hard to probe the fight out of him. "Or maybe you don't care what happens to her."

Low blow? Maybe. But it was necessary, even if he didn't

82

quite deserve it.

"Why would you think that?" he asked, and I wished he'd start yelling. Cussing. Anything to show me there was a living being with genuine emotions behind that frozen-looking face of his. "What do you think I'm doing here?"

I shrugged and glanced at the card we swiped in the cafeteria to get our daily food ration. "Enjoying free room and board?"

He was fuming in his own understated way. I could tell by the way his eyes narrowed and one of them twitched just a little. "That's not why I came." His voice was so steady. I would die if I had to keep such a tight lock on my emotions. I guess that's why I'm the screamer and he's the deflector, but man, I hate the way he tenses up whenever I get upset. It's like he just wants the fight to be over so he'll say anything he thinks I want to hear. Drives me insane.

"All I know is you didn't come here for her. If you did, you'd actually hold her when you went to the NICU instead of sitting around playing stupid games on your phone."

"It's how I de-stress." His voice was getting whiny, which is how I knew I was about to lose my head.

"Stress? You want to talk about who's stressed?" One of the men in scrubs was staring at me, and the weary-looking mother gave me a sympathetic half-smile. The mommy equivalent of the black power salute. "I just squeezed a six-pound child out of my vagina," I told Jake. "It was bloody. It was messy. It hurt worse than passing a golf-ball-sized kidney stone while getting your wisdom teeth yanked out with no anesthetic. Then I got loaded on a jet and flown here where I'm stuck until Natalie gets better. And the doctors are pushing for something that I don't think she …"

"Wait, what did you say?" Jake's eyes had lost their glazed-over shine, and he leaned toward me.

"I said the doctors are a bunch of idiots full of …"

"No," he interrupted. "About her. What did you call her?"

I hadn't realized I'd let it slip. It was Jake's fault for getting me so worked up in the first place. "Nothing."

"No," he pressed, "you called her something. What did you say?"

I leveled my eyes at him. "Nothing."

If he knew anything, he'd shut up, but no. He had to keep poking. "Natalie. You said Natalie. I heard you."

Well it sure beats Patricia, I wanted to yell at him, but something stopped me. He'd caught me off guard. I wasn't ready for this conversation. Wasn't ready to share her name with anybody yet, not even her father. But I couldn't deny it. Then I was the one staring at my plate like a guilty child caught copying down her foster parents' ATM pin number on a piece of unfinished homework. I wasn't sure what he'd say. He'd been pushing me to name her Patricia since we found out she was a girl, but I could never bring myself to agree. Whenever he brought it up at the Ronald McDonald house, I just pretended to be too tired to think about it. *We'll name her when she's ready to come home,*

I said. A defense mechanism. Like a stray dog you bring in off the streets and your foster mom warns you not to settle on a name because someone's going to come and claim him, and the minute you give him a name the harder it will be to let him go when the time comes.

So I thought I'd hold off on the naming thing until she got discharged. Everyone in the NICU was happy with calling her *Baby Girl Franklin*, so that's what I was going to do, too.

Then I had a dream one night. You probably think I'm some kind of psycho by now, some bat-crazy chick who sees visions in her sleep and hallucinates while Holy-Ghost grannies stand up and testify on Open Mic Sunday. But I'm serious. It was one of my first nights at the Ronald McDonald house, and I went to bed wondering if it would have been better if my baby had died. If she hadn't survived the brain hemorrhaging. Because she was so weak and frail, and she didn't even open her eyes. She was just knocked out all the time, and the neuro guy told me her brain scans were crazy irregular and it would take a miracle for her to recover from that extensive of an injury. I may not have a science degree, but I know that when a medical specialist uses a word like *miracle*, things aren't looking that hot.

So I went to bed that night thinking about how much easier life would be if she had just died while we were still at County Hospital in Orchard Grove. Easier for her, I mean, because most of the doctors assumed she was going to die anyway, and she couldn't be very comfortable in the NICU with all those tubes shoved down her and poking into every major part of her body. Well that night I had a dream. Jake was there, and he was all excited because the doctor had just called and said they'd found a cure for our baby. The only catch was he had to take her to the hospital right away. It's funny, looking back, because she'd been in the hospital her whole life by then, but in my dream we were home in Orchard Grove. So I let him take her, and the hospital was only a few minutes away, so I sat around the trailer waiting for Jake to come back, and I wondered what it would be like once our baby was cured.

And then there they were, since in a dream you don't have to wait for anything, and Jake handed me this beautiful smiling girl. He was all excited, but the minute he put that kid in my arms, I got this creepy feeling start to zing up my spine. "What's this?" I asked, and he was grinning as big as a fool and said, "Don't you recognize your own baby?"

I said, "This isn't my baby."

And Jake said, "Of course it is. See? The doctors healed her." He looked all happy like a puppy about to get a treat, but I couldn't shake that feeling of spiders crawling up my skin.

"What do you mean they healed her?"

Jake stopped smiling and put on his best mansplaining expression and said, "Well, when I took her to the hospital, the doctors took a blood sample to get out some of her DNA, and they cloned her. They used a special solution so she developed to the right age, and they made sure there wasn't any brain hemorrhage this time. Isn't it great?"

I couldn't even hold the thing anymore, that smiling Gerber baby with the fat legs and chubby cheeks. I dropped her in Jake's arms and said, "Where is my daughter?" Because even though this was a dream and even though Jake obviously thought I was an idiot when it came to scientific reasoning, I understood that just because you make a clone that doesn't mean the original stops existing. He said he didn't know what I was talking about, and I got frantic. I was screaming and clawing at his face and screeching, "Where is my baby? Get me my baby!"

Then I saw her. Don't ask me how, because I was still with Jake in the trailer, and she was in the hospital. But I saw her, just lying there in a black plastic trash bag in a grimy bathroom, and she wasn't crying because she wasn't cured and didn't have the lung capacity to let out the faintest little whimper, but I could sense how scared she was. How terrified and lonely. She was cold. Cold and abandoned, and even though I could see her there clear as day, I couldn't get to her because I was stuck in that stinking trailer. I was punching Jake by then. I've never done that in real life, not to him, but in my dream I was whaling on him, and I don't even know what he'd done with the cloned baby by then because I didn't care about her. I just wanted my daughter. And I was screaming to try to get to her.

Natalie!

Natalie!

Natalie!

I couldn't tell you how or why that name popped into my

brain, but I woke up and was still screaming it in my mind. My heart was probably going a hundred and forty beats per minute. I had sweat on the back of my neck and under my boobs, and for a minute or two I was so disoriented I thought I was still in the dream and my baby had been dumped into a trashcan in a hospital bathroom. But then I talked myself down from freaking out. Reminded myself that Natalie was in the NICU being taken care of by a team of competent nurses, and I'd go over first thing in the morning before they changed shift and get a full report about her night. But something changed after that. I stopped going down all of those what-if bunny trails. You know what I mean. What if Natalie hadn't stopped breathing? What if I hadn't been living in the middle of nowhere and had delivered her in a real hospital where there was a NICU ready to rescue her if something bad happened?

What if I hadn't messed everything up?

What happened to my daughter was a tragedy and a mistake, and if I ever figure out that the doctor or the hospital did something wrong, you can bet your leather-bound Bible that I'm going to sue the shirt off their backs. I guess in a way, that dream helped me come to terms with the fact that my baby girl was sick and that there was no such thing as a miracle cure. But it did something else, too. All day I kept thinking about the way I'd screamed her name when I saw her lying there all cold and abandoned.

Natalie. Where in the world had my mind come up with that? I didn't know anybody called Natalie. I can't even remember any movies or TV show characters with that name. But from then on I thought of her as Natalie, which is how I got in trouble with Jake.

Of course, when I slipped up and used her name while we were having dinner, I didn't tell him about the dream or anything like that. I tried to play it down and just said something like, "I don't know. It's just something that's kind of been growing on me."

I was expecting him to whine about how he really thought we should name her Patricia after his mom, who I hadn't even met by then, but he didn't. He had this strange expression on his face, so for a minute I almost expected him to start blubbering. Instead he pulled himself together and then reached for his phone. I rolled my eyes. It was so like him to give up right in the middle of an argument and hide behind that tiny plastic screen. I was still mad, but I didn't have the energy left for a proper fight, so I just planned to finish dinner and get back to Natalie's bedside by shift change. But after swiping a few things, Jake said, "Here, I want to show you something."

He passed me the phone, but it wasn't one of his stupid candy games. It was some kind of note-taking app. And just a quick glance was all it took for me to see that he'd made probably a hundred different entries in the past two weeks.

"I started writing her letters," he told me. "I was going to make a record about her time at the hospital, and when she got discharged I was thinking of having a copy printed. Maybe give it to her for her sweet sixteen or something."

Every once in a while, even now that we're married, I look over at Jake and have this kind of freak-out moment like *Holy cow, I don't even know who this man is.* It happened to me there in the cafeteria. The letters he wrote our daughter were really private. I couldn't bring myself to read a full paragraph. He had all kinds of pet names for her, ended just about every single sentence with one, actually. *Honey, princess, baby girl.* But then something caught my eye.

"Natalie?"

He was blushing now and squirming in his seat across from me. "I didn't know what name you'd settle on, so I figured I'd just throw something in there, and then when she came home I could replace it with her real one."

"So you picked Natalie?" I had goosebumps on my back again, except they weren't the creepy sort this time. He looked at me, and something passed between us, which sounds silly to say, but there's no other way to describe it. We didn't talk about the surgery anymore that night, but the next day when the gut guy came by to pressure me yet again about the surgery, I told him I'd go ahead and sign the consent form.

And then I went over to the HUC at the front desk and asked her to change my baby's ankle tag from *Baby Girl* to *Natalie.*

CHAPTER 15

Patricia is cleaning the dishes after lunch, which is always a fun little skirmish. It usually involves me offering to help and her refusing three or four times, each of us on our best behavior. The ritual inevitably ends with her complaining about how she's the only one who does any work around the house. Of course, in true Patricia style, she never actually complains, and she manages her not-complaining in such a polite, gracious manner that if you get mad at her or annoyed, you're the wicked witch instead of her.

"It will be nice for Tiffany when your daughter gets big enough to help out around the kitchen." She's not really talking to me, but she's not talking directly to Jake either, so neither of us respond. Unfortunately, Patricia doesn't take easily to being ignored. "When the twins were born, my mother had already died, and my mother-in-law never ate properly so was too sickly to travel. I sometimes wonder how young people manage these days without any outside support."

Of course, we all know she doesn't really wonder that, because when Jake and his sister were born, Patricia's husband spent his eighty hours a week at the office (not that I could blame the poor fool), and there was nobody else around to help her out.

She lets out a dramatic sigh. "It's a good thing I've been taking calcium since I was a teenager. My sister never got in the habit, so now her osteoporosis is so bad she has to hire a girl to do her cleaning for her."

In Patricia's mind, any housewife who hires someone else to do the cleaning for her, whether by choice or laziness or sickness, isn't even worthy of her title. Neither is a mom who sends her kid to daycare. Fortunately, this is one of those times when Patricia is just happy to have a captive audience. We don't have to engage with her or even agree as long as we let her vent.

"That's what I've been telling Abby ever since she got so serious with that computer science boy." Abby is Jake's twin sister, who thankfully is enough of a black sheep that she absorbs the bulk of Patricia's ire. Not that I get how a first-year law school student could turn into such a disappointment while Jake the convenience store cashier is Patricia's pride and joy. Or maybe she complains to Abby just as much about him. It wouldn't surprise me.

"I told her that she needs to focus on her studies. That boy is nothing but an unhealthy distraction." This rant is familiar enough that I already know about *that boy* and how he's doing some sort of postgraduate work in computer science and probably has a higher IQ than me, Jake, and Patricia combined.

"They've only known each other for three semesters, and they're already talking about getting married once she's out of law school." Her eyes are wide as she shakes her head in convincing bewilderment. I find this somewhat humorous given the fact that Jake and I hooked up, shacked up, got pregnant and then hitched all in the same calendar year.

I feel sorry for Abby, truth be told. From what I gather, Patricia pegged her daughter as the smart one and Jake as the disappointment before the kids were toilet trained. Patricia pushed Abby, which explains the first-year law student status, and basically ignored Jake, which explains the nine-dollar-an-hour cashier job. The downside to being the genius in the family is that Abby will never live up to Patricia's expectations. I've never even met the poor girl, but I see it so clearly. Eventually Abby's going to marry and have kids, whether with this computer science genius or someone else. And Patricia will shake her head and cluck that overused tongue of hers and say, "It's just so sad that Abby has to be away from the children. When the twins were that little, I refused to work outside the home." And if by some insane chance Abby postpones her law degree or takes time off work to be that stay-at-home Martha Stewart wanna-be that Patricia expects of her, there will be just as much headshaking and just as much tongue clucking, except this time it will be, "When I was raising the twins, I kept up my nursing license. I didn't put my whole life on hold. That's the reason why so many children are growing up spoiled."

Thankfully, Patricia isn't as talkative today as she can sometimes be. When the dishes are done and my kitchen is scrubbed senseless, she reminds me that it's almost time for my daughter's tube feeding, then she takes Natalie and retreats to her room, and I can finally breathe again.

CHAPTER 16

It's like kicking off your sneakers and unsnapping your bra after an eight-hour shift at the old-people's home. That's how I feel when Patricia takes her once-a-week nap. She's not religious or anything. I'm sure that woman would find fault with Mary, Joseph, and the baby Jesus if she got the chance. But every Sunday, she sets her timer and takes an hour-long nap. Not fifty-nine minutes. Not sixty-one.

It's the most relaxing hour of my entire week.

Natalie's had her formula and is quiet for the most part. She's got her apnea monitor on, and I don't expect her to need anything for another thirty minutes or so. That's usually when she has to be suctioned out after a tube feed. The doctors think she has some reflux, which is bad for her long-term lung health, but there's not much they can do about it right now. We have her in her car-seat insert by our bed so Jake's mom can nap quietly in her room. It's funny how fast we stopped calling it the nursery as soon as Patricia moved in.

Jake and I are snuggling under the blankets. He's the big spoon, even though I'm two inches taller and about twenty pounds heavier. At least I am right now, but that will change eventually.

There's no rush. If I can wear my swimsuit by Fourth of July, I'll be content. Maybe I'd be a little more freaked out about things if Natalie hadn't gone through what she did, but when you've seen your kid at all the possible variations of blue-gray on the spectrum, that extra baby fat doesn't seem like the death sentence you once thought it would be.

Jake's quiet, and I'm quiet, and it sort of reminds me of the night before Natalie's G-tube surgery. It had been a pretty hectic day. When I told Sandy about the procedure, she dropped everything and flew from Boston to Seattle. I don't even want to guess what she paid for a last-minute ticket like that. I don't know how she managed it on her husband's pastor's salary, but she came by that afternoon and rented a car. I hadn't said anything to her about it, but she must have known that after three weeks staying at the Ronald McDonald house with no way to get around I could use a shopping spree. I don't even remember what I got that day. Pads and underwear, I'm sure, and some cereal and things we could keep in our room for easy snacks. But I wasn't used to that kind of running around, plus I was worried about Natalie's surgery in the morning. Sandy was staying with a couple she and her husband met all the way back in their seminary days, so Jake and I had the evening to ourselves. I was so tired I don't think I even made shift change that night.

"You worried?" he asked me, and his breath was hot on my shoulder while we spooned.

"A little." I hated the thought of Natalie having that procedure. Hated the thought of her getting knocked out by some anesthesiologist. I already regretted signing those papers. Maybe it wasn't just the surgery itself, either. Maybe it was because putting in the G-tube was a permanent solution, and I was still stupidly hoping for a quick and easy cure. A drowning sailor will hold onto anything he can get his hands on, right?

"I worry about her, too." It sounds like the regular sort of stuff two people would say when their child's about to have a major operation, but it really struck me that night because Jake didn't talk much those days. I mean, he doesn't talk much now, but it was worse back then, which is why I sometimes tried to drag him into an argument. I figured if I gave him a good fight to get all that extra stress out, he'd be a lot happier in the long run. Maybe his brain's just wired differently because it never worked.

But that's why the conversation we had that night stands out to me. He opened up a little. Shared some of his fears. Not about Natalie dying. Neither of us were ready to talk about heavy stuff like that yet. But about what had happened. And how guilty he felt.

"Do you ever think this is God's way of punishing you?" he asked me while we cuddled.

I was pretty surprised. Jake had never mentioned God before. His mom raised him without any religion, boasting that when he got older he'd have the freedom to choose any path of faith he wanted, but of course it just meant he didn't choose any path. As far as I knew until that night, he didn't even believe in God at all.

"I don't think it works that way," I lied. I didn't want to tell him about my own guilt and shame. About the David and

ALANA TERRY

Bathsheba reference I'd read from Elder Tom. About those chastity pledges I took back in high school, years after I'd lost my virginity. That's the problem with those things. Your youth leaders tell you not to sleep around until you get married, make it out like that's the most sure-fire way to book your one-way ticket to hell, but they don't tell you how to do it. How to handle the boyfriend who keeps reminding you that if you don't put out he'll find someone who will. Seriously, I mean these people are so pro-life and all — and so am I — but if I'd gotten pregnant in high school, I probably would have had an abortion in secret just to keep proving to everyone at that church I was still on God's side. How backwards is that?

I guess you don't have to grow up in a real churchy foster home to pick up on that whole guilt thing. Jake was feeling it too, maybe even more than I was. "Sometimes I think God's mad at me." And he buried his head between my shoulder blades and I swear he started to cry. It was quiet so I couldn't hear him, and I acted like I didn't notice at first, but there were definitely tears. After a few minutes, it was stupid for me to keep pretending when both of us knew what was going on, so I rolled over and tried to cheer him up.

"Come on," I said. "You're like the most solid guy I know. You couldn't do anything to make God mad. You're too good a person for that."

He buried his face in his hands then, and that's when I started to get that worry pit growing deep in my gut. And I knew what he

97

was going to say before he said it because it sort of felt like I was floating up above our heads when he yanked the blanket over his face so he wouldn't have to look at me when he admitted, "I cheated on you."

I don't know if you've ever had someone come up to you and just throw their fist into your gut when you're not expecting it, but that's how it felt. I yanked the blankets off him. If he'd done something that horrible to me, he was sure as anything going to look at me when he confessed. "You did what?"

"I cheated on you." And he was sobbing, and the whole story came out, and it's not even that juicy. It was when I was on bedrest, he was stressed out because he was worried about the baby, and there was a girl from work, Charlene, who by the sound of it took advantage of him in that situation. She came over one night, brought some beers, *blah, blah, blah.* It's not that I wanted to hear the whole story, but after a statement like that, I was going to make him tell me every stinking detail.

But really, that's all there was. He said afterward he felt so bad that he sent her a text. Said some horrible things to her to make sure she'd never come around again. In a way it was a relief. It was the first time I'd seen him act like a jerk to anyone. It made me feel like I was dating a regular, normal guy, not some saint I didn't deserve and certainly could never hope to keep. Even the fact that he cheated on me wasn't as upsetting as you might think. Maybe if Natalie hadn't been about to undergo a major operation because the doctors were convinced she was so brain-damaged she'd never learn to swallow on her own, I might have been more upset.

Everything's relative, right? Besides, I'm no Mother Theresa. *Let him without sin cast the first stone*, or however that Bible quote goes.

"What about you?" Jake asked.

"What about me?"

"Have you ever … Did you ever want to …"

"No."

"No?"

"No." And the conversation ended there.

Thank God.

CHAPTER 17

Jake's sound asleep. He's just like his mom, Sunday naps and all. He's snoring loudly enough that there's no way I could drift off even if I wanted to. I've always hated naps though. What's the point when they make you feel so groggy and disoriented when you wake up?

It's two hours before Natalie needs another feeding, and my trailer is clean enough that the Queen of stinking England could stop by to use the toilet and I wouldn't feel embarrassed. I don't know what Patricia's got planned for dinner, but I can guarantee it's going to have a golden top, it's going to be served along with plain brown rice, and she isn't going to need or want my help.

Who would have thought being a new mom could be so dull?

I bundle Natalie up. It's not too cold out, mid-forties. The snow's falling pretty hard. It's probably stupid of me to have her out in weather like this, but I can't just stay cooped up in this trailer forever. Something about that church service today has given me cabin fever. I've got to get out. Patricia will pitch a royal fit if she sees me with Natalie tramping about in the middle of winter, but I checked the clock before she lay down for her nap. I have exactly thirty-seven minutes. Plenty of time to stretch my legs and get Natalie and myself both some fresh air.

I can't believe I'm walking around the trailer park in a snowstorm just for the fun of it. Do you remember when power walking used to be all the rage? I never understood it before, but it's starting to make sense now. The walking around outside part, not the whole *ball your fists and bend your arms at a ninety-degree angle* junk. Natalie's got this cheap stroller one of my co-workers at Winter Grove passed down to me. Her kids are all teenagers now, so that will tell you how old of a model it is. Nothing fancy like those ones you can strap a car seat into or anything, but it works. I wish it weren't so cold. I swear I've felt Natalie's forehead and cheeks at least five times since I left.

I'd love a more visually appealing neighborhood to walk around in, but it's over half a mile just to get out of the trailer park, and I only have thirty-two minutes left to get home, stash the stroller somewhere, and get Natalie out of her winter things. I feel like Cinderella keeping her eye on the clock before she has to rush back to her wicked step-mother's.

I suppose if I was like Jake and grew up with Patricia, I wouldn't see all her faults. I wouldn't care so much. I mean, I know he's not the sharpest crayon in the box, but I'm pretty convinced Jake thinks his mom is nice. *Nice* as in he's lucky to have someone like her. And the way she berates him, never directly, never right to his face, but man. I wouldn't put up with it for ten minutes if I were him. If it were my trailer and she were my mom, I would have thrown her out on her middle-aged *Buns of Steel* butt before the end of that first week.

Fish and company both stink after three days. I forget which one of my foster parents said that, and seeing as how I was a foster brat and therefore more like company instead of family, I wonder why she told me in the first place. I've got my cell phone in my pocket, and part of me thinks about checking in with Sandy. She's called me a few times lately, but that trailer's so small and the walls are so thin I never feel comfortable talking to her when Patricia's around. I should call her, but I know I won't. She's busy. She's got that little boy she adopted to take care of. I guess that makes him my foster brother. Not that those labels mean anything.

I check Natalie's cheeks one more time to make sure she's not getting too cold, and I think about those three days Sandy spent with me at the hospital when Natalie was having her G-tube surgery. It was like we'd only been apart for a week or two, when it was more like three years and I'd gone from a foster kid in Sandy's modest home in her perfect little suburban paradise to an unemployed welfare mom in a trailer park.

How's that for moving up in the world?

It's funny because by the time I was a senior in high school, I was so sick of Sandy babying me. It was always *tell me about your day* and *you look tired, are you sleeping all right*, and I hated that attention and smothering. Fast-forward three years, and all of a sudden I can't get enough of her mothering. I fell asleep on her shoulder once in Seattle. Can you believe that? It was the morning Natalie went in for her surgery, and the nurse told me I could wait at the Ronald McDonald house and they'd call me when it was over, but I didn't want to be that far away, so Sandy and I sat in the surgery area for four stinking hours. At one point, she said I looked tired and wrapped her arm around me, and the next thing I knew I had drool on my cheek and the nurse was there to say Natalie was in recovery and the surgery had been a success.

Man, I miss Sandy. I'd probably go postal if I tried to live with her again, but it would be nice to at least be in the same town or somewhere nearby. I just hate picking up the phone and calling someone. It feels so arrogant, like I expect her to drop everything and talk to me about all my stress and worries just because I made a little device of hers ring a couple times. And I know if I call she'd want to know about Natalie, and what is there to say? *She's not dead yet.* But there's been no measurable progress. She's not even gaining weight. The poor little thing weighs eight ounces more than she did at birth and that's all.

No change.

I wonder if that's going to be the story of Natalie's life, as long or as short as it is. She'll be eighteen years old, but instead of ordering her cap and gown or worrying about college tuition, I'll be pouring predigested formula down her G-tube. Measuring out her anti-seizure meds that knock her out for twenty-three hours of the day. Suctioning out her throat whenever she starts to choke on her own drool.

Thinking about the suction machine reminds me that I left it at home. And by the time I've turned around, Natalie's grunting in her sleep because her airway's getting clogged. If I had that Yankauer with me, she'd be comfortable in two seconds flat. As it is, I've got to rush all the way home in the snow, and now I'm the one who looks like a stupid power walking maniac.

At least I'm getting my exercise for the day.

Count every blessing, right?

CHAPTER 18

I arrive home before Natalie's breathing gets too wet, and I throw on the suction machine. It's so loud I'll probably go deaf before her first birthday. After I clear out her airway, I take a quick picture of her because she looks like a little Eskimo in her downy winter wrap-up. Once she's unbundled, I put her on her little buckle-in chair in the living room and plop down on the couch to post the photo online.

I'm trying to think of a grabby caption when my phone beeps. It's a message from Sandy. *How's my sweet girl today?* I'm not sure if she's asking about me or Natalie, so I tell her we're both fine and send her an attachment with the photo I just took.

What a tiny thing. Is she gaining weight? Sandy asks, and I have to love her for not lying through her teeth like most of my friends will when they see the photo. *She's getting so big! She looks so healthy! You're doing a great job!*

I give Sandy a brief reply because I really don't feel like having a long, drawn-out conversation over messenger. It's just such a pain waiting for someone's response, not knowing if they're in the middle of typing something or maybe they've gone out partying for the rest of the afternoon and won't get back to you until tomorrow night. Not that Sandy's the partying type. In fact, she's the most straight and stable person I know. I met her when I was fourteen, and I lived with her until I was eighteen, and that whole time I only saw her and her husband fight once. I mean, they bickered quite a bit, but most of that was good natured and just the way they interact with each other. But this was a real fight. I'm sure if Jake had been there he would have crawled into the corner and peed his pants.

I'm trying now to remember what it was. Something about one of their adopted daughters. Blessing, I think her name was. She was already out of the house by the time I moved in, but she still gave Carl and Sandy a ton of grief. Always either strung out on drugs or in recovery, and I probably shouldn't judge her because when that anonymous savior rescued me from the trash bin and I started my journey as a foster brat, I figure most people wouldn't have expected me to grow up and become anything more than a crack queen or heroin addict myself.

Well, Blessing had checked herself out of whatever recovery center she'd been in, and Carl and Sandy didn't know where she was. They'd already tried tracking her down in the usual spots, her no-good friends who were more than willing to shoot her up again or that uncle who pimped her out for drug money from the time she was in a training bra. But they couldn't find her anywhere. Carl's the nicest guy you can ever hope to meet. He's a pastor, so I guess he has to be kind and loving, but he was a professional football player for a couple years before that. Nice as he is, he's no pushover. I don't know too much about his upbringing, but he survived being a black kid in the South way back when, so you know he's got to have some street cred.

He was telling Sandy that Blessing was an adult now and responsible for her own actions, and if the two of them rescued her every single time she went off the deep end she'd never learn to take care of herself. Sandy wouldn't hear it. I'm sure in her mind, Blessing was still the scared little pre-teen who came into their lives so many years earlier with her trash bag full of hand-me-down clothes over one shoulder and a lifetime of emotional trauma sitting on top of the other. And Sandy was freaking out. I mean, that woman can yell when she sets her mind to it. But Carl's not the kind to stand hen-pecking either. And man, the two of them went at each other's throats. When they finished, Sandy knocked on my door. It was past bedtime, but I think she figured I was still awake. She came in and found me crying and asked, "What's the matter, sugar? Were we being too loud?"

I didn't know how to express how terrified I felt right then, because Carl and Sandy's home had felt like heaven to me. And Sandy sat down on my bed and started rubbing my back and said, "Talk to me, pumpkin," and I'm sure it took ten minutes for me to get out one coherent sentence, but I finally managed to tell her what I was scared of.

"You're going to get a divorce, and then I'll have to find a new home."

Sandy kept rubbing my back and explaining how she and Carl

made a promise before God to always love each other and always stay together, no matter how much they disagreed. And one day God would bring a Christian man into my life, and we'd make that same promise, and I had to remember that even when things got hard not to give up on our relationship. She made it sound simple. I'm surprised I wasn't so jaded by life at that point that I didn't laugh in her face. But I wanted to make Sandy happy, and I wanted to believe that it was true, that two people who fought could make up afterward and still have a pleasant marriage that didn't result in cracked ribs or ER visits or their foster kids getting whisked out of the home in the middle of the night. I wanted to believe Sandy when she said one day I'd meet a wonderful man, and even if we disagreed from time to time, we'd love each other just as much as she and her husband did.

See, I told you I was naïve.

CHAPTER 19

I sometimes wonder how Sandy did it. Took in so many of us foster kids, I mean. You've already heard what kind of person she is, how she's just so good and strong and loving. I don't think she yelled at me once the whole time I lived with her. Sure, there were the regular things, like I had to clean up my room or I couldn't go out paintballing with the youth group, and I got grounded a couple times for talking back, but if those things got her angry at me, it never showed.

It's funny, because I thought that in order to punish somebody you had to be mad at them. It sort of makes sense when you think about it, right? But Sandy punished me all the time, usually just for little slip-ups. Like if I didn't finish my homework on time I couldn't watch TV on the weekend. That kind of thing. And you might have grown up in a home where that was just the way it was, but the way I grew up, you didn't punish somebody unless you were really ticked off at them.

Sandy was different. That's why I feel like such a pathetic mom these days because even though Natalie hasn't done a single thing wrong in her entire life, I'm mad at her all the time. I don't yell or anything, and I'd never shake her or hit her. I'm not that much of a deadbeat. I'm just so upset with her for getting sick even though that's stupid because it's not her fault.

It's mine. My fault entirely. I'm the one who was so scared of a simple surgery. I mean, nobody's said it to my face, but I think it's pretty clear by now that if they'd cut Natalie out after the first ten or twenty hours of labor, she wouldn't have been in the birth canal long enough for her brain to start bleeding like that. The strange thing is that she was being monitored the whole time. There was no way for any of us to know there was a problem.

I've looked online a little bit at medical malpractice and stuff. I could probably find someone to try to sue the doctor who delivered her. But I signed the forms myself, put my signature right there on the page that said I was declining a C-section, so most likely it would just be a long, drawn-out process without any real results.

There are other reasons too, other things I've done that I wonder if they contributed to my daughter's problems, but I'd never ask a doctor. I don't want to admit it for one thing, and if it really was my fault, there's no chance I'd want to know. I'd take a settlement, though, if someone offered me. A stinking big one. The first thing I'd do is move out of this neighborhood. I mean, we all know the jokes about trailer trash, right? Maybe I shouldn't be so snobby after growing up in the foster system and everything, but I really don't think I belong here.

I've been looking at duplexes. Nothing too outrageous. I think a place with three rooms would be perfect, one for me, one for

Natalie, and an extra room I can use as my office. I don't see myself going back to work as long as Natalie's this fragile, so I've been looking into some online jobs, maybe transcription work or something. I don't know. I'm not that great with computers, but I could figure it out if I had to.

Then again, if I got a big enough settlement, I wouldn't have to work at all. I could stay home with Natalie or maybe even hire a nurse to take care of the suctioning and some of the tube feeds. Because God knows once I had a place in my own name I'd have Patricia out the door in ten seconds flat.

Probably less.

Speaking of Patricia, I know her hour-long nap is about to end. This is my last five minutes of quiet for the rest of the day. I check my phone to see if anyone's commented about my picture of Natalie in her little snowsuit. Not many likes yet. I guess the photos of sick babies do a better job getting people's attention. Just one comment. I click and see it's from Sandy.

She's such a precious little thing. Just like her mom.

Sandy's not really into social media or anything, so I think it's cute that she tries to keep in touch this way. She's even included a few stickers with hearts and smilies and cheesy stuff like that. It was good of her to come be with me while Natalie was having her surgery. I'm not sure what I would have done otherwise. There were some days in the NICU when I was under so much stress I thought I might literally lose my head. I even thought about calling my OB back in Orchard Grove, ask her if she could prescribe something just to take the edge off my nerves. I hate the idea of taking medicine for a mental problem like that, but I was sort of desperate.

I still feel that way every once in a while. Like I need a pill or something. I took this depression screening online, and I've got like thirteen out of the fifteen warning signs. I've been telling myself it's just baby blues. All the mommy magazines said it's normal, and most folks don't have to go on meds for it. But I wonder if I'm always going to feel like I'm in this fog or if it's just going to miraculously disappear, sort of like the morning sickness did right after I made it to thirteen weeks.

What to Expect when you're Postpartum. That would be a good book for someone to write one day.

It's times like these I wish I were more like Sandy. So loving. So maternal. It's like she was made to be a mom and a pastor's wife and that's about it. Part of me thinks I'd go crazy if my life were that boring, but part of me envies her. Wonders what it would be like to have so much love to share with others.

Of course, Sandy comes from a really good upbringing. Rich Southern folks. Family money, all that junk. From what I can tell, the only real big stresses in her life were when her parents freaked out that she married a black man and when her adopted daughter Blessing turned into such a big disappointment.

I should mention she and Carl have kids of their own, too. Bio kids, I mean. And they just keep adding to the family, like I already told you about the little boy they recently adopted. They would have adopted me, I'm sure of it, but there were paperwork issues and I guess I wasn't *legally free* or whatever you call it. I should have been. I mean, I don't remember that I've ever met my bio mom face to face. I'm sure I must have a couple times when I was a baby because that's just what happens in the system, but I don't remember any of it. I don't know. Maybe someone just dropped the ball on my file.

Sometimes I wonder if it would have made a difference. If Sandy adopted me officially. On the one hand, there's no way she could love me any more if I were legally her daughter. That's just the kind of person she is. But sometimes I wonder if we would have stayed in touch better. If I would have started to call her Mom. I mean, I'm already planning to teach Natalie to call her Grandma Sandy, but that's more like a title than an official name.

I couldn't do it, all that fostering and adopting she does. And I wonder how she finds the patience to take care of all those kids but also how she gets over that constant fear of loss. I mean, I'm Natalie's birth mom and I already know that I'm keeping her at a distance. At arm's length. Like that stray puppy I wasn't allowed to name. I know any day Natalie might leave me, and the stronger our bond, the harder that's going to be.

So I sort of mother on autopilot, which I hate about myself. *But how else do you do it*, I want to ask her. How do you take these kids into your home knowing that most of them are going right through that revolving door and walking out of your life forever? How do you keep from either dying from grief or turning into a robot mom?

I sometimes think about the girl who delivered me. Wonder if she's even alive. I know I could find her name and stuff if I dug into the records, but part of me wants to think the paperwork's lost completely. Part of me wants to think that's the real reason why Sandy never adopted me. Besides, I don't have any reason to go digging too deep into my past.

It's normal, I guess, to think about the woman who gave you birth when you become a mom yourself. Man, I had no idea how scary it must have been to drop a kid in a dirty high-school bathroom. Sure, she was stupid. Stupid but incredibly brave.

Which makes you wonder why she just left me there when all was said and done.

I still don't know the story of my rescue. Was it another student who went in to check her makeup? Did a teacher hear a strange noise and go in to see what it was? I don't even know if it happened during school hours or not. What if it was the night janitor who found me?

I shouldn't wonder these things, but I do, even though knowing the answers won't change a thing. Maybe I'm more sentimental than I like to admit.

I hear Patricia stirring in the bedroom, so I shove my phone into my pocket and grab a bottle of formula so it looks like I'm being productive. Natalie's next feeding isn't for a while yet, but at least I look like the doting, attentive mother I'm never going to be.

CHAPTER 20

Patricia comes out of her room with a cross sleepiness hanging on her face. I offer a smile. Every once in a while, I try to be friendly just to keep her on her toes or to prove to Jake that I'm not the witch she claims I am behind my back.

Patricia doesn't return my smile. "I already fed her," she says.

"I know." I stare at the bottle in my hand. I turn it around and squint at the fine print on the label. "I was just checking the ingredients."

Patricia comes over and picks Natalie out of the bouncy chair. "And how's Grandma's little precious?" she asks in that sing-songy voice people use when they want to make a fool out of themselves. The funny thing is Patricia's not the adoring grandmother she tries to sound like. She only uses that tone of voice with Natalie when she's upset with me and wants me to know that she's grand enough to love my child even though she can't stand the fact that her son chose me for his baby mommy.

"Did you have a nice nap?" I ask.

Patricia's making cooing faces at the baby, which is pointless because Natalie's eyes aren't even all the way open. She's tired. I wonder why Patricia won't leave her alone.

"Oh, it was fine." Patricia sits down with Natalie in a dining room chair with a dramatic sigh. I wonder if she ever took acting classes. Probably not. She doesn't strike me as the type to put much stock in theater or the arts. "Did you have a nice afternoon?" she asks, staring down her nose at me and then glancing around the living room, probably to see what chores I could have been doing if I hadn't been so lazy.

"Not bad," I reply and wonder when Jake will wake up. It's bad enough he leaves me alone with her for six hours a shift when he goes in to work. Thankfully, he's been working nights lately, so most of the time he's gone I can be in my room and at least pretend to be asleep. It's harder during the day, when there's nowhere for me to go, nowhere for Patricia to go, and an entire afternoon and evening stretched out before us until we can part company and shut ourselves up in our rooms. Maybe I should learn from her and go take a nap.

"Is Jake asleep?" she asks.

I nod, wondering what biting remark she'll make next. She smiles a little. The expression looks so unpracticed on her wrinkle-free face. I know I'm not going to look that good when I'm her age. But hopefully I won't be as mean-spirited either.

"That boy would never nap for me when he was little." This is one of Patricia's favorite subjects, how she raised the twins without any outside help. But she doesn't go there. Not this time. "I remember putting him in his crib one day and letting him cry for half an hour. I just needed time to myself."

We're in new territory now, territory where Patricia's not setting herself up as the monument of ideal motherhood. I'm nervous, like I felt the time that one foster dad came into my room except he wasn't drunk.

"Yeah." I try to offer a little chuckle. It's as unpracticed on my vocal chords as that smile was on her face. "I bet that was hard."

"You have no idea." Her features are soft, but I'm still waiting for the claws to come out. The barbs to poke through that gentle exterior. "I begged Jake's dad to spend more time at home, but even on his day off, he was behind that computer screen of his ten or twelve hours."

"I would have gone batty." I don't know why I tell her this. Warning bells clank and clatter in the back of my brain. I'm not supposed to open up. Not supposed to let my guard down. Not with her.

"Yeah, well, I suppose that's the upside of Jake's not working more hours, isn't it?" The haughty look is back in her eyes now. I think I imagine her straightening her spine. Throwing back her shoulders. This is the Patricia I know. This is the Patricia I've grown to despise.

"I guess not," I say, hating myself for that thirty seconds of almost-closeness.

She's got the point for this round, but I know it's nothing but a single battle. A single battle in a war that will go on raging as long as the two of us have to coexist under the same roof.

CHAPTER 21

"Well, I didn't mean it like that. All I'm saying is you've got your schoolwork to focus on." Patricia's on the phone with her daughter, Jake's twin. I've never met Abby, but at this point, I'm not sure how well we'd get along. I mean, I can only imagine all the junk Patricia's told her about me, and heaven knows I've heard enough about her to fill a whole two-page spread in a tabloid.

"He's a distraction. And you and I both know you don't need another one of those in your life. Not after Ian."

I don't know all of Abby's history, but I've put enough pieces together to understand that she was engaged to this Ian dude, but something happened and the wedding was called off, and not even Jake can come up with a satisfactory explanation about what went wrong.

I'm bored listening in to this phone call, but Patricia's cleaning up the kitchen after making us all chicken pot pie for dinner, and I'm stuck here watching Natalie in case she needs to be suctioned. Believe me, you can't talk on the phone and handle a suction tube at the same time. Once I had to spend an hour on hold with Medicaid. There was some problem with Natalie's paperwork. One of the therapists wrote down her number wrong, and the state was threatening to make us foot the entire bill.

As if.

I was on hold so long, and Patricia went out to pick up Jake from work, and Natalie started to choke so I turned on the machine to slurp all her gunk out, and that's when the service rep picked up the line. Of course.

Anyway, now Jake's in the shower, and Patricia's been yakking at Abby for half an hour. The kitchen's perfectly spotless, cleaner than it was the day Jake and I moved in to this trailer park, but she'll be going at it for another sixty minutes, I'm sure. Jake might be in the shower that long, too. I swear, out of all the things Patricia picks to gripe about, I wish one of them was my husband wasting so much of our hot water.

"Oh, she's as good as you could expect, all things considered." Patricia lowers her voice and slips her back to me. *Subtle, lady.* I wonder if they're talking about me or the baby. "No, she'll probably have that tube her whole life."

The baby.

It's funny. In theory, I agree with Patricia completely. Even if we end up finding that miracle cure for Natalie, I still act like she'll have that feeding tube until the day she dies, and that way I'll never end up disappointed. So it's not the words Patricia's using, it's the way she's saying them. Like she actually believes that since she was an LPN working at a plastic surgeon's office back in the nineties, it makes her an expert on newborns with brain injuries. I wish there was somewhere I could take Natalie, but my bedroom is so messy there's nowhere to sit, and she's asleep anyway, so I don't want to bother her.

"Ok, well, I need both hands now. You want to talk to your brother?" Patricia yells for Jake, as if she couldn't hear the shower water running for the past twenty minutes. "Jake!" she shouts again, and I wince at the grating sound. "I think he stepped out."

She catches my eye, and I feel a groan about to escape from the pit of my gut, still uneasy from that saltless pot-pie dinner and unseasoned rice. Before I can grab the suction tube and look like I'm in the middle of something, Patricia thrusts her cell in my face. "Here's Tiffany," she shouts to her daughter.

I stare at the phone as if she's just handed me a fat, hairy tarantula. Why does Jake have to spend so stinking long in the shower?

"Hi, Abby." We've talked once before, a day or two after the wedding. She called Jake up to congratulate him, told him she was happy for us both, then actually asked to talk to me. It wasn't an awkward conversation at all. Maybe if it weren't for the way Patricia insists on poisoning us against each other, the two of us could be on good terms.

"Hey, Tiffany. How are you?" She doesn't know that everyone calls me Tiff, and I don't bother correcting her. It's not like we're going to turn into the kind of sisters-in-law that talk regularly or anything.

"Pretty good. Tired." I laugh. For a second, I feel somewhat normal. Aren't all new moms sleep-deprived?

"How's the baby?" she asks, and her voice is hushed and sort of pitying, the same tone you'd use at a funeral home.

Still alive. That's what I feel like telling her. But even though Patricia's got her back to me and is scrubbing the inside of my microwave, I can almost see her ears sticking out from the sides of her head, straining to hear what I'm saying.

"She's doing well," I lie. "Getting a little stronger bit by bit." What else am I supposed to tell her? Natalie hasn't changed since the day we brought her home, and that was two months ago. She hasn't gained weight, hasn't cried, hasn't met any of those baby milestones the mommy magazines tell you to watch out for.

"I'm glad to hear it." Abby's voice is stuffed with false cheer, and I wonder if she hates her mom as much as I do for forcing us to chat like this.

There's an awkward pause, like Abby doesn't know what else to talk about with someone whose baby is as fragile as mine. I feel sorry for her and ask how school's going.

"Busy," she says, just the way she's supposed to. Like I'm supposed to say I'm tired when she asks me how I feel.

Another pause. I wonder what she's thinking. You know, I heard all these things growing up about how twins are supposed to be so close. Like you hear these stories where two twin sisters marry two twin brothers and they all live together in the same house? Someone should turn that into a sitcom. I think it has

121

potential. But even in real life, stuff like that happens. Or you hear stories about one twin who maybe lives a thousand miles away from his sister, but the day she gets into a really bad car accident is the day he coincidentally decides to show up for a surprise visit, and he ends up donating his kidney to save her life or something dramatic like that.

Anyway, Jake and his sister aren't like that at all. I mean, they're polite when they talk, but they usually only call each other on birthdays or holidays or things. And then they chat for ten or fifteen minutes and go back to their separate lives. Abby's so busy with school and now this boyfriend her mom hates but who sounds like a decent enough guy as far as boyfriends go. Part of me wants to find someplace private to talk, tell Abby she shouldn't feel guilty for being with this computer whiz because he's smart so he'll probably make plenty of money. And if she's a lawyer ... all I have to say is that's a family that would never have to wait an hour on hold with Medicaid to get a seven-hundred-dollar medical bill covered by the state.

Jake turns off the shower and steps out, and I glance down the hall at the steam following him from the bathroom. Man, he looks good today. I mean, he's no body-builder or anything, but that's never been my type. I want him to look up at me, give me his little cheesy grin that used to get my insides quivering like that glass of water in *Jurassic Park*. But instead he shoots me a questioning kind of glance, like he's not sure if he's going to be mad at me or not when he finds out why I'm on his mother's phone.

It's your sister. I mouth the words to him before he turns around. I stare at his back as he disappears into our room and shuts the door behind him.

CHAPTER 22

"Did you have a good day?" Jake asks.

I'm curled up against him, nestled beneath my electric blanket. Patricia's out watching some cooking show, so Jake and I went to bed early.

"It wasn't bad." I've been thinking about that granny lady in church now that everything's quiet and there's nothing to do. Patricia will sleep in Natalie's room, so she'll cover the night feeding and the suctioning, and she'll take care of the apnea monitor if it goes off.

"I'm opening tomorrow, so I've got to get up early."

I hate it when Jake works days.

Jake must sense that I'm upset, because he snuggles up a little closer. "Sorry I won't be here to help out."

It's sweet of him to say, even though he never helps with the baby anyway. I swear, that boy can go three or four days without even touching his own daughter. I think he's afraid, actually. Afraid that he'll make a mistake. Part of me thinks he still feels guilty for what happened in the delivery room, like he should have noticed sooner something was wrong. Really, if he hadn't been there, I probably would have gone on sleeping. I wouldn't have woken up at all. I've never told him this. We haven't ever talked about that day, truth be told. I think eventually we will, and I'll be sure to tell him it's not his fault. But if I were to bring it up now, it would make things worse. Open old wounds that should probably be left alone. What are adults always telling kids?

Don't pick your scabs.

I like this, though, this closeness and warmth. Of course, a lot of that's from the electric blanket, but some of it — that sense of security — comes right from him. I nestle my head into that spot between his shoulder and chin, that soft place that feels as warm and inviting as the smell of Sandy baking her famous homemade cookies. It's warmth and security and peace all wrapped up with something else. Something I don't necessarily want to put a name to. Because if I'm wrong ...

"Did you and Abby have a good talk?" His voice is distant, like he's asking me about his sister but he's thinking about something else. Heaven knows what. Maybe what time he has to wake up tomorrow. Or how long until his mother turns off the TV and stops polluting our home with that ridiculous, canned noise. Or a pouty-lipped, busty co-worker named Charlene he slept with while I was stuck in a hospital waiting to deliver his baby.

"Yeah," I tell him, but my mind's somewhere else, too. Shame in the pit of my core. Terror that one day I'll let it slip and he'll find out what I've done.

He kisses me on the cheek. It's soft. Friendly. Like we're a married couple sleeping side by side in a nursing home, all romance and passion distant memories in the past.

I hate that I'm thinking about him right now. Hate that I'm thinking about him that way. Because I've resigned myself to the fact that nothing's going to happen as long as his mother is staying here. The funny thing is I feel more prudish around his non-religious mother than I ever did around Sandy, and she's the picture-perfect pastor's wife who probably didn't even kiss a boy until the day she and her husband got married.

Back when I lived with Sandy, I went to one of those girls-only lock-ins at her church. You know, the kind where they get these cute, perky college-aged women to tell you why you've got to save sex for marriage. The pathetic part was they acted like we were so pure to start with. Like we weren't the kind of girls passed around from foster home to foster home where some of the guys we met were ok and some weren't. And these abstinence cheerleaders kept going on and on about not wanting to give your husband *hand-me-downs* on your wedding night, and I signed the abstinence pledges, and I wore the purity rings, and all the while I was sneaking Lincoln Grant in through the bedroom window. Because those twenty-year-old virgins didn't understand girls like me. Girls who would give up their breasts and fallopian tubes to know what it felt like to be clean. Pure.

Whole.

Hand-me-downs on your wedding night. It's a dumb phrase

for me to be thinking about right now, but some things are harder to forget than others.

"What time do you have to get up in the morning?" I ask Jake, but he doesn't answer. He's already asleep.

CHAPTER 23

Well, I made it through the day with just Patricia and me. And Natalie, of course. She did well, actually. I don't think we had to suction her quite as much as usual. I wonder if that means her swallowing is finally improving. If she's able to swallow her saliva, then one day she might be able to handle real food ...

I can't get ahead of myself, though. Best to assume she'll have that G-tube for the rest of her life. But days like this, it's sometimes hard to remember my resolve. I held her for a while this afternoon while Patricia was out grocery shopping. That woman always complains we don't have enough fresh fruits and veggies on hand. She doesn't know we're on food stamps because Jake's too embarrassed to tell her, but the one good thing about Patricia bunking in with us is she buys most of the groceries. Otherwise, I don't know how we'd afford the extra food. Not that she eats much. That woman is skinny as a flagpole and about as feminine.

Anyway, while Patricia was out, I was online for a little bit, but there wasn't much for me to say, so I took Natalie out of the crib and held her for a while. She stayed awake for a full twenty minutes or so. I wasn't watching the clock real close, but I think it's the longest she's gone. And that whole time she was with me, I didn't have to turn on the suction machine once.

Hashtag blessed, right?

Part of me wanted to jump online right away and tell everyone how well she was doing, but another part of me wanted to keep it to myself. Something special just between my daughter and me.

My daughter. That's so stinking weird.

Jake came home from his shift around two, and I think maybe once we're in bed tonight I'll tell him about Natalie's good day, but right now he's tired and kind of grumpy. That's ok. He gets that way when he's hungry. He probably went the whole shift without eating. He does that to save money, which I guess is nice on the one hand because we need every penny we can scrape up. But on the other hand, I'd rather him come home in a slightly better mood, so it's something of a lose-lose.

Patricia's setting lunch on the table right now, so at least I won't have to put up with his bad attitude for long. I swear that boy gets hormonal when his blood sugar drops too low.

It's funny because Patricia makes this big stink about eating together, to the point where if Jake doesn't get off work until eight or nine at night she'll actually hold dinner until then. But it's not like we're this big happy family feasting around the table and sharing our deepest thoughts or even talking about our days. Mealtimes are quiet. Patricia will sometimes offer some sort of unsolicited advice she picked up from her heroic efforts raising twins without a living soul in the universe to help her out, but other than that we don't really say anything.

Now that I've met Patricia, I feel like I understand Jake better. Why he's so quiet. It used to trip me out back in the NICU. We'd eat dinner together every night before he'd head back to the Ronald McDonald house and play Candy Zapper on his phone and I'd return to the NICU to talk to the night nurses as they were starting their shifts. We'd sometimes go an entire meal without saying anything more than, "You ready?" when we were done.

I asked him about it once, asked him why he was so quiet. I had just said goodbye to Sandy the day before, and if there's one woman who doesn't know how to eat a meal without yakking someone's ear off, it's her. I think that's why I noticed how silent Jake was in comparison.

"Just thinking," was all he said, and I wanted him to tell me more. Don't ask me what I was expecting. Some sort of big share-fest where he'd reveal all the things he was afraid of and I'd tell him all the things I was sorry for but hadn't found the guts to bring up yet. And we'd cry because we were both so relieved to get certain things out in the open, and then I'd hug him and tell him how glad I was he came to be with me in Seattle because once Sandy left, I realized even more pointedly how much it would suck to be out there totally alone.

But I kept chomping on my fries, and he kept poking at his Jell-O, and neither of us said anything until we were finished eating and I asked, "Ready to go?"

And that was it.

I used to think it'd be so romantic to fall in love with a perfect stranger. To trust those emotions so well that even if you didn't know his name you could look at him and be convinced that he was the one for you. It sounds sweet and dreamy, but what you don't think about is how lonely it is to fall in love — or at least think you've fallen in love — with someone you know, only to find out months later that you're nothing but strangers.

CHAPTER 24

It's Wednesday morning, and I'm at the pediatrician's office with Natalie. Roberto screwed up Jake's schedule, so he's at the store working day shift. Again. Which means I had to wake up at 4:45 to drop him off so I'd have the car. It also means I'm here with Patricia because it takes two people to haul Natalie anywhere, one to drive and one to sit in the backseat with the suction machine ready in case she chokes.

Dr. Bell's running late, but there's no surprise there. She's the only pediatrician in Orchard Grove, and unless you're filthy rich or your kid has a complicated medical history, you have to see one of the family doctors instead. I like Dr. Bell, though. She's pretty young. Low thirties I would guess, but she's got nice skin, so she could easily pass as a twenty-something. She's thorough and methodical, which is nice when you're in the office with her but a real pain in the butt when you're stuck in the waiting room.

At least she keeps a lot of magazines out here. Right now, I'm skimming an article called *Ten Hot Tips to Spice up your Love Life ... Even after Baby!* Unfortunately, the writer doesn't mention anything about intrusive mothers-in-law or apnea monitors prone to go off at all hours of the night.

Patricia's reading a food magazine, which strikes me as mildly ironic. With as many cooking experts as that woman follows, you'd think someone would have introduced her to the concept of salt by now.

I'm still mad at Jake for rushing to the store just because Roberto needed him. I know he wants to work as many hours as he can get, but it's been two weeks since we've seen Dr. Bell, and he should have known that Patricia's the last person I'd want to tag along on a trip like this. Today's the day I'm going to tell the doctor I'm taking Natalie off the apnea machine, and I could use Jake there to back me up.

Jake texts me while I'm thumbing through the winners of the last month's photo contest. One of the babies is only a month older than Natalie but can already sit up on her own in one of those funny little rubbery chairs. She's smiling too. It's no wonder the editors picked her. I should send them a picture of Natalie just to see what they'd do. Find them a photo from one of her first few days, when she's got an IV in her forehead and tubes shoved down her throat. I'd like to find that printed up and put alongside all these fat Gerber babies who've never seen the inside of a medevac jet.

Talked with the Dr. yet? Jake wants to know. I roll my eyes. If he expects Dr. Bell to be on time, he's even dumber than his mother thinks he is. I don't even bother to answer. I remind myself of all the things I want to talk to Dr. Bell about. The fact that Natalie hasn't gained a single pound since we've had her home.

The fact that she still hasn't cried. The fact that the apnea monitor we've got is a waste of everybody's time.

Or is it?

I don't like to admit it even to myself, but I'm still thinking quite a bit about that weird thing that happened to me at church on Sunday. That hallucination or Jesus trip or whatever it was where I saw Natalie on God's lap. Even now, I have no doubt it was her, just like I have no doubt that if it weren't for her brain injuries she would look exactly like that image in five or six years, missing teeth and all.

The problem is I still don't know what it means. Is she going to be healed? Or will she die? How am I supposed to figure out anything when that's my range of possible explanations? I can't shake the feeling that the vision is supposed to tell me something. Am I too stupid to figure it out? Too scared? And what if I get it wrong? What if the vision means she's going to be just fine, but I don't have enough faith, and so I take her off the apnea monitor and something bad happens?

But then there's the other side of it too. Like what if the vision means she won't be healed until she gets to heaven, but I hold on too long and make her suffer when I'm supposed to let go so she can see Jesus sooner or whatever? I've been thinking about Sandy too, wondering what she'd say the vision means. I should talk with her, but how do you start a conversation like that? *Hi, Sandy. I'm calling because some Holy Ghost lady stood up in church, and while she was talking, I was wigging out and saw my daughter on*

Jesus' lap, only now I don't know if that means I'm supposed to take her off her apnea monitor and let her die or if it means that she's going to be just fine and I need to have patience.

I'm trying to guess what Sandy's reaction would be when Dr. Bell's middle-aged nurse calls me back. I can never remember her name. Trixie or Marge or one of those other names you'd expect to call a waitress at an old-school diner. But she's all smiles, and she even takes the suction machine so I have both hands free to carry Natalie in her car seat.

"How's the little miracle baby?" she asks. I try to remember how long it's been since I've had a face-to-face conversation with anyone besides Jake or his mom.

"She had a really good day Monday," I tell her.

Nurse Smiles beams down at my daughter. "Good for you, little angel."

We get into the room, and I see her name tag now. Barb. That's right. She flips through some pages on a clipboard. "Oh," she says. "They must have given us the wrong forms."

I can't figure out why she's fidgeting so nervously as she takes out some stapled pages and tosses them on the counter. "Never mind," she says and holds her pen ready over a blank page. "Why don't you tell me how she's been since the last time you brought her in?"

I frown. "Not too many changes, really. I'm a little worried she hasn't gained any weight." I go on and wonder why I bother since Dr. Bell is going to ask me the exact same questions in a few minutes. While Nurse Barb scribbles away on her pad, I steal a glance at the discarded packet on the counter.

Four month well baby check. There are Natalie's name and birthdate written on the top in curvy feminine handwriting where you'd almost expect to find a heart dotting the *i* in Natalie's name.

I look at the questions on the form. *Does your child sleep through the night?*

Yeah, and ninety percent of the day, too.

Does your child transfer a toy from one hand to the other?

She might if she had any clue what her hands were for or how to use them.

Does your child smile and make eye contact?

Screw this.

Nurse Barb's telling me what vaccinations Natalie's due to get today. Poor thing. I have to step out of the room whenever they do it. I can't stand to see the way she scrunches up her little face, her own silent version of crying.

Barb wraps up all her questions, and she leaves me and Natalie alone to wait some more. There's a mural of sunflowers and cute oversized bumblebees on the wall. Each room has a different theme. Last time we came here, our room sported an underwater setting with little orange Nemos and blue Dori fish. All the paintings are signed *J. Bell* at the bottom, but I don't know if that's the pediatrician or maybe a relative of hers or something.

I gave Natalie her tube feeding right before we came here. I hoped it would give her a few extra ounces on the scale, except now she's making that grimace like she's uncomfortable, and her breathing's gotten really noisy. I power up the suction machine, wondering if the family the next room over can hear it.

Ever since we got out of the NICU, I've only met one other mom with a suction device like ours. It was when we were still in Seattle, still getting set up with specialists and making sure Natalie would be healthy enough for the drive back to Orchard Grove. We were in the waiting room at the lung doctor's, and this boy with glasses shuffled in. He was older, maybe nine or ten, and he looked perfectly healthy except he kind of rocked side to side when he walked. Anyway, his mom was lugging a suction machine with her. Exact same make and model as mine. Even the same gray carrying case.

She sat down right across from me, and I made it a point to give Natalie a suction even though her airway was clear at the time. I don't know what I was expecting. This strange woman to reach over and give me a hug and tell me how everything would be just fine. It was stupid of me, but when I first saw her I thought maybe we could become friends. Not the kind to get together for play dates or anything. Her son was way too old for that, and Natalie and I were headed back to Orchard Grove in a day or two. But maybe we'd connect online. Maybe I could ask her some of those things the nurses don't think to tell you, like how to keep the collection canister from reeking when you use the machine fifty times a day but Medicaid only lets you order one replacement a month.

Well, she didn't say anything to me. It's funny because I'd been worried about taking Natalie out into the real world, worried about all the strange stares we'd get when people saw me shoving a tube down her throat. They'd be curious. They'd gawk. They'd feel sorry for me and my baby.

I learned that day there's something I hate even more than being pitied.

It's being ignored.

CHAPTER 25

I've been on my phone looking at the same posts for half an hour or longer when Dr. Bell finally steps in. I get this sense she's a fascinating woman. You'd think that somebody nerdy enough to get all the way through medical school wouldn't waste too much time on things like fashion or makeup, but Dr. Bell could probably pose for one of the articles in the mommy magazines she keeps in her waiting room. She's not gorgeous, not the kind of woman you wouldn't trust your boyfriend around. More like the big sister you look up to but know you'll always stay stuck in her shadow no matter how hard you try.

Dr. Bell smiles and shakes my hand. It's not formal when she does it, and when she's done she gives my shoulder a short rub. "How are you today?" That's the difference between an actual pediatrician and all those specialists we saw in Seattle. The specialists never think to ask the parents how they're doing.

"Pretty good," I answer automatically, afraid she might not believe me. It's stupid and immature. I feel like the new kid in junior high all over again, just hoping the pretty girl takes pity on me and asks me to sit at the cool table in the lunch room.

Dr. Bell's got these soft eyes. I think that's part of why she looks so young, that and her fabulous skin. If we were friends, I'd ask her what products she recommends, how she keeps her complexion so smooth. But that's not the kind of relationship we have, and as she flips through Natalie's chart, I fill the uncomfortable silence by saying, "You know, she had a really good day Monday."

Dr. Bell sets down her clipboard. "Tell me about it." I find myself wondering if she has a husband. Maybe a dark, sexy boyfriend. Heck, for all I know, she might have both.

"Well," I begin and pray that I don't yak her ear off and make a complete fool of myself, "she was awake for half an hour or more in the afternoon. I mean, she still doesn't make eye contact or anything, but she stayed pretty alert. More than normal, at least."

I can hear the hopefulness in my own voice. It's pathetic really. That's what I was so excited about? That's the progress I couldn't wait to tell her?

"Oh, and she didn't need to be suctioned that whole time." I'm saying this, but all I'm thinking about is how pretty Dr. Bell must have been as a teenager, how all the boys probably had crushes on her and all the teachers adored her and all the girls wanted to be just like her. Even the way she holds that pen. She's so poised and confident. That's why I say she could be in one of those mommy magazines.

"Still three or four times an hour on average?" Dr. Bell's

looking at me, and I have to rewind what I just heard to figure out she's asking me how often I suction Natalie these days.

"Yeah, about that. It gets worse after she eats."

"Immediately after?"

"No, about half an hour."

"So you give her a tube feeding, and then about thirty minutes after that is when she needs the most suctioning?" Now you know what I mean when I described her as being thorough.

"Yeah. That's about right." I like this conversation, this back and forth we're having. I realize I don't have anyone in my life to just sit down and talk with.

"Now tell me about her eating habits. She's still taking 95 mLs six times a day?"

"Yeah." I'm amazed at the way she remembers the number without looking at Natalie's chart.

"Well, let's go ahead and increase that to 105 mLs. See if we can get her weight up some more. And those six feedings, is that spread out just through the day, or does she need a snack at night too?"

I love the way she talks about Natalie as if my baby understands concepts like snacks or hunger. With the G-tube, she doesn't even have to be awake to get fed. In fact, most of the time she's dead to the world.

"She gets a feeding at night, but that's just because it's the schedule she's on."

Dr. Bell nods. I wish I could have her over to my house. I have the feeling that if she saw Natalie there, she'd be even more understanding. More sympathetic. I want to sit with her in my living room over coffee. Talk about our jerky ex-boyfriends or what med school was like. I don't even know if doctors still have to practice on corpses or not. There's no way I can picture her covered in sweat and grime and dissecting some dead stiff.

Dr. Bell's writing on the chart. "Let's try this. Let's stick with six feedings a day, but let's do them every three hours starting first thing in the morning. I want you to try it and call me Friday to let me know how she's handling it. What I'm hoping is it will give you a chance to sleep straight through the night for a change."

She looks at me with so much compassion that I wouldn't tell her that my mother-in-law takes care of the night feedings even if I had to testify under oath.

"And what about you?" Dr. Bell asks me. "Are you getting the support you need? It's not easy to ask for help, I know that, but sometimes it's the best thing you can do for you and your baby."

Now she sounds like she could write a mommy magazine article in addition to modeling for one. It's kind of funny in a sad way how she thinks that my biggest problem is not having enough help.

"We're managing ok."

"I know it's a lot of work," she says with a soft smile, "but it's really paying off. I don't know if Barb told you, but she's gained four ounces since last time she was here. I think increasing the formula's going to help a lot too. Good job, Mom."

I'm pretty used to medical professionals calling me *mom* by this point. That's basically all I went by with the nurses in the NICU. But part of me's afraid I'm about to say something really cheesy like *Call me Tiff. It's what my friends do.* Thankfully, Dr. Bell turns those kind eyes away and writes something on her clipboard.

"Just hang in there. This new schedule will hopefully get you some of that rest you need. And don't forget, it's perfectly fine to take a nap. I know some parents in your situation get nervous about that, but that's why we got you the apnea monitor."

I meet her smile this time and decide then and there that I'm not going to bring up the DNR today. Dr. Bell thinks I'm doing a good job. I'm not about to burst her bubble.

CHAPTER 26

The pediatrician spends another half an hour asking me questions and examining Natalie. I feel pathetic when I realize it's the most relaxed I've been in weeks, and I'm not at a spa or a five-star restaurant or even the mall. I'm at the stinking doctor's office.

When Dr. Bell acts like she's ready to wrap our meeting up, I realize I don't want to go home. It's time to pick up Jake from work, so at least I won't be stuck alone with Patricia. But it's not like he adds much to the family dynamics. He'll run straight to the couch and be glued to his phone until dinnertime, I'm sure of it.

I wonder sometimes why I'm still with him. If I could afford a place of my own, would I have ditched him by now?

Dr. Bell gathers up all her papers. "Well, if you don't have any other questions ..."

I'm wracking my brain. Anything to get her to stay with me, even if it's only another two or three minutes. I feel so pathetic, starved for friendship. It reminds me of the NICU and how I could go a full week with the nurses the only people besides Jake I talked to face to face.

"Oh." She's staring at my intake paperwork, and my heart

lodges itself near the base of my throat. I know what she's going to ask, and I don't want to hear it.

"It says here you wanted to talk to me about the apnea monitor?"

I feel my face flush and hate myself for it. I glance at the clock behind her head. Natalie still has to get her shots, and Jake can get grumpy if I'm late picking him up.

"Are you having issues with the monitor?" Dr. Bell prompts.

"No, it's not that." My hands are clammy. This isn't the time. She's been so nice, so patient listening to me talk about my daughter. She's the only person in the world besides Sandy that I feel so comfortable with.

I can't tell her I want my daughter to die. What was I thinking?

I swallow. It's so loud I can hear the saliva work its way past the lump in my throat. "We're just having a lot of false alarms and I was wondering if that was normal."

Dr. Bell smiles. "Unfortunately, it is." She sighs. "I can only imagine how hard that must be, especially when you're trying to catch up on your sleep."

She has perfectly round eyes. Doe eyes, except the kind that make you look warm and feminine. Not the kind that make you look stupid or too trusting.

"Some parents with DNR forms decide that the apnea monitor isn't worth the hassle ..." Her voice trails off. She's inviting me to agree with her without actually forcing me to say the words. God bless her.

"No." I try to make myself look confident, put together, even though I'd never pull it off as convincingly as she does. "But you know, speaking of the DNR, my husband and I decided that we don't need it after all."

Her eyes have softened even more now, and I know I've said the right thing even though I'm lying through my teeth.

"So, umm, I was just wondering if there's anything we need to do. You know, to cancel that order or whatever."

I can't meet her gaze. She's the kindest woman I've met in the state of Washington. I can't believe I wanted to tell her my little girl would be better off dead.

She's hugging the clipboard. She reminds me of Sandy right now. Of course, Sandy's a few decades older, but she and Dr. Bell both have that same kind of quiet gentleness that hangs around them like a halo or one of those beautiful crocheted shawls you can buy online.

"Well." She's talking slowly, and I think that maybe we'll get an extra ten minutes out of this interview, not just another one or two. "If you and your husband both agree that this is the way to go, I'll make a note here in your chart, and that's as formal as it needs to be."

I meet her smile this time, certain I've made the right choice. It's a good feeling, one I'm not sure I've experienced since Natalie was born.

Dr. Bell's hand is on the door knob. "Why don't you make an appointment to come back and see me in two weeks, and I'll let the nurse know she's ready for those shots."

I'm a little disappointed she doesn't use Natalie's name, but I gush out my thanks and feel stupid afterward for being so sappy. So needy. When did I grow into such an emotional sponge that I've latched on to my daughter's pediatrician, some woman I only see twice a month?

Natalie's half awake, but she's not fussing at all, so I leave her in her car seat and wait. I hate when she gets shots, I really do. Maybe if she was healthy to start with I would have become one of those anti-vaxxers. I don't know. It would sure beat putting her through so much torture every month or two. But she's so sick I figure she needs all the immunizations the clinic can give her. It may not be ideal, but I guess a baby with a little mercury in her bloodstream still beats a baby who's died from whooping cough or that RSV virus that sounds so scary.

I glance at the time. Knowing the way this clinic works, it will be another twenty or thirty minutes before we see the nurse, and by then I'll be late to pick up Jake. He'll be in a bad mood, and Patricia will blame me. Make her sour-lemon face and comment something about how she always made sure the house was clean and a hot meal was on the table when Jake's father came home from work. Of course, they've been divorced now for twelve or thirteen years, and there's been another failed marriage between then and now, so I'm not about to take marital advice from the likes of her.

I flip on my phone. None of my friends have posted anything interesting online, so I switch to YouTube. I'd be embarrassed to show you my video feed. I'm way too addicted to those talent shows, you know the ones where people sing in front of famous judges or things. I don't have time to watch them on real TV, so this is how I get my fix.

There's a new video today, a twelve-year-old girl belting her little heart out. She's doing a Whitney Houston song, the one from that really old *Bodyguard* flick. Gutsy move. Didn't someone say the song was forbidden now that Whitney's dead or something like that? I study the girl's face, wondering how someone so young could pretend to know about that degree of loss and heartache.

She does a knock-out job though. Gets the confetti and everything. Of course she starts crying, and her mom backstage starts crying, and I just wonder if anyone in this happy little universe knows about babies who could die from a simple flu virus because their lungs are so compromised and their frail little bodies so weak.

Another video pops up in my recommended list, a clip from *Dancing with the Stars*. It's that adorable teen girl from the hillbilly show, and she's dancing a routine to some of the old-school Disney movie songs.

A whole new world ... I swear there's a lump in my throat the size of her right dimple. It's the hormones. It's got to be the hormones. I'm biting my lip or else I swear I'd start blubbering. It's just that she's so young. Young and pretty and healthy.

The tears are still streaming down my cheeks when Barb

comes in with her tray of torture devices. "Is the little angel ready?"

"Yeah." I wipe my cheeks when she isn't looking. "I'm going to step out of the room. Just let me know when you're done."

She doesn't make me feel bad that I have to bail. If I were a good mom instead of a wimp, I'd be in there with my daughter. I'd hold her and comfort her while the nurse injects her with poisons that all the anti-vaxxers are convinced will cause autism or cancer or sterilization.

But I can't. It's not that I can't handle her crying.

It's the fact that I know my daughter won't even make a sound.

CHAPTER 27

"She did great." Barb comes out just a minute or two later with a smile, as if she weren't some sort of twisted sadist who just finished injecting my baby girl with live viruses. "She slept right through it, tired little angel."

I assume she's trying to comfort me.

"Oh, before I forget," she adds, "the woman you were here with, she wanted me to tell you that she went to pick your boyfriend up from work and they'll be back to get you in just a few minutes."

My boyfriend. Of course, with different last names and still no ring, I can't blame Barb for her mistake. In fact, it was probably Patricia's fault to begin with. She's been living with us two months. Two stinking months, and she's never once mentioned the fact that we're married. I swear, if Jake and I make it to our fiftieth anniversary and she's alive and kicking, that woman will still refuse to acknowledge me as anything but her son's live-in partner.

I plaster on a forced smile and thank Barb for telling me. No use shooting the messenger, right?

I go back in the exam room. Barb has strapped Natalie into her car seat carrier, and my daughter's as oblivious as Sleeping Beauty. I grab my phone and lug Natalie back into the lobby to wait.

I'm not in the mood for mommy magazines anymore. I'm sick of reading about what my baby should be doing as a healthy four-month-old. Because she's not healthy, but the idiots who publish the junk don't know that. They think I'm the typical brand-new mom who's worried about things like stretch marks and a diminished libido and how much longer until my little girl starts to crawl.

I wonder how long ago it was that Patricia left. How long I'll have to wait here. After being shut up in the trailer for weeks at a time, it's exhausting to go out. This is my first time leaving the house since Sunday.

Jake and I haven't talked about the church service at all. I don't know if he's planning to go back this weekend, and if he is, I don't know if I'm planning to pitch a fit and refuse or if I'm planning to go back with him in hopes of catching a more precise heavenly message. But I feel settled for the first time since that granny started talking. Like somehow I got the answer to my question about the vision after all. I feel really good that I canceled the DNR, and I don't think it's just because that's the decision Dr. Bell wanted me to make.

Maybe in five years my daughter will look like that little girl with the missing front teeth. Chocolate skin and almond eyes. That's how I always pictured the kind of baby Jake and I would make.

I wonder if we'll still be together when Natalie's that age. I wonder which one of us will be the tooth fairy and sneak into her room to hide the coin under her pillow. I wonder if she'll run to me when she's hurt or to her dad. I wonder if I married Jake because I was in love with him or because I was so scared of losing Natalie that I latched onto anything reminding me of her.

Sandy sent me an article a few weeks ago about grief. It's funny because until I read it, I didn't think I had anything to mourn over. I mean, my daughter was sick, but at least she was alive. Well, the article was written by a special-needs mom. Her baby didn't have a traumatic birth like Natalie. I forget now what it was, but I think it was one of those chromosomal things. Not Down Syndrome, but one of the less common types that are kind of similar. And in the article, she was talking about how she had to grieve the loss of the healthy daughter she and her husband hoped to have.

So I guess that means I'm grieving too, and I know people say you're not supposed to make any big decisions while you're in that sort of mental state. You know, big decisions like getting married.

Live and learn, I guess.

I can't say that I regret my choice. I'm just waiting to see how it all pans out. If Natalie dies, I really can't picture staying with Jake after something that traumatizing. Which means I probably married him because of her, which probably wasn't the brightest idea.

But what if she doesn't die? And what if she's not a vegetable her whole life? What if she really grows into that smiling girl I saw sitting on Jesus' lap? Chocolate skin and almond eyes.

It could happen, right?

"Miss Franklin?"

I look up, and Barb's there smiling at me. I stand automatically before I know what she wants.

"You left the suction machine in the exam room," she tells me. I wonder why she didn't just bring it out, but I pick up Natalie in her car seat and follow Barb down the hall back to the bumblebee room.

Dr. Bell's in there, and I'm afraid she's going to lecture me for not having the machine with me. I've been doing a good job. I mean, I haven't forgotten it anywhere until now except for that time when we went on a walk and I left it at home, but we were never more than three or four minutes away from the trailer. I feel like I should apologize or something when Dr. Bell asks me, "How long have her secretions been that color?"

I pull back the cloth carrying case so I can see the collection canister. My face immediately wrinkles up. I try to remember when I last cleaned out the receptacle. Patricia does it, or at least I assume she does, because it's empty every morning when I wake up. Of course, if I tell that to the doctor she's going to think I'm the most negligent mom in central Washington, so I say, "Not that long. Maybe a day or two."

I study the can, trying to decide what label I would give it. I've always admired the way crayon companies come up with so many different synonyms for the same shade, and I wonder what Crayola would call this. Maybe *swamp green* or *marshy muck*.

Dr. Bell is frowning. "What was her temperature when she came in?" she asks Barb.

"Around normal, but I'd have to get her chart to be sure."

"99.1," I tell them both, thankful for the chance to prove my maternal attentiveness. I glance from one worried face to the other. "Is that bad? Is something wrong?"

A nurse in Looney Tunes scrubs leads a mother and two little kids down the hall. Barb shuts the door to give the three of us more privacy.

Not a good sign.

"Is that too high?" I ask. I seem to remember one of the mommy magazines explaining that it's not technically a fever until your temperature's over 101. Or was it 102?

"You were planning to come back in two weeks, right?" Dr. Bell asks. I nod, even though I haven't scheduled anything at the front desk yet.

She looks at Barb. "Let's see if we can get her in this Monday." She glances at the marshy muck secretions in my daughter's canister and says, "Actually, we don't want to wait the whole weekend." She nods to Barb, who is poised and ready to rush out of the room and schedule an appointment for my 99.1-degree daughter.

Dr. Bell's face is grim.

"Let's get them back here first thing Friday morning."

CHAPTER 28

When Jake finally pulls up, I can't tell from where I am if he's mad or not that he had to wait at work. I've got the bulky car seat in one hand and the even bulkier suction machine in the other, and in the back of my mind I hear Sandy's husband lamenting about how chivalry is dead.

I slip into the backseat and make sure the car seat clicks in place. The suction machine's on my lap, but now that I've examined its contents, I'm a little worried about some of that marshy muck spilling onto me if Jake hits a bump or takes a corner too fast.

Patricia's sitting primly in the passenger seat like she's the stinking Queen of England, and all I can do is fixate on the worry I heard in Dr. Bell's voice when she told Barb to bump up our next appointment.

They're anxious about infection. I guess that's what the green color can mean, but Natalie doesn't have a runny nose or a cough or anything like that. And she was bundled up even though the heater in the clinic was on, so that might explain why her temperature was a tad high.

I know I'm going to feel like this — like I just downed a four-shot espresso with about a cup of extra sugar — until I get back to Dr. Bell's on Friday.

"How'd the appointment go?" Jake asks, and I can tell by his voice he's not ticked off about waiting. Good. I couldn't add one more stress to my day.

"Wants us to come back Friday morning. Her secretions are kind of green, so she just wants to make sure it's cleared up by then." I know Jake's an even broodier worrywart than I am, so I try to sound casual, like I'm talking about a girlfriend who wants to stop over for a cup of coffee. It helps having some reason to pretend I'm not about to die of panic.

Patricia twists around in her seat like a yoga guru. She's got that lecturing professor look on her face. "Green could mean infection."

I don't bother to tell her she might have shared that useful information as soon as she noticed the change in the color of Natalie's secretions. It would only turn into an argument about how she handles all of Natalie's care and I'm the ungrateful mom who's too lazy to parent my own kid. Like she doesn't realize I'd be more than willing to rinse out the saliva canister each day if she didn't always beat me to it.

I try to change the subject. "The good news is we can start feeding her every three hours during the day and cut out that feeding in the middle of the night." Nobody responds. I'm glad Patricia isn't droning on about how much sleep she missed when she was nursing the twins.

I want to ask Jake about his shift, but I feel so stupid here in the back seat. I've only driven a car a handful of times since the doctor put me on bed rest. I don't even know how many months it's been. I already told you how I can't keep it in my head that we're already in December. Christmas is in what — about a week? Heck if I know. The mommy mags make it out like baby's first Christmas is just as exciting as the first word or the first step or all those other firsts that Natalie may never achieve in her lifetime. As for me, I just want to get past Christmas and on to New Year's. My resolution? Get Patricia out of our house.

I know she's pitching in with the baby and all, but seriously. She's been here two stinking months. Time to pay rent if she's going to stay. My vote would be to keep on living dirt-poor but at least have the trailer to ourselves again.

I haven't thought of a Christmas gift for Jake. I haven't thought of a Christmas gift for anyone. I wish I could look back to Natalie's delivery day and find someone besides myself to blame. A million-dollar settlement sounds pretty good right about now.

CHAPTER 29

It's evening, and we're all sitting around the TV watching one of Patricia's cooking competition shows. I hate to admit it, but I find the cutthroat challenges mildly entertaining. The host just made one of the contestants trade in all her spices for a five-pound chunk of sea salt and a cheese grater.

The funny thing is I bet her dish will still have more flavor than Patricia's.

A commercial comes on, reminding us that it's time to buy diamond jewelry for the ones we love. I wonder if Jake and I will ever get around to finding each other rings. It's not like we sat down to actually plan our wedding. He asked me on a Monday morning, and we arrived at the courthouse with our paperwork that Thursday.

Just the kind of romance every girl dreams about, right?

I still don't know why he did it. Asked me to marry him, I mean. We'd had this major fight the night before. A big one. He yelled, so you know it had to be huge.

It was a week after the G-tube surgery. He'd been in Seattle for nearly a month, and Roberto gave him an ultimatum. Either come home and get back to work or find another job.

For a little while, we talked about leaving the trailer and finding a place in Seattle. Jake was looking for work out there, not going from business to business or anything, but he was checking online to see if anything popped up.

I was all for the move. There wasn't anything tying me down to Orchard Grove. I hated the trailer park. I'd fallen out of touch with all my co-workers from the assisted living home. I still got together sometimes with Jake's friends from the store, but that was about the extent of our social lives. I hadn't even met Dr. Bell yet.

But Jake's a creature of habit, and even though Roberto treats him like a soiled diaper, Jake's comfortable there. Knows the people, knows the job. Sometimes I wonder if that boy has an adventurous bone in his entire body.

Anyway, he needed to get back to work. Roberto had been bugging him for a couple weeks but said he'd wait until after the surgery. Now there were no other excuses. Of course, Jake didn't tell me all this while it was happening. He waited until his mind was already made up.

"I think I need to head back home soon," he said. We were out walking because I needed fresh air. I tried to force myself outside two or three times a week, take a little walk to unwind. Jake didn't always come, but he wanted to this time. It was pouring rain, typical Seattle weather, so we were walking all the levels of one of the parking garages. Real romantic setting, as I'm sure you can imagine.

I thought Jake was just making small talk. He'd mentioned going back to Orchard Grove before, but I never thought much about it. Jake isn't the proactive type if you haven't figured that out yet. Doesn't find the gumption to do much if it takes him out of his little comfort bubble.

And at that point, at least as far as I knew, his comfort bubble was with me and Natalie in Seattle. Not that I was going to get on my knees and beg him to stay or anything. But I didn't think he was all that serious until he told me, "Roberto put me on the schedule for Tuesday."

I no idea if Tuesday was in one day or six, but he was obviously talking about a definite date sometime in the coming week.

"Really?" I tried not to sound upset. I didn't want him to think I couldn't handle being here with Natalie on my own. In fact, I figured it might be nice to hoard that thirty-four-dollar-a-day Medicaid meal voucher all to myself. "How are you going to get back there?"

"Marcos is in town visiting his sister. He's driving back tomorrow."

"Tomorrow." The word fell flat on my lips. Would he come back? What if Natalie never made it to Orchard Grove? What if Jake never saw her again?

"Kind of sucks, doesn't it?" He let out this little laugh, like he thought it was a stupid idea too, but Roberto said he had to so what choice did he have? Jake's such a yes boy. I'm sure Patricia made sure of that when he was still in diapers.

"There's one more thing," he said quietly. Like he was scared of me. I hate it when he does that. Makes me feel like I'm some ogre he's got to tiptoe around.

"What?" I knew it wouldn't be good news from the tone of his voice.

"Charlene's going to be driving with us, too."

CHAPTER 30

I'm proud to say that I didn't freak out immediately. Heaven knows I could have. I mean, what kind of man ditches you and your dying infant to spend four hours in the car next to the woman he cheated on you with?

Charlene? Seriously? Out of all the women Jake knows, she's not even that high up there on the hot scale. I mean, she's got the hourglass thing going on, but she's at least twenty pounds overweight, and she's got this sleazy aura about her. Like you could catch an STD or a canker sore by just looking at her.

I held my tongue at first. I mean, it wasn't Jake's fault he couldn't afford anything more than a lemon and had to rely on other people to drive him to and from the city. But still, he'd done so much to convince me earlier that he and Charlene were done with. That he'd been so rude to her there was no way she'd have anything to do with him again. And now they were about to spend four hours together driving over the scenic North Cascades in the fall when everything's gorgeous and vibrant?

Man, I hate that woman.

You can call me a hypocrite if you want. I probably wouldn't argue with you. But seriously, how would you feel if it was your boyfriend who'd been with Charlene and now was planning to catch a ride with her, leaving you and your sick baby behind in Seattle with absolutely no one?

Well, we didn't say much for the rest of the walk. It was a stupid idea anyway, trekking up and down that parking garage. If the point was to get fresh air, I should have picked a location that didn't stink of car exhaust. I don't know if you've ever paid much attention to hospital parking garages, but the cars get more and more flashy the closer you get to ground level, since that's where all the doctors park. I remember looking at those red Porches and Audis and imagining what it would be like to have a buttload of money like that.

When Jake and I got back to the hospital, I told him I was going to see Natalie.

"I'll come too," he said, which was weird because he usually headed back to the Ronald McDonald house early to play his stupid candy game on his phone. I wasn't going to argue, though. I didn't want him to think I was mad at him for bailing out on us. I didn't want him to think I was scared senseless to imagine being left in Seattle alone.

When did I grow to be such a big baby?

"You're pretty quiet," he said when we got into the elevator.

I shrugged. The more he talked, the madder I got.

"Are you upset about Charlene?" Man, how dense could he be?

"What do you think?" I snapped.

I don't think he was prepared for me to jump on him like that. He got this look like Bambi's mom before the hunter blows her brains out. He reached out and tried to grab my hand. Not the smartest move he's ever made. "I already told you, there's nothing between us."

"Yeah, I got that part pretty clear by now. But thanks for the mental image."

I didn't want to look at him. Didn't want to see his pathetic expression, his futile attempts to calm me down at a time like this.

"You know what I meant."

I got out of the elevator and kept walking. I wasn't about to listen to him whine.

"Come on." He hurried to catch up. "I need that job to make rent this month."

I laughed in his face. As if he didn't know how much I hated that trailer park. I'd be happy if we got evicted. I'd be happy if the whole stinking lot burned to the ground.

"Please, it's not like anything's going to happen …"

He still thought this whole thing was about Charlene. I didn't want to hear his arguments. I needed to go see my daughter. I walked ahead, but he grabbed my hand.

Hard.

"Come here and talk to me." He'd never spoken to me like that. Forceful. Almost threatening.

I snapped my head around to face him. At least he'd lost the doe-eyes. Now he looked mad. Now he looked ready for a fight. Too bad I wasn't in the mood.

"I'm going to the NICU." I tried to pull my hand loose, but he didn't let go. It was getting late, and the hospital wasn't very crowded or I'm sure he would have never dared.

"Let go of me." I pried my hand free and walked away, but he yanked me by the back of my shirt. And that's when I flung around and hit him. Not that hard. Not in the face or anything, just in the shoulder. Enough to stun him so he'd let me go.

He swore at me. I'd never heard those words come out of his mouth before, not before and not since. But at least I was free.

I stomped ahead confidently, certain he wouldn't dare follow me. I kept my hands in fists in case he was watching me storm off, but I couldn't keep this ridiculous smile off my face.

Who would have thought that Jake had a pair of balls after all?

CHAPTER 31

I've already told you how much I despise being ignored. I would much rather be hated than tossed aside and abandoned. That's why I felt a little thrill of victory when I finally managed to make Jake angry. I was acting like a witch. I'll be the first to admit it. But for weeks, I'd been trying to get some reaction out of that boy. Like when you're a kid and you keep poking at the jellyfish in the aquarium because you just want to see it do something.

I'm sure if I had a psychologist or therapist they'd tell me how messed up that is. Tell me it's immature try to make someone mad at you because you're attention-starved and insanely hormonal.

They can take all their book learning and shove it down their throats. What do they know about me, anyway?

I got to the NICU that night, and there wasn't much to do. Natalie was asleep. I usually held her at least once a day. It's this skin-to-skin thing where you take off your shirt and wear a hospital gown and you put the baby right up against you in nothing but a diaper. Yeah, I was weirded out by the sound of it at first too, but I guess they've got all kinds of science to prove how effective it is at enhancing your kid's health. Who knows? Maybe that's why Natalie survived her NICU stay in the first place. I don't know.

But I didn't want to hold her that night. I'm not into New Agey mumbo jumbo kind of stuff, but I was fuming mad, and I was worried that somehow I could transfer all that negativity to my baby if I held her in that state of mind. Honestly, with me being so ticked off at Jake, I just didn't feel very warm and squishy toward his daughter, know what I mean?

So there wasn't much for me to do except wait around for the night shift to show up so I could hear the reports from the nurse. Maybe I was more upset about Jake taking off than I realized. All I knew was I was sick and tired of the NICU. Natalie had recovered from her surgery. She still couldn't swallow, but that might never improve. I couldn't see any reason for her to stay there. I'd watched the nurses taking care of the suctioning and tube feeds and was sure I could figure it out.

That's what got me so upset about the whole thing with Jake. He could leave any time he wanted. But what was I supposed to do? It's not like I could go back with him to Orchard Grove and mail Natalie my breastmilk from there. I was trapped. Four weeks of bedrest during the torture of a central Washington summer. After that Seattle for a month, and all this for a daughter who might never know or care who I am.

I don't mean to sound like an ingrate, but come on. How much junk is one woman supposed to put up with?

Jake could up and quit any time he wanted. He could hide behind his stupid minimum-wage job as a lousy store clerk. Well, what about me? When would I get a break? When would I get to leave?

The whole Charlene thing was just a convenient focal point for my rage. What I hated most was the fact that he was free to walk away. Would I ever see him again? There's no chance the Orchard Grove hospital could care for someone like Natalie. Would it even be safe for me to take her back there? Maybe I'd stay in Seattle. Except without Jake, that would mean I'd have to find a job, pay my own rent, foot all the bills. How was I supposed to do any of that when Natalie would need round-the-clock care?

Why is it always the mothers who get tethered to the kids and not the other way around? I earned more at the Winter Grove assisted living home than Jake made slaving for Roberto. Maybe I should go back to work at Winter Grove and let him stay home with Natalie. At least then I wouldn't have to worry about his path crossing with Charlene's anymore.

Charlene. We were friends once, in a casual sort of way. She had a thing for Jake from the beginning, but seriously, I always assumed he was too much of a good guy to do anything other than a little harmless flirting.

Learn something new every day, right?

I know I shouldn't be so self-righteous about it all. Jake doesn't know the half of what I've done.

Thank God.

CHAPTER 32

Jake wasn't at the Ronald McDonald house when I got back. I wasn't surprised, and I was too exhausted to waste any energy wondering where he went. He could have been at a bar getting drunk with Charlene for all I cared.

I needed to think. Ask myself if it was right for me to stay mad at him. He shouldn't have cheated on me. That was stupid. But he felt bad about it, and he came clean. Which is more than I've done. I've got my secrets, and I plan to keep it that way. What Jake doesn't know won't hurt him.

Except there's the guilt, too. Part of me thinks that Elder Tom's right. God's punishing me for my sins by making Natalie suffer.

I can't change what I've already done. That's why we call it the past. But after our fight, I started wondering if I should tell Jake about what happened. Maybe it would give Natalie a better chance at survival. I would have done anything to leave the NICU. I would have confessed to murder if it could have gotten me and my daughter out of there an hour earlier.

People say a mother will do anything for her kid. Well, I honestly didn't feel all that maternal toward Natalie back then. It was sort of nice cuddling when we did our skin-to-skin time, but she still didn't know who I was or act like I was any different than the dozens of nurses who took care of her.

Maybe I did have that protective instinct but just didn't know it. That's the only way I can explain what I did next.

I wrote Jake a letter. I knew if I had to do it face to face, I'd wimp out. So I got it all out on paper. I didn't even type it. Wrote it all by hand. Gave my wrist a pretty bad cramp, too.

I left it on the bathroom counter, so if he came back that night he'd see it before he went to bed. I didn't want to change my mind and tear the paper up or anything, so I sent him a text to let him know I had something important to say to him and there was a letter waiting in our room.

And then I tried to fall asleep. Which obviously wasn't very easy. I might have ruined everything. If my relationship with Jake had even an ounce of potential to work out, I probably destroyed it in one impulsive note.

Oh, well. I couldn't take back that text I sent him. It reminded me of my labor, actually. Once the water breaks, it's not like you can change your mind and decide to wait another week or two. Once it's all set in motion, there's not a whole lot more you can do besides hold on and wait for everything to pass.

Unless you're a chicken like me.

I don't know what time it was when I finally got out of bed, but I tore up the letter and flushed it down the toilet. Jake didn't need to know. Who was I kidding? Getting rid of my own shame and guilt wasn't worth sabotaging everything good between us. It wasn't fair to him.

Of course, I'd sent him a text that there was a letter waiting for him, so I had to do something. I ended up writing him this really dumb note about how I forgave him. I was feeling so guilty about my own past I think I even apologized for getting mad that night, and I told him the truth. At least the part about me being scared to be alone in Seattle. Stupid of me, I know. But from my text, I knew he'd be expecting something kind of significant, so I had to give him that.

After all the lies I'd told him already, it was the least I could do.

CHAPTER 33

The stupid cooking show is finally over, and Natalie's tucked in her crib for the night. The rest of us are out here in the living room being lazy. Patricia's flipping through a *Taste of Home* magazine, Jake's playing Candy Zapper, and I'm staring at my phone, scrolling through my friends' posts, hoping to find something interesting.

"What time do you work tomorrow?" I ask Jake.

"I open tomorrow and Friday. Then I'm back to nights."

I don't even want to think about being stuck for the next two days with Patricia in the house. "That's not going to work," I tell him. "We've got to take Natalie back to Dr. Bell on Friday."

He shrugs and doesn't even look up from his screen. "Guess you'll have to drop me off again."

I roll my eyes. He could take his bike or something if he wanted. I mean, he'd have to get up earlier and ride in the cold and dark, but it's either that or he and I both have to get up at the crack of dawn.

I think about Dr. Bell, how kind she was to assume I'm sleep deprived because I'm caring for Natalie all night. How good it felt to talk to someone who doesn't know I'm living in a trailer park with the mother-in-law from the pit of Hades.

"I thought her appointments were every two weeks now," Patricia comments, and I grit my teeth. I swear, if the next few words out of her mouth are *When I was raising the twins*, I'll go postal all over her smug little face.

I glance at Jake. I've spent my day trying to downplay the green secretions without making him all antsy and nervous. Because if he gets antsy and nervous, I'll get even more antsy and nervous, and it's going to be a miserable couple of days.

I'm sure Natalie's fine. Sometimes your snot and drool turn green. Maybe she's fighting a cold or something simple like that. Her temperature wasn't that elevated. Not even an official fever. I'm sure we have nothing to worry about. Nothing at all.

"I think a big part of it is Dr. Bell wants to check up again since we're changing the feeding schedule," I say. It sounds so much nicer than admitting the pediatrician thinks something might be wrong.

At the mention of night feeds, Patricia squares her shoulders and straightens her spine. It's like that woman's taken it as a personal insult that she no longer has to set her alarm for 2:00 am to pour formula down my daughter's feeding tube. The less she does around the house and the less she does to take care of Natalie, the less leverage she gets to lord over me. That's the only reason she's ticked. If I didn't know her better, I might hope that Patricia's sleeping through the night would mean she'd be easier to get along with, but I'm not that naïve anymore.

Jake's still staring at his phone when he says, "Natalie had a pretty good day today." I don't know if he senses the tension and is trying to change the subject or if he's just filling the silence with drivel. It doesn't matter as long as it keeps Patricia from bringing up her herculean success raising twins singlehandedly. I'm surprised she didn't do it barefoot in the snow too.

Uphill both ways.

"Yeah," I agree mindlessly.

"I should hope so." Patricia's still sitting like there's a flagpole shoved down the back of her bra, and she's got her hands folded on her lap like she's some sort of stinking beauty-queen washout. "She's getting Tylenol with each of her feedings."

"She's getting what?" My voice is seething. I know it must be bad because even Jake glances up.

Patricia tilts her chin up and slightly to the side. It's her Japanese-American version of a shrug. "I knew she was due for her shots today. I always gave the twins Tylenol when they had theirs."

I've got my hands clenched into fists, and I'm envisioning what it will feel like when that angular, Botoxed jawline connects with my knuckles. "You can't just give my daughter medicine without telling me." Did you catch that? *Telling me.* Not *asking me.* Two months, and she's already got me partially trained.

Just not trained enough.

She makes this ugly little laugh, like she's the witch in her candy house and Hansel and Gretel just accused her of eating helpless children. "I might have asked you to give it to her if I thought you would remember." She lets out a sigh worthy of an

Academy award. "You know me. I don't mind a little extra work." I'm on my feet. It's not like I'm about to do anything stupid. I just need to engage my leg muscles. This isn't a fight I can take sitting down. "I didn't ask for your little extra work." My vocal cords are sore. Strained. I'm not used to yelling anymore because I've walked on eggshells ever since she moved herself into my house.

Patricia pouts as if she has a dozen cameras pointed at her and she wants to give them each her best sympathetic expression. "If I had known it would upset you, I would have let you measure the medicine out before I poured her formula in." Another shrug. This time it's both her chin and her shoulder that are involved. "I'm very sorry," she apologizes, as if I'm mad because I didn't get to squirt the Tylenol into Natalie's tube myself. She's either a stinking genius of deflection or the biggest idiot in the history of mothers-in-law.

I grab my hair. Anything to keep myself from decking her. I'm closer to her now. Close enough to reach if I wanted. "She. Is. My. Daughter." I'm punctuating every word like they're each an individual sentence. "You don't give her anything without my approval."

She opens her mouth, but I take a step forward and cut her off. The chin lowers a degree or two. I think she finally realizes I'm royally ticked off, and I outweigh her by forty pounds.

I stare down at her. "I don't care if you're a nurse. I don't care if you raised twins. You could have squeezed out eight babies at once like Octo-Mom, and I wouldn't trust you near my child."

The almond eyes widen for a split second before narrowing. The skin across her face is completely taut, like she's tensed every single muscle. I can feel the heat of her wrath, but I'm not intimidated. What's she going to do? Bleach my bathtub?

"You're lucky." Her voice is completely controlled. And in between sentences she's smiling at me, her lips tight like she's got them sewn shut. "You're lucky that raising twins taught me patience and self-sacrifice. It's a lesson I hope you learn one day. For my granddaughter's sake, I hope you learn."

I want a yelling match. Part of me hopes she'll stand up and confront me. Fine with me if this turns physical. *Bring it on, Grandma.*

Instead all I get is a sermon from a woman perfectly calm and rigid like she's taken lessons from Queen Elizabeth herself.

She does stand up, but it's not to confront me. She doesn't even look in my direction but goes and faces her son, who's just sitting on his butt and gaping at the two of us like some kind of braindead vegetable.

"I told you she wasn't fit to be a mother." Patricia's voice is quiet. Subdued. She may as well be reminding him to brush his teeth before going to bed.

I know just what she's doing. Trying to pit him against me. Two against one. It's the only way the odds will ever lean in her favor.

"I'm going to bed now," Patricia says. "I hope that by morning you'll both realize how much I've sacrificed for that child of yours."

CHAPTER 34

You would think that in a situation like this, Patricia would storm out of the room. Except she doesn't. It's more like gliding, like she's taking classes at charm school and balancing ten stinking books on her head.

I'm so mad I don't even look at Jake. Obviously, he wasn't the one who gave my kid Tylenol without asking me first, but if he wasn't such a pushover, there's no way the mother-in-law of Frankenstein would still be living under my roof.

I should have kicked her out that first week she was here. *Fish and company both stink after three days*, right? Of course I'm mad at her. And it's not even the Tylenol. That's just the final blow. No, what gets under my skin is the way she presents herself as so selfless and faultless. Like she's a stinking martyr. Nobody asked her to put her life on hold to live in a trailer and suction out a sick baby round the clock. Nobody asked her to scrub this place senseless just to prove she works harder than the rest of us. Nobody asked her to make us bland casseroles every night and complain that our regular diet doesn't give us enough fiber or vitamins.

The thing is, if I were to go to Jake and list all the reasons why he has to kick Patricia out, I wouldn't have anything to say. That's why I sometimes think she's a literal genius. That woman hasn't done anything but bend over backwards to help us out since she arrived on our doorstep. At least that's the way she sees it, and that's the way Jake's bound to look at it, too.

Man, I wish I could get some settlement money out of the OB. Get a house in my own name. Patricia's like a vampire. And no, I'm not talking about the sparkling types from those stupid teen romances. I'm talking about the old-school kind of vampire you have to invite into your home or they can't get in. This is Jake's trailer, so he did the inviting, but now there's no way to undo it. Not unless he mans up and confronts her about her behavior.

But like I said, what behavior?

Take the Tylenol, for example. In Patricia's mind, she was trying to help. And I'll be honest with you. I never knew about giving your baby Tylenol before her shots. I never read about it in any of the mommy mags, and it never crossed my mind. Heck, Patricia might have even saved Natalie a lot of discomfort today by keeping her drugged up. Who knows?

I can't hate her for giving Natalie the medicine. But it's the stinking principle of the thing. Natalie's my daughter. Mine. If anyone is going to be making decisions about her medical care, it's going to be me.

Sandy told me once that you don't just marry a person. You marry their whole family. At the time, she was trying to show me how it probably wouldn't be in my best interest to marry Lincoln Grant. Talk about messed-up families. His dad was in jail on child porn charges along with Lincoln's older brother. He had a sister who was arrested multiple times for solicitation, and his mom was a raging drunk.

So when Sandy gave me that advice, I thought she just meant you shouldn't marry someone with that much family drama. Family psychosis might be a better way to put it, at least for the Grants. I should have listened better, and maybe I would have understood that even if your mother-in-law's not a streetwalker or a druggie, she still has the ability to make your life an absolute nightmare.

Of course, I didn't realize any of that when Jake proposed to me in the Ronald McDonald house. It was the morning after I wrote him that note where I told him I forgave him for what happened with Charlene.

At least that's what I intended the message to be, but I spent about one sentence on Charlene and four paragraphs on how scared I felt about him going back to Orchard Grove. I think I was trying to stroke his ego or something. Assuage my guilt over those things Jake never had a clue about. He still doesn't have a clue, by the way. I've never told him what I was going to say in that first letter, and I never intend to. But that's probably why the second one turned out mushier than I planned.

I woke up at the Ronald McDonald house with Jake kissing me on the eyelid. He had the letter in his hand, and before I could even stretch myself out, he sat down on the side of the bed and started rubbing my arm. "Thank you for your note," he whispered. For a split second, I thought he was talking about the first one, the one where I confessed everything. There's nothing to wake you up like having your heart literally stop dead in your chest.

Then I saw the letter in his hand and remembered the original was now swimming with the fishes or slowly dissolving in chemicals at some water treatment facility. I still felt guilty though, so I put on my best behavior and gave him a smile. "You're welcome, babe."

And he kissed me again and stroked my forehead, and I don't remember that he'd ever been that tender or loving with me since Natalie was born. Ripping up that confession was definitely the right call.

"I'm sorry I was a jerk," he said. "I thought you were mad about Charlene. You could have told me sooner that you wanted me to stay here."

I don't know if it was the stress from not sleeping well or the postpartum hormones or how wretched I felt knowing that he had nothing to apologize for compared to what I'd done, but I felt myself getting ready to cry. "I just don't want to be alone." I know I wasn't the most truthful of girlfriends, and I'm definitely not the most truthful of wives, but that may have been the most honest thing I've told Jake in my entire life.

The tears were burning my cheeks by that point. Real ones. I'm ok at acting, but I can't muster up tears on command. And Jake wiped every single one of them away.

"You don't have to worry," he said. "I'm not going anywhere. I already texted Roberto and let him know."

I sat up in bed and hugged him and cried on his shoulder. He probably thought I was relieved and that's why I was going at it. Really, I was crying because I knew that if I told him everything, there's no way he'd stay with me, letting me sob into his chest, saying such nice things and trying to comfort and soothe me.

He would never forgive me if he knew the truth.

CHAPTER 35

He proposed to me ten or fifteen minutes later. It wasn't all that steamy or romantic, but I guess that's not what either of us needed at the time. My tears had stopped, and we were just talking. I don't even think we were cuddling or anything at that point. Jake's got his faults, but he's a really good listener. He'd have to be after growing up with someone like Patricia. Back when she was raising her twins like a boss, I'm sure Jake couldn't get a word in edgewise against her. Come to think of it, he still can't today.

Anyway, that morning he wanted to know exactly what I was feeling. I swear, if that boy applied himself, he could become a stinking shrink or something.

"Did you think I was walking out for good?" he asked. Because, of course, he assumed all those tears were about him.

I should warn you that this isn't going to be the most romantic of stories. But I loved Jake. Messed up as I was, I loved him. And he was right. I was scared of being abandoned. You think about my past — what happened with my birth mom, all those foster homes — and maybe you'll cut me a little slack. So maybe I've got a small chip on my shoulder. Who doesn't?

"I don't think I can do this without you," I told him. Like I was a stinking princess locked away in the dungeon, unable to lift a finger to save myself.

"Do what without me?" he asked. As if he couldn't fill in the blanks. I think he just wanted to keep me talking. I'm not sure. Isn't that what a shrink would do?

"I don't know. Everything." I wasn't going to spell it all out for him. Not because it felt like I'd just eaten a whole slice of humble pie and it was turning into little dry cement crumbles in my mouth. But because all of the scenarios were so horrible. Why didn't I want to be left alone? Because Natalie might die. She might have to stay in the NICU for months. She might catch an infection. She might end up on a ventilator again, and I'd have to decide to pull the plug or not.

That's why I didn't want him returning to Orchard Grove.

He put his arm around me and said, "I'm not leaving you. We're in this together."

When I lived with Sandy, she started taking me to this counselor dude, some Christian therapist who went to her husband's church. I don't even remember his name. I only saw him a handful of times. But he told me something that I haven't forgotten. We were talking one afternoon — he had this office where everything smelled like leather — and he said my problem was I sabotaged my relationships. Instead of letting people hurt me, I was trying to regain some sense of control and destroying relationships on my own terms before others had the chance to abandon me.

It made sense. It's that control I'm always looking for. Did I tell you that after that guy assaulted me when I still worked at the convenience store, I actually went on a date or two with him? Not my brightest moment, but I think it's the same idea. Once you agree to go out with someone, everything that comes after is on your terms, not his. You're not powerless anymore.

Man, I hate to feel powerless. I think that's why I came so close to telling Jake about what I'd done. I knew he was going to leave, but if I destroyed our relationship before his foot was out the door, our massive falling out would be in my hands.

But I didn't want to be like that anymore. It was a miracle that Jake was still with me, that we were still a couple. And if we ever broke up, there's no way I could find someone else who would see Natalie as anything more than a vegetable. So when all of a sudden I heard Jake mention marriage, I said yes. I was sick of sabotaging myself. I was sick of ruining the best things that ever happened to me. I was terrified of being left alone, and if Jake and I got married, I wouldn't have to worry so much.

Besides, if he ever discovers what I did, it will be that much harder for him to leave.

CHAPTER 36

Patricia hasn't stirred since her regal exit to her room, and I haven't heard a peep from Natalie, either. Now that I think about it, I have no idea why I ever agreed to let Patricia sleep in my daughter's room. Was I so thankful for the chance to have someone else take charge of all the night suctioning and tube feeds that I was willing to risk my baby's well-being? I mean, who knows how Patricia is trying to poison her against me? I swear just that grumpy aura alone could probably turn the sweetest Gerber baby into a colicky monster.

I know I've got to talk to Jake about her, but he's avoiding me. Which is silly when you consider that our elbows are only an inch apart from each other. It's amazing what kind of armor one small smartphone can set up between two people. He's slaughtering colorful pieces of candy, and I'm cyber stalking a girl I knew back in high school. She was one of the snotty ones from Sandy's church who started the rumors about me and Lincoln Grant to begin with. Is it wrong for me to secretly rejoice that she's now divorced?

At least I've got a husband, *chica.*

For now, anyway.

But this Patricia thing has got to stop. Did you know that the Chinese symbol for *trouble* is a picture of two women living under the same roof? I'm not making it up. I read it on this random fact website I sometimes go to when I'm bored.

I've already decided that Jake and I are having the Talk tonight. It can't wait until morning because he'll leave for work before I'm even awake. When it comes right down to it, Jake has to make a decision. Mommy or me. And based on past events, the odds aren't too hot in my favor. But I can't go on like this indefinitely, can I? You can't blame me if I'm at the end of my rope. No, not even that. It's more like I ran out of rope weeks ago, and now I'm at the bottom of a thousand-foot cavern with no footholds or ladders or even a little bucket on a pulley to get me out.

So Jake's got to man up and make the call. Either Patricia goes, or I go. Only now I'm thinking about sabotage and wondering if this is my way of ruining my marriage intentionally. If Patricia stays, that means I'm out of here, me and Natalie both. And then where would we go? It's bad enough my baby and I live in a trailer and get Medicaid, WIC coupons, and food stamps. Like a stinking statistic.

I don't know. Maybe I should sleep on it. Things always look clearer in the morning, don't they? Except Jake's waking up at 4:30, and if I have to spend the entire morning alone with his mom without talking any of this through, I'm going to kill her.

I swear I'm going to kill her.

"You almost ready for bed?" I ask.

"Mmm." His eyes never leave his screen. It's a wonder that boy hasn't pulled a muscle in his forearm yet from popping all those stupid gobstoppers and bubble gums.

"I'm sorry I yelled at your mom." The words are painful coming out of my throat, but I need to do something to get his attention. *Desperate times*, right?

Jake zaps an entire row of purple-grape gushers. "Yeah, it was just Tylenol."

I bite my lip and carefully plan out my next words. "I know, but on the other hand I think it's more than that. Have you noticed how she's kind of taken over all of Natalie's care?"

"She's just trying to help." It's my husband talking, but it's his mother's voice in my head. *Somebody around here has to step up and pitch in.*

I need Patricia's help about as badly as I need a double mastectomy. "I just thought that when she came, she'd only be staying for a week or so. It's been two months now." Even though I'm skillfully avoiding eye contact, I feel Jake's body tense next to mine, so I add, "She shouldn't have to put her own life on hold this long. We can take care of Natalie at this point."

He's frowning, but I think it's because he's got too much red on his screen and none of those donut bombs to get rid of them all at once.

"What do you think?" I prod. It takes every ounce of self-control in my body to keep my voice down. He's lucky I don't take his stupid phone and hurl it against the wall.

You can tell he's got more white in him than his mom because he shrugs with his shoulders in typical American style. "She'll probably go home sometime after Christmas."

I have to mentally walk my way through the calendar to figure out how far out in the distance he's talking. About a week?

God bless me if I haven't strangled her by then.

CHAPTER 37

It's the morning after that blowup about the Tylenol, and I'm lying in bed. I woke up half an hour ago when Jake got up for work, and now I can't go back to sleep. The sun won't rise for a few more hours. I'm not even sure God's awake this early in the day.

Jake and I didn't say anything to each other before he left. I don't even think he noticed that his stupid alarm woke me up.

Some days I'm so glad I married Jake. Other days I don't have a clue what I was thinking.

We went to the courthouse the morning he proposed. We had no idea there were waiting periods or anything like that. We thought you could just show up and get it done. The clerk told us we could fill out the paperwork that day but we'd have to wait for Thursday to actually go through with it.

Knowing me, knowing how I hate feeling close to someone who might end up abandoning me, you might think I spent those three days on pins and needles. Or maybe I secretly planned ways to sabotage my own happiness like that counselor accused me of doing.

It wasn't like that. I can honestly say we were happy. Heaven knows I had enough reasons to be literally depressed, except I wasn't.

I couldn't believe it was really going to happen. I was really getting married. And to someone like Jake.

If you had asked me back in high school, I'm sure I would have told you my dream man would be like Lincoln Grant. Dark skin. Super sexy. Deep voice. Hard abs. The works.

Man, I have to laugh when I compare Jake to that. But there was something that felt so right about everything at the time. Like I was making the mature decision for a change. I was doing what was best for my daughter. I was providing her with a stable family life. I wasn't going to be a *woman of the world* anymore. I was done sleeping around. Done living irresponsibly.

God would be happy with me if I married my baby's father, right? Doesn't that kind of go with the whole purity philosophy?

I sort of saw this marriage as my way to get back on the right foot with God. I mean, I knew he hadn't ever left me, but I also knew my choices weren't doing anything to make him happy. Who knew? Maybe if Jake and I made our relationship official, God would turn away whatever wrath he was pouring out on our tiny, helpless baby.

If I'd studied the Bible more thoroughly, I might have realized that even getting hitched hadn't worked out too well for David and Bathsheba and the child they conceived in sin. But that's the God of the Old Testament, right? The God of the New Testament's all about mercy and grace.

Thank heavens.

I've been thinking more about God since that Sunday service.

I'm glad Jake forced me to go with him. It's kind of like after you eat real healthy for a day or two, and it kick starts something in your body where you want to keep up the good work. That's how I've been feeling spiritually.

I'm married now, and ironically I'm abstinent, at least for as long as Patricia's been here. That's got to count for something in God's eyes, right? And I was really ticked at Jake last night, but I didn't even yell at him. We had a civil discussion, I let him know my opinion, but I didn't raise my voice or anything.

Isn't that how the Bible says women are supposed to behave with their husbands?

And I've got a date in my head now. Jake said his mom would leave after Christmas. I think that's his way of telling me, *let's not rock the boat right before the holidays, but after Christmas is over, I'll tell her she's got to go.* It's the best choice, really. He's right to not kick her out this week of all weeks. That would be cruel.

But now that I see a light at the top of the mother-in-law pit of Hades, I'm starting to think about what it will be like when Jake's at work and I'm the one taking care of Natalie. I want to be the kind of mom in those magazines, the kind of mom Dr. Bell thinks I am. I'll get a library card. Start reading her stories like I'd been planning to do all along. It just feels so awkward to hold a book and read to a baby who doesn't even notice you, but I'll make myself get used to it.

I feel good. I mean, if I'm going to be taking care of Natalie, I've got to get past this parenting autopilot I've been on and start engaging with her. I should sing songs to her. I've got a pretty good voice. She'll love it. Maybe we'll watch *America's Got Talent* together. Maybe she'll be the youngest winner. Maybe one day my baby will become world famous. With that chocolate skin and those perfect almond eyes, I'm sure it could happen.

I get up and do some stretches. I'm not like some girls, you know, who go overboard into fitness, but I like the way my body feels when I'm done. If I'm going to make myself a better person, I'm going all out. That's why I'm out of bed hours before my usual wake-up time. I've got a house to clean. Breakfast to make. Christmas to plan.

I'm shocked to hear myself say this, but I actually think it's going to be a good day.

CHAPTER 38

"How was work?" I ask as soon as Jake gets home.

"Not bad." His voice is uncertain, like he doesn't know why I sound so cheerful. He glances over my shoulder, and I peck him on the cheek.

I'm all smiles. This is exciting. Like handing someone a surprise Christmas present. Jake doesn't know about this change in me. I'm glad he's a little off-guard. It means my metamorphosis is dramatic enough for him to notice.

He's looking at me sideways, like he doesn't trust me. "Where's my mom?"

I almost laugh. Is he afraid I strangled her and dumped the body in my perfectly bleached bathtub?

"She wasn't feeling well today. She's coming down with a cold or something." Which is amazing, given how many hundreds of dollars she spends a month on health supplements. That's one thing Patricia's got going for her. She married into money and hired a good lawyer when she got divorced.

Both times.

Jake frowns, and I wonder if he'll be on edge until he sees his mom alive and kicking. Or at least alive. I've never witnessed someone succumb to a common cold that dramatically. Like she's Wonder Woman one day and Madonna in that musical *Evita*, wallowing on her deathbed the next.

It was perfect timing, which is partly why I think God might have noticed my desire to be a better person and he's blessing me for it. I mean, I'm not happy that she's sick, but I went into the day hoping for the chance to prove that I can care for Natalie by myself, and that's exactly what came about. I got all her tube feedings in on time. She never had a soiled diaper for more than five or ten minutes before I was there to clean her up, and I even got lunch ready by the time Jake got home. It's chicken soup from cans, but I did add a few frozen vegetables. And guess what? I'm serving rice, but I actually put it into the soup.

I also added salt.

Let's watch Patricia's blood pressure jump fifteen points after the first bite.

I follow Jake into the kitchen. "You still didn't tell me about your day."

He takes the lid off the pot and gives it a confused expression like he's never seen brown rice in broth before. Then again, maybe he hasn't.

"Work was fine."

"I'm glad to hear it." Any other day, I would have pressed him for details. Assumed that since he wasn't talkative, there must be something he was trying to hide from me. Not today. Today is a fresh start. A New Year's resolution a little bit early. I'm not going to be the sulky, nagging wife I've been. I'm not even going to complain about Patricia living with us, at least not until after Christmas. But by then, my husband says she'll be gone anyway.

I grab the spoon and make myself look busy. "Hey, can you tell your mom that lunch is ready?"

Jake's still staring at me like I've just morphed into one of the mutants from the X-Men, but he leaves the kitchen and I hear him knocking softly on Patricia's door.

Natalie's breathing is a little gunky, so I leave the soup simmering to suction her out. I'm glad that Jake and his mom come down the hall while I've still got the Yankauer in my hand. If this doesn't prove to them that I've got what it takes to care for my child, nothing will.

Patricia looks awful, like she's gotten into a fight with a hair dryer and lost. I understand now why she spends that forty minutes putting on her foundation and concealer every morning. I'm sure I would too if that's what I looked like without any makeup. I don't know how to describe her hair. It's not exactly frizzy, because I don't think many Japanese women have that problem. All I can say is it gives me some small satisfaction knowing that my mother-in-law gets bedhead and tangled hair just like the rest of the world.

"I made you some chicken soup." I force humility into my tone, reminding myself of my resolve to finally become the person God would want me to be. The kind of person Sandy would be proud to call her daughter. I give Patricia a smile.

A real, literal smile.

I can tell Jake's on edge because he's shifting from foot to foot like he expects me to turn myself into that attack bunny from *Monty Python*, jump across the room, and sink my teeth into my mother-in-law's neck. Before long, he'll be used to the new me. We'll look back on our first few months of marriage, realize all our problems were due to hormones and all that anxiety over Natalie, and we'll laugh about it, thanking God those days are over.

We'll be regular churchgoers too. And not just the kind who show up every so often on Sundays. When I set my mind to do something, I do it all the way. I'm talking about prayer meetings, Bible studies, the works. Heck, people can even come here for a home group if they don't mind being cramped. Patricia's scrubbed the trailer spotless, so when she leaves it won't be too hard keeping it presentable.

I serve up the soup and take the bowls to my husband and mother-in-law at the table. I smile at my daughter, who's asleep in her bouncy chair and doing fine now that her throat is clear. I steel a quick glance at the ceiling, hoping God notices how good I've been. Hoping he sees how hard I'm trying.

Hoping it will be enough for him to overlook all the mistakes I made in the past and choose to save my daughter.

CHAPTER 39

Patricia goes right back to bed after we eat, but she thanks me for lunch first. And even though I detect what I think is a hint of criticism when she tells me how *interesting* the soup tasted, I don't let it get to me.

Jake helps me clear the table, which I haven't seen him voluntarily do the entire time we've been together. Maybe my positive attitude is contagious.

Maybe we do have what it takes to make this marriage work.

"That was nice of you to get lunch ready," he says.

I start loading up the dishwasher. "I don't mind. I kind of enjoyed it."

If Jake's going to think I'm ready to take care of Natalie by myself, I've really got to sell it.

"You enjoyed it?"

I shoot him another smile, certain my cheeks will be sore by the end of the day. "Yeah."

We don't say much after that. Once his dishes are cleared, Jake goes to the couch, but even the stupid music from his Candy Zapper game doesn't bother me like usual. He needs a way to unwind. We all do.

Natalie's making noise in her sleep. It's not quite snoring. It's more like gurgling, like some of that drool's getting stuck in the back of her throat but she's breathing right through it.

"Aren't you going to suction her?" Jake asks from the couch.

I try to ignore how accusing his tone sounds and remind myself it's good that he worries about our daughter just as much as I do.

"It's not that bad." I figure if I show him how confident I am, he won't be so anxious. I grab a rag and wipe the table, inwardly gloating when I find a single grain of rice Patricia dropped onto her chair.

Jake's still frowning at our daughter. "I really think she needs to be suctioned."

I turn my back so he won't see me roll my eyes. "She's fine." I walk by the bouncy seat to prove to him I'm being attentive. "That's just the way she sounds sometimes when she sleeps."

I toss the empty cans of soup into the trash and rummage around in search of the Tupperware. Patricia's moved things around since she took over the kitchen, and I have to open four different drawers before I find them.

I start to load the dishes, wondering what I should do when I'm done with the kitchen. It won't be that long until Natalie needs another feeding. I'm glad Dr. Bell switched her to a three-hour schedule. It gives me more to do throughout the day. More ways to be productive.

More ways to prove I'm mom enough to care for my own child.

I spill Jake's half-filled coffee cup from this morning while I'm reaching for the soap brush. It makes a mess all over the counter. I grit my teeth. If I can get through an eighty-six-hour labor, I can take care of a sink full of dishes.

I take a deep breath. I read on this self-help website once that at least nine-tenths of your daily stress can be relieved by breathing. Don't ask me how it works. I'm not even sure I believe it, but at least the action gives me something to focus on besides the old coffee dripping onto my kitchen floor and the cold stain soaking through the front of my maternity pants.

I make it through the first half of the dishes without further incident, but I stop when I hear a loud droning from the living room. Jake's bending over the bouncy chair, Yankauer tube in hand.

"What are you doing?"

Of course, he can't hear me with his ear right next to that stupid suction machine. I wonder if we need to worry about Natalie's hearing. It can't be good for her having that thing go off three or four times every hour so close to her little ears.

I'm in the living room now. I guess you could say I stomped over here, but that's because I'm worried about Natalie. Jake hasn't suctioned her once in her life, not as far as I remember. I turn off the machine as he's sticking the tube in Natalie's mouth.

"What the heck?" he demands, straightening up.

I square my shoulders, hands on hips, and face him.

"What was that for?" he whines.

"I told you she's fine." I grab the Yankauer out of his hand.

"She needs to be suctioned."

"No, she doesn't." Except now that I'm closer to her, I can hear it too. That wet noise in her throat.

Jake tries to snatch the Yankauer back. We're like two little kids playing keep away from each other. Except neither of us is laughing.

"Listen to that." Jake thrusts a finger down at our daughter.

I try not to wince at the sound. It's not snoring, really. More like a cat purring or water percolating in an old-fashioned coffee maker. Not the noise you ever want to hear coming from your own child's lungs. It reminds me of this foster brother I once had, Eliot Jamison, and his horrible asthma I used to tease him about. Man, I was merciless too.

"She needs to be suctioned." Jake's voice is softer now. More subdued. I can tell he's trying to keep the peace. He doesn't want to fight. Neither do I.

"I guess you're right." I hate to say the words. It's like they're physically painful creeping up from my throat. But they don't kill me, and I turn on the machine.

"I'll do it," Jake says and crowds into my space.

"I got it." I try to elbow him out of the way without it coming across like I'm manhandling him.

"I said I'd do it." He yanks the tube out of my hand. I swallow the curses I want to shout at him. It's not worth a big blowup. I should be glad he wants to be involved. Another week, as soon as

Christmas is over, it will just be Jake and me taking care of all these things. We may as well learn to share responsibility now.

I sigh and head back to the kitchen. Apparently, this is my place for the time being. I've got to watch out or resentment's going to grow and fester until we have a major eruption. That's why I prefer one or two smaller skirmishes a day. Otherwise you're just saving all that negative energy up for the really big ones.

But I'm going to learn. God's going to help me. I'll be the kind of woman I always pictured I'd grow up to be when I was at those youth retreats.

I realize now that even if the Grandma Lucy lady wasn't specifically telling me the future, she still inspired me. Made me realize that my daughter's beautiful and that she deserves a mom who loves her. A mom who's willing to work hard to protect her.

A mom who's not about to roll over and let her die without putting up the fight of her life.

CHAPTER 40

Patricia's still under the weather, but she dragged herself out of bed at five in the afternoon like a stinking martyr, hellbent on making us our daily casserole. It took Jake and me a full ten minutes to convince her to go lie down some more.

We decided to work together to make spaghetti for dinner. Jake's watching the pasta, and I'm browning the hamburger meat for the sauce. It's nice, just the two of us in here. Our kitchen's small. I've seen walk-in closets on TV with more space that this, but Jake's not that big of a guy, and we work comfortably side by side.

It's been a quiet afternoon. While Patricia napped, I spent some time online and Jake did his phone thing, but it felt different. Like we were more connected even though we weren't actually talking. It reminded me of the lunch we had as soon as we signed the marriage license. We decided to walk to this little seafood stand just a few blocks from the courthouse.

It's hard to describe how peaceful everything felt. It was one of the only perfectly clear days we had that entire six weeks in Seattle. The seagulls were out, and man were they loud. Jake held up a French fry, and one swooped down and grabbed it right out of his hand.

We stayed there for a little over an hour, just munching on our food and sometimes sharing a little with the gulls. I thought about what it would be like in a few years if we brought Natalie here, went for a walk like this, the three of us.

"I can't believe we really did it," Jake said.

"Yeah, I know." We both laughed. We laughed a lot that day, like two kids who finally mustered up the guts to go doorbell ditching at the grumpy old neighbor's house and couldn't stop giggling afterward. Like they couldn't seriously believe how audacious they'd been.

"I'm so in love," Jake said.

"Me, too." And I don't know if you get this way, but every time I get too happy, like too many good things seem to happen all at once, it turns everything bittersweet. Like I can't fully enjoy the fact that life is so stinking perfect because I know eventually it has to get worse. Eventually, I'd have to go back to the NICU and confront the fact that my month-old daughter might never leave that place alive. That she might never know who her mommy and daddy are or how much we love her.

"What are you thinking about?" Jake asked, and I didn't want to spoil everything so I said I was thinking about Sandy and how she'd gush and be so surprised when I shared the good news.

"I'm really glad you have someone like that in your life," he said.

"What about you? Did you tell anyone yet?"

Jake shook his head, and I thought I could detect a hint of that melancholy I'd just been feeling in his posture.

"Not even your mom?"

I didn't know much about Patricia at the time. Jake's so full of daddy issues he's like a walking cliché, but he'd never said anything against his mom, so I figured they must be on decent enough terms.

"Nope."

"What do you think she'll say?"

Another shrug. I could sense some kind of cloud passing over the sunshine of our joy, so I shut up. Didn't push it anymore. What and how Jake told his mother was his own business.

At least that's what I thought.

That evening at the hospital, Jake's phone rang while we were enjoying our first dinner as husband and wife.

"Please don't tell me you just eloped with some drug queen you hardly even know." The voice was so shrill and loud I could hear it from across the cafeteria table.

Jake turned the same color as a Santa Claus hat and stood up. "Hi, Mom. Now's not really a good time." He shot me an apologetic glance. I don't think he knew I had heard every word.

The stupid thing is Jake blamed me for it all. I was so excited to tell everyone I posted it online as soon as we got back to the hospital that afternoon. He said I should have waited until he had a chance to tell his mom himself. We had a big fight about it in the cafeteria, and we were both still fuming hours later when I got back to the Ronald McDonald house after spending the evening in the NICU.

"How was I supposed to know you didn't want it public?" I demanded after he went on moping about it.

"You should have asked."

"So what was I supposed to do? Wait a few weeks for you to find the courage to tell you mom you'd gotten married?" Except I didn't use the word *courage*. In fact, I may have included an anatomical reference that questioned Jake's manhood.

"I can't believe how selfish you are," he exploded. "Was that the only reason you wanted to get married? So you could see how many likes and stickers and *OMG, I'm so happy for you* comments you can get? Are you really that much of an attention whore?"

I could tell he regretted his words as soon as they left his mouth, but I slapped him anyway. Call it reflex if you want. I didn't deserve to be treated like that. Not on my stinking wedding night.

"Don't you dare talk to me like that," I told him, waving my finger in his face as he rubbed his cheek. "Don't. You. Dare."

"You know I didn't mean it. I'm sorry." Jake's such an expert at apologizing, it's a good thing he's not abusive. I could see a lot of immature girls running back to him and forgiving him over and over just because he sounds so stinking humble when he says he's sorry.

I was tired and ready to be done with the fight. None of it was my fault, but if he was ready to kiss and make up, I wasn't going to stop him.

"Next time, just tell me if there's something you don't want your mom to find out so I can be more careful."

"Ok." Jake gave a sheepish grin. "Next time we get married, I'll be sure to remember that." He patted the spot beside him on the bed. "I'm sorry we had a fight."

"Don't worry about it," I said and sat down next to him. "Every couple does it."

"Yeah, but I think a lot of them wait until they've been married a week or two."

We both smiled. Jake's got a really nice jawline. It's kind of square and angular. He gets that from his dad, but he's got Patricia's smooth, tanned skin. And his hair's gorgeous. I don't remember if I mentioned that yet or not. He doesn't wear it too long, just long enough that you can detect a hint of curls. You should see him in his high-school graduation photo. He wore his hair down past his shoulders, and oh man. I don't know a single girl — white, black, Asian, or otherwise — who wouldn't die for hair like that.

I started playing with it while we were sitting next to each other, running my fingers through those loose curls.

"What are you doing?" he asked.

"Just enjoying your hair. I think you should grow it out long again."

"No, why are you looking at me like that?"

"Like what?"

Jake gets embarrassed about stupid things. Sometimes it's annoying, but sometimes it's cute and endearing. He let out a little giggle before I kissed him, right on the spot below his ear.

"What are you doing?" he asked again.

I kept one hand on his hair and ran the other up his leg. "What does it look like I'm doing?" I kissed him again on the neck, that little indent right by his shoulder.

He grabbed one of my hands. "We shouldn't. We can't."

"It's ok," I tell him. "We're married now, remember?"

"Yeah, but don't we need to wait a few more weeks? I don't want to hurt you or anything."

I freed my hand and let it creep up his shirt. My lips traveled down his jaw to his chin. "It'll be fine," I mumbled. "Don't worry about me."

"I'm always going to worry about you."

That melancholy feeling came back then. Squeezed my heart until I felt so full I literally hurt. Times like that make me think that God had to be as loving and gracious as Sandy always said he is because there's no way I'd done anything to deserve a husband like Jake.

CHAPTER 41

I'm sitting here staring at my phone, except I'm not paying attention to anything online. I don't even have any browsers or apps open. I'm just staring.

I know I don't deserve to be happy. It makes sense that these past few months were as horrific as they've been. I've got to do my penance, face my consequences, reap what I've sown, all those stinking clichés.

I'm thinking about right after Jake and I got married, how gentle he was, how scared he was of hurting me, how he promised to take care of me. We didn't talk about Natalie that night, but I think once we got married we started loving her even more. I know I did. Because we were a family now. She wasn't just this little sick girl who popped out of my body. She was my own flesh and blood, the tangible result of my relationship with my husband. So maybe we didn't do things in the right order. Maybe I was as tainted as those abstinence cheerleaders said I was. Maybe all I had to give Jake that night in the Ronald McDonald house was *hand-me-down love*, but you know what?

It was beautiful.

The problem is I know it's not going to last. I'm not talking about sabotage or anything like that anymore. I know that's my tendency, but this is something different. It's not false guilt, either, and no self-help guru or psychologist can convince me otherwise.

I've done such a good job fighting these memories whenever they try to surface. I've done such a good job ignoring the shame that will probably suffocate me if I ever let it take full reign of my emotions. I've stuffed that guilt into such a small hole in the center of my soul that I hoped I might lose it there forever.

But there it sits, and I can feel it getting bigger. Pressing against the constraints of my conscience. It takes an iron will to contain it. Keep it buried where it belongs. And I'm so tired. I've been up since 4:30 and cleaning or cooking or suctioning out my daughter the entire day. I'm not used to this kind of schedule.

I'm not used to this kind of strain.

I don't know why this demon from my past is trying to escape now of all times when things have been going so well. I feel like I should do something. Pray against it. Fight it. But how? It's like trying to stop a tidal wave and all you've got is a trash can full of shredded paper.

I bite my lip and jump online. There must be someone I can stalk, someone who can get my mind off this demon. If I ignore it completely, it's bound to go away eventually, right? Like the stray cat you refuse to feed, no matter how persistently he cries at your front door.

A distraction. That's what I need.

I don't recognize the profile picture at first glance. Elder Thomas? What in the world is he doing on my news feed? Then I see that Sandy's replied to something he wrote, and since the internet's semi-omniscient, it assumes I want to see it, too.

It's some pro-life meme. Anti-baby-killer meme, I should say. At least it's not one of the ones that shows the dismembered fetus, but it's not much better.

And all of a sudden I'm not sitting on the couch looking for something to slow my racing brain. I'm not in my trailer waiting for Natalie's next feeding time.

I'm five months pregnant, I've driven all the way to the Spokane Women's Clinic, and I'm about to kill my baby.

CHAPTER 42

"Have you had an abortion before?" the nurse asks me.

"No." I'm shaking. I shouldn't be shaking. This is a safe procedure. Everything I've read online promises me that it's safe. And I'm not alone. Something like twenty or thirty percent of all women in America have done what I'm about to do.

It's no big deal. Like getting a tooth pulled. Uncomfortable for a short time, but then the problem's taken care of for good.

I shouldn't be here. I wouldn't be here if I hadn't gotten into that big fight with Jake.

He'll never forgive me after this.

"Are you ready?" the nurse asks.

I nod my head and sign the form she's holding on her pink clipboard.

It's silly for me to be thinking about my foster mom. Not at a time like this. I haven't talked to Sandy in years. Haven't thought about her in years. So why am I so worried all of a sudden about what she'd say?

I could always change my mind. I already signed the form, but what's the nurse going to do? Strap me into the stirrups and force me to go through with it?

211

I could get up and walk out right now. If I weren't so stinking mad at Jake, that's exactly what I'd do.

"All right," the nurse tells me before she bustles out of the room, "all I need you to do is hop into this gown, and I'll be back in a few minutes to check up on you."

My relationship with Jake is never going to recover from this. And that's the only reason why I'm here.

CHAPTER 43

The nurse said *a few minutes*, but I guess she meant fifteen or more. I'm tired. I drove all the way to Spokane, and I haven't even had coffee today. I've been trying to cut back on caffeine because I read online that it's healthier for the baby.

There's some irony for you.

Jake's texted me about fifty times. Wants to know where I am. Why I stormed off like that. When I'll come home. Reminds me he's working tonight and has to have the car back by six. I don't reply.

He can ride his bike.

I'm proud of myself that I made this decision. I should have done it months ago. It would be infinitely easier for everyone involved if I had. But I wanted to pretend it would all work out, that Jake and I could learn to be that little picture-perfect family.

Who was I kidding?

I just wish I'd done it before we got that ultrasound. Before I learned it was a she. That makes it harder. That and the fact that I've already felt her kicking around some.

On the drive out here, I passed a car with an *Abortion is Murder* bumper sticker on it. Made me wonder for a minute if it was a sign. It was right by an exit, too, so I could have gotten off the freeway if I wanted. Turned around and gone home.

Then when I got to Spokane, I passed this church with a billboard in front. *Before I formed you in the womb, I knew you.* It was some Bible verse, and there was a picture of a cute little Gerber baby with squishy cheeks and triple elbows and huge stinking dimples when she smiled at all the passers-by. The sign had the address for some kind of pregnancy center offering abortion alternatives. I know what that means, and no, I'm not giving my baby up for adoption, thank you very much.

Once my mind is set, nothing changes it. Not even a message splattered across the sky. That's why I hope the nurse comes back soon. I want to get this taken care of and move on.

I still don't know what I'll tell Jake. He loves this baby already. It's embarrassing the way that a grown man humiliates himself singing songs and making goofy faces at my belly.

He'll be crushed, but he'll get over it.

He'll have to.

CHAPTER 44

I'm drifting off to sleep. Seriously. I thought this would be a quick in-and-out procedure, but I guess it's far enough along it's going to be a little more complicated than that.

I knew I should have come here sooner.

The nurse has been in and out, in and out, and now I'm waiting again. Waiting for those silly sticks she shoved up in me to do their work. It's been such a stressful day, first that fight with Jake, then the drive all the way out to Spokane. I don't know if I even have enough gas money to make it back to Orchard Grove. If Jake didn't need his stupid car back, I might stay here for good.

In the bathroom at the clinic was a number for a shelter for battered women. Even have a free shuttle that will come pick me up. Jake's never hit me, but they're not going to turn me away just because I'm not bruised up enough.

Even a woman's shelter would beat that stupid trailer park.

I forget how long the nurse said I had to wait before we could go on with the procedure. I'm just so tired and stressed out. Why in the world did I think it would be a good idea to give up coffee?

I've got to rest my eyes. I won't fall asleep or anything. I just need to give my brain a break. Slow down. Unwind.

I've been living the past five months for someone else. It's time to take care of me for a change.

CHAPTER 45

I'm in some big room I've never seen before. Almost like a ballroom. Tons of open space.

It's depressing here. Lots of black and gray, with just a tiny ray of light streaming in from the far window. If this were a movie, I'd say the director was trying too hard to be dramatic.

There's no one here. It's totally empty except for me. There's something up front on a little platform. Maybe this isn't a ballroom. It reminds me more of a church or something but without the pews or places for people to sit. And there's no podium for the preacher to stand behind, just a wooden box. Like they're getting ready to do a Christmas pageant but the only prop they've built so far is the manger for baby Jesus.

That's what it is. A manger. I go up to it. I think I hear a sound coming from the stage. My footsteps are slow. It's like I have to wade through four feet of Jell-O. It takes me forever to get to the front of the room, but I'm finally there.

And then I realize I'm not alone. There's some old woman who just appeared out of nowhere. Is this part of the Christmas pageant? Is she supposed to be some sort of angel?

She's bending over the manger, and she's got her hand on a baby.

I think maybe she's singing a lullaby. I get closer and can see that the baby's a girl. And the old woman's not singing, she's praying.

Except it's not quite a prayer, either, because she's not talking directly to the Lord. She's talking to the baby. *You're a blessed child, a living miracle. Your life is evidence of the power of the great God Almighty.*

I glance down the at the baby. So little. So helpless. Chocolate skin and almond eyes. And then she smiles at me. She's gorgeous. So stinking gorgeous.

And then the old woman meets my gaze. I'm expecting this gentle granny type, but her whole expression flashes with anger and power. Like that elf chick in *Lord of the Rings* who gets tempted to steal the ring from Frodo and starts talking in that super creepy voice.

That's what the old lady sounds like when she looks me square in the eyes and tells me, "What God has ordained, let no mortal dare terminate."

My heart's literally stopped in my chest. I'm covered in sweat, and I'm breathing as fast as if I'd just spent ten minutes in a boxing ring with Patricia.

I'm not in the women's clinic anymore. I'm not in Spokane. I'm in my living room. Jake's glancing up at me from his phone.

I haven't thought about that dream in months. I have no idea why it stole its way into my head now of all times.

But my hands turn cold, and my whole stomach twists itself

into a giant pretzel and tries to squeeze my abdominal cavity into its iron grip.

I've tried my hardest to forget Spokane. Forget about what I almost did that day to my daughter. But now I know why that Grandma Lucy lady at church looked so stinking familiar.

She's the woman from my dream.

CHAPTER 46

Jake's looking at me like I'm batty. Who knows, maybe I am.

"What's wrong?" he asks, and I wonder if I made a noise in my surprise without even knowing it.

Grandma Lucy. Is my mind playing tricks on me? I've gone so long avoiding all my memories from that women's clinic. Is that why the Holy Ghost lady at church looked so familiar, or am I just confused? Traumatized?

That's a thing, you know. Post abortion stress disorder. It's like PTSD, but for women who have abortions. I looked it up once online.

"You're kind of tripping me out," Jake says.

I try to shake reality back into my body and brain. I'm not in Spokane. A flashback. That's all this was. Maybe I do have that post-abortion thing even though I didn't go through with the procedure.

After I dozed off and had that dream in the women's clinic, I told the nurse I had to get something from the car. She looked a little suspicious, so I said it was my inhaler. I don't have asthma, but I lived with this foster kid once who did. Eliot Jamison. I've had tons of foster siblings, but he's one of the only ones I remember in any sort of detail. Maybe because I teased him so bad. Anyway, I got dressed, and the nurse said she'd walk me to the car, but I told her I could go myself.

I think she still suspected something, either that or she didn't want the clinic to get sued, because she followed me out anyway.

I should have just told her. Let her know I changed my mind, but she'd already prepped me for the procedure by then, and I was afraid she'd say it was too late.

So she trailed me to Jake's car, and I had to make it look convincing that I was digging around for some imaginary inhaler, and then when I was all the way inside where she couldn't get to me, I shut the door and locked myself in.

She knocked on the window, more scared than angry, and you could tell she was worried about getting fired or something. But I was done with the women's clinic, and I wasn't ever going to look back.

I never do.

Five minutes later, I was in a gas station bathroom, pulling out those dilator thingies. I was sure by now the people at the clinic were going nuts, but I hadn't used my real name on the intake form or given them anything but a made-up phone number and address. There was no way they were going to see or hear anything from me again.

I flashed those little cinnamon-looking sticks down the toilet, prayed to God it wouldn't clog, and jumped back in the car.

I was going back to Orchard Grove. Back to the father of my baby.

CHAPTER 47

Jake's probably at home worrying about me right now, but I can't help that. He's always going to worry about me. Said so the day we got married.

I left the trailer in a kind of a whirlwind. Told him I had to go to the store to buy some tampons. It was the only excuse I could think of. Instead of heading to Walmart, though, I drove three miles in the opposite direction, where I've been parked for the past ten minutes, trying to work up the nerve to walk up to the door.

There's no use asking what I'm doing here. Have you ever felt so compelled to do something you couldn't even explain it to yourself? Maybe that's why the salmon always travel up those streams to spawn. They probably don't have a clue why they're doing it. They just know that if they don't, something inside them will break or they'll die a terrifying, violent death.

I'm staring at the sign of Orchard Grove Bible Church. It's got one of those changeable message boards where preachers can put little wisecracks. This one says *Honk if you love Jesus. Text while you drive if you want to meet him.* I wonder if it was the pastor who came up with it or someone else.

I feel like the biggest idiot in the history of the world. I don't even know what I'm going to say once I go in. But I feel even more stupid sitting out here in the parking lot, so I finally get out of the car and head up the walkway. The church has two entrances. I wonder if I'm supposed to use the big one that leads straight to the sanctuary or if they want you to use the side door on weekdays. Does it matter?

I try the smaller door, but it's locked. So is the main one. Great. There's not any way for me to get in. I'm about to go to the car and run to Walmart since there's absolutely nothing else for me to do here when a man comes out of the little house beside the church.

"Can I help you?"

It takes me a few seconds to recognize him without the fancy shirt and tie. He's in athletic pants, the kind that swish when you walk, and an LA Lakers hoodie.

LA Lakers? Does he know what decade we're in?

I'm so startled to see him like this, I don't know what to say. I'm about to stammer something about forgetting my Bible here on Sunday when he comes towards me and stretches out his hand.

"I'm Greg. Is there something I can do for you?"

I'm staring at the ground. The pastor's wearing faded faux leather slippers in the snow.

I take his hand, feeling a swoosh in my stomach like I haven't experienced since the first few months of the pregnancy.

"I was actually looking for somebody." My face is hot. I remind myself to be assertive. There's nothing in this world more annoying than a mousy woman. I square my shoulders. "That old lady who spoke after the sermon. Your, umm, your grandma. I mean, your grandmother-in-law. Is she ... Does she happen to live here with you?"

The pastor squints his eyes at me. I'm almost certain he's got some Native American heritage, but there's a small chance it's Hispanic. Or maybe a little of both.

"Grandma Lucy?" he asks.

I nod my head, trying to convince myself that he probably has two or three people a month show up in front of his house wanting to know the same thing.

"She's not actually a relative," he explains. "That's just what people in the church call her. She lives down on Baxter Loop. The big farmhouse there with all the goats running around."

Goats? I don't know what part of town he means, but I guess that's what GPS is for.

He tilts his head to the side.

"Did you need her for something?"

I force myself to laugh. "Oh, nothing serious. It was just that, well, she said something I've been meaning to talk to her about."

He nods his head. Maybe he does get regular visitors stopping here asking about her.

"I'm sorry to bother you," I say.

"It's really no trouble. I've got to salt this walkway anyway."

I wonder if he's going to change into winter boots first. Or at least shoes that are designed for outdoors.

"Be careful not to slip," he tells me as I make my way back to the car.

Safe inside Jake's Pontiac, I open up Google Maps.

I've got to find this Baxter Loop.

CHAPTER 48

The farm the pastor mentioned is impossible to miss. As soon as I turn onto Baxter Loop, I see the signs leading the way.

Safe Anchorage Goat Farm. 2 miles.

Raw goat milk, cheeses, and soaps. 1.3 miles.

Please drive slowly. Goats ahead.

I think this last sign's a joke until I literally have to brake for three goats stripping bark from a tree on the side of the road. I follow about half a dozen colorfully-painted arrows up a winding driveway until I stop in front of a bright red farmhouse. I feel like I've jumped back in time at least sixty or seventy years.

A middle-aged woman in one of those old-fashioned aprons — I think you call that pattern calico even though I've never been a hundred percent sure what calico actually means — stands on the porch and waves at me.

"Welcome to Safe Anchorage!" she calls out as soon as I step out of the Pontiac. "Are you here for milk, cheese, or to meet the animals?"

It's been a couple months since I've talked to two strangers in a single day. I glance around, half expecting Grandma Lucy to appear like a phantom at my elbow. "I'm here looking for someone." At least now my voice is competent. I don't even want to know what that LA Lakers fan boy pastor thinks about me after that show I gave him. "Is this where Lucy lives?"

The woman's smile broadens, a feat I wouldn't have imagined possible.

"Of course. Come right in. Grandma Lucy will be delighted you stopped by."

I know for sure this woman's too old to be anyone's granddaughter but for lack of better alternatives, I follow Calico Lady through the swinging double doors of the farmhouse entrance. Some bells tied to the knob chatter merrily as we enter.

"Who've you got there?" An old man with a potbelly and Santa Claus beard glances up from his recliner by the fireside. I'm half afraid that if I get close enough to glance at the newspaper he's reading, I'll find that I've somehow stepped back into the 1950s.

"Friend of Grandma Lucy's," the woman replies. "Grandma!" she hollers up a flight of stairs, and I try to guess her age.

I feel like a kid being sent to the principal's office for truancy when Grandma Lucy appears at the top of the stairs, her spectacles falling halfway down her nose. Her shock-white hair reminds me of the icing on the gingerbread houses Sandy and I used to make with some of her younger foster kids.

"Hello, dear," Grandma Lucy says. Like we've been neighbors for decades and I've stopped by for our regular afternoon chat.

"I'll heat up some tea," chatters Calico Lady, and I'm left alone at the bottom of the stairs watching Grandma Lucy descend.

Before I know it, my hand is clasped warmly in hers and she's smiling into my eyes, saying, "Now remind me, my dear, where it is that we had the privilege to meet."

I bite my lower lip. I can stand my ground in a room full of medical specialists whose total net worth must be in the tens of millions or more, but I feel uneasy in front of an eighty-year-old granny.

"I was at church on Sunday. I was there when you ..."

Grandma Lucy nods sagely and sucks in her breath. "Rachel." She says the name with absolute certainty.

I hate to correct her. "No, I'm Tiff."

Grandma Lucy's led me into a little greenhouse room with a view of the backyard. She still hasn't let go of my hand. "No, my dear. Rachel, the mother weeping for her children."

It's been a few years since I've been a heavy partier. I'm not used to this feeling, this racing in my chest. "I guess that's me," is all I can say.

Grandma Lucy sits me down in a gaudy upholstered loveseat with giant rose patterns splattered all over in dizzying masses. She pulls up a rocking chair and sits across from me so close our knees touch.

"Now, tell me about your baby. I want to hear everything."

CHAPTER 49

By the time Calico Lady brings us in some tea, I've spilled out the entire story. How Jake and I conceived a baby out of wedlock. Grandma Lucy doesn't look too shocked at that part. I didn't leave out any of the details about the fight that led me to Spokane, and I told her exactly what happened there.

The only thing I don't mention is the dream. The dream where she appeared to me and prayed over the child I was about to abort. I just explained that I got to the women's clinic and changed my mind in the exam room, and that was all.

And over tea, I tell her the part that terrifies me the most. "I think that maybe if I hadn't had them put that stuff in me to get me ready for the abortion, she wouldn't have gotten sick."

"What makes you say that?" Grandma Lucy isn't smiling anymore. Part of me's afraid she's going to stand up at any minute and kick me out of this peaceful home because I nearly killed my own child.

I swallow. Whoever said that confession is good for the soul was an idiot. I feel horrific having the ugliness of what I've done stare me in the face. But somehow I can't stay silent. I have to tell this woman everything. When I'm done, part of me thinks she'll transform into a bird or something and fly away, and then I'll wake up and realize it was only another dream.

"They put this stuff in me before they started the procedure," I tell her. "It's supposed to make it easier for them to take the baby out. Well, I left the clinic and removed it myself, but I think that's maybe why Natalie had all the problems she did."

There's still a hint of a frown on Grandma Lucy's face. I knew it. She's going to kick me out, scream that I'm a baby murderer and that I don't deserve to be a mother.

"Tell me about what problems you mean," is all she says.

I tell her about the pre-term labor. It was a few months after my trip to Spokane, but I still wonder if it's related. I didn't tell anyone about those sticks, not the doctor at Orchard Grove County, not the people in the NICU. Grandma Lucy and I are the only two living beings in the world who know.

"I was on bedrest," I say. "I had to stay in the hospital four weeks, and even then she still came a little early."

"And that's why she has health problems now?" Grandma Lucy asks.

"No," I answer. "At least, I don't think so. She was fine at first. Everything looked perfect. But it was a really long labor, and she had bleeding on her brain, and ..."

I stop myself. I'm perfectly capable of telling a woman I've just met about how I went in to have an abortion, changed my mind, and was too ashamed to consult a doctor or anything after I removed the dilator sticks myself. I can tell her about the research

I did online, about how I'm convinced that's why I went into preterm labor and got put on bedrest to begin with. But I can't tell her what happened in the delivery room that morning. Not in any sort of detail.

"She stopped breathing and got transferred to Seattle right away." My story ends there.

Grandma Lucy's rocking slightly in her chair. Her body is so relaxed I wonder if she's about to fall asleep. Then Calico Lady enters the room with a tray full of dainty snacks and two flowery mugs she fills from a petite lily-patterned teapot.

I wait for something magical to happen now. For Grandma Lucy to quote a Bible verse that will wash off all the stains of my past. For her to pray for my child and tell me I can go home now because Natalie's perfectly healed.

Instead, she smiles and says, "Have a snack, my dear. You look hungry."

CHAPTER 50

From the greenhouse room, I can see the sky turn that shade of pale violet you only see in the winter. The sun will be setting any minute now. I've got to get home or I'll be late fixing dinner.

So much for turning into Supermom who can take care of the cooking, cleaning, and child-rearing. I didn't even last a full day.

Grandma Lucy and I have finished our snacks. She's sipping her tea, rocking slowly back and forth, back and forth, like I'll be here all night and well into the morning. People like that make me uncomfortable, people who don't realize some folks follow something called a schedule.

I don't feel any better after telling Grandma Lucy about Natalie, and I wonder why I bothered to come at all. The urge that tugged me so strongly here now feels immature and irresponsible. Patricia's sick. Jake's not used to suctioning out the baby. Natalie was due for a tube-feed an hour and a half ago, and if Patricia didn't drag herself out of bed, we'll have to make it up sometime tonight when we all should be sleeping.

I set my flowered plate on the arm of the hideous loveseat. "Thank you so much for the tea," I say. "Everything was delicious."

Grandma Lucy doesn't respond. I'm not even sure she can hear me.

I make a move like I'm about to stand. "I better get going. It's close to dinner time."

No response. Great. The old woman's having a stroke. My plan is to go find Calico Lady to let her know something's wrong, but before I can sneak past her, Grandma Lucy reaches for my hand.

"Your daughter will live." She's speaking the words so softly I'm only half sure I heard right.

"What did you say?"

"Natalie will live." She's got such conviction in her voice. Such finality. Like a judge handing down a sentence.

How do you know? That's what I want to ask, but for some reason I can't form the words. I should demand more information. Make her tell me exactly what she means and how she can be so certain, but something stops me.

Because in the core of my being — that place deep within my soul where if I venture too long I might lose myself forever — I know Grandma Lucy is right.

233

CHAPTER 51

You'd think I'd be high as a kite since I left Baxter Loop and drove back to the trailer park. Either that, or you'd think I'd dismiss what Grandma Lucy said as the words of an old woman whose sanity is already in question.

I don't doubt her at all, though. As soon as she told me my daughter would live, it's like I'd known that from the beginning. I just needed someone to teach me how to have that faith. I've never been into signs and wonders and junk like that. Even when I lived with Sandy, her husband's church was way more subdued. You wouldn't find white-haired grannies standing up and making proclamations or prophesies directly from the Lord. But even though this kind of faith is so far out of my comfort zone, it fits me. It suits me.

The irony is that my soul is even heavier now than it was when I went in search of Grandma Lucy. Because now that I've told someone the whole story start to finish, I'm even more convinced that everything that happened to my daughter was my fault. The preterm labor. The bedrest. Who knows, probably even the brain hemorrhage — they're all my fault for going to that clinic.

I'd been holding onto a shred of hope that maybe the two things were unrelated. I didn't go through with the abortion. And for a little bit, I was smug enough to think that made me a decent mother.

If I was a decent mother, I would have never driven myself to Spokane in the first place. I would have never allowed that nurse to insert those stupid sticks up inside me. And I would have gone straight to a doctor instead of driving home to Orchard Grove once I took them out.

A thought flashes uninvited through my mind. I could sue the abortion clinic. They didn't tell me what would happen if I left early. But in order to do that, I'd have to let Jake and his mom and the whole world know what I did. I'd have to sit there while a lawyer proved that my daughter would be perfectly healthy if the clinic hadn't prepped me for an elective abortion.

Nothing's worth that amount of torture. Not even a settlement large enough to buy a dozen trailer parks.

I'm pulling onto our street. It's so ugly here. Ugly and colorless. No wonder I'm unhappy all the time. It'd be different if I lived in one of those cute little rustic homes on Baxter Loop.

Safe Anchorage Farm is less than ten minutes away. I wonder if I'll ever go back and visit with Grandma Lucy again.

I doubt it.

Something's wrong. My brain registers danger before my eyes tell me what they're seeing. I speed up.

Red strobing lights.

Strangers on my lawn.

An ambulance in front of my house.

CHAPTER 52

I swerve up and slam on my brakes behind the ambulance. I have to get in. Have to make sure my daughter's safe. I haven't even told Jake that I don't want the DNR anymore.

What if I'm too late? What if everything Grandma Lucy told me was a lie?

I'm breathless. Breathless and dizzy and like I'm about to throw up. My legs can hardly support my weight. "Where's Natalie?" I demand before my brain has the chance to focus on any of the faces I'm seeing. "I'm her mom. Where's my daughter?"

"Everything's fine."

I don't recognize the voice. I can only vaguely make out the man's features. Why won't someone tell me what they've done with my child?

"I'm her mom," I repeat. Maybe I'm trying to remind God. I don't know. Didn't he just promise me through some eccentric old lady that Natalie would be fine?

Someone's got their hand on my shoulder. They're leading me to the baby seat in the living room. What's that? Is it her? I scoop my baby up and clutch her to my chest. Why did I leave her alone for so long? What was I thinking?

My eyes still aren't processing everything. It's pixilated, like when your internet clogs up when you're streaming a movie. I have to examine my daughter with my fingers to try to determine where she's been injured since my eyes won't focus.

You can't do this God, I pray. *You can't tell me one minute she's going to be healed and the next minute take her away from me like this.*

"What happened?" I demand.

"Everything's fine, ma'am." My vision narrows in on a man with a stubby blonde beard. It says Captain on his name badge. Good. Someone I can trust. "Your husband was suctioning out your daughter, and he nicked the back of her throat with the Yankauer. It's absolutely nothing to worry about."

Nothing to worry about? Then why is there an ambulance parked in front of my house?

"She bled a little, so he gave us a call. He did the right thing, but it's nothing serious. She's got a scrape in the back of her throat. Might be uncomfortable for a little bit, but she's perfectly healthy."

Perfectly healthy? He's a horrible liar.

I sink onto the couch, still holding my daughter. My mind is racing as the paramedics get ready to leave. It takes forever. Like back in Massachusetts when Sandy would invite thirty people over for Christmas Eve dinner, and from the time the guests started to say goodbye until we had the house back to ourselves again it could be two hours or longer.

Someone's asking me about the car. Telling me to move it. I hand the keys to a man without a face. I don't know if it's Jake or not. I can't take all this noise and motion. I can't take all these strangers. I need them out of my house.

"Tiff? Tiff?"

My eyes barely manage to focus on my husband. I don't know if I'm supposed to be mad at him or not.

He's rubbing my shoulders. Gives Natalie a kiss on the top of her head. I can't remember the last time he's touched her.

"I'm sorry. I know I should have texted you, but she was bleeding, and I thought I'd punctured her windpipe or something, so I called the ambulance. I'm sorry to scare you like that."

"It's ok," I answer before I know if I'm telling him the truth or not.

He plants another kiss on Natalie's head and then one on my cheek.

"I'm just glad she's ok. Know what I mean?" He's scared too. I can hear it in his tone. I'm about to tell him it's not his fault, but a grating, fingernails-on-chalkboard voice jumps in ahead of me.

"Of course, none of this would have ever happened if you hadn't just run off without so much as a word about when you'd be back."

CHAPTER 53

"It's not her fault."

It's cute the way Jake is trying to protect me from his mother. I need to start giving that boy more credit from time to time.

"Nobody said it was her fault." Patricia is sitting at one of the dining room chairs, swollen bags under her eyes. Her skin is some shade between yellow and gray, and her hair hangs in ragged, sweaty clumps around her neck. "All I said was if she'd had the common courtesy to tell me she'd be gone for so long, I could have been out here to suction the baby myself."

"I know how to take care of my own daughter." Jake's talking so fast my brain can't keep up in time to form a response of my own.

"Nobody said anything about knowing how to do it." She's lecturing her son like he's a six-year-old asking why Daddy has so many late evenings working with his pretty blond secretary. "I'm talking about experience. You haven't had the chance to practice as much, so I was just …"

"How am I supposed to get the practice if you're always here doing it for me?" Jake demands. This is new, hearing him go at it with his mom. I wonder if he feels nervous. Scared.

Or maybe exhilarated.

I keep my mouth shut.

Patricia forces her lips to turn upward, but her eyes are as cool and calculating as ever. "You're a good boy, Jake. I'm sorry life hasn't given you the rewards you deserve."

He doesn't say anything, but I can see the tremor racing up his arms from his clenched fists.

"It's kind of you to care so much about your little girl." Patricia's voice drips with sweetness. Like poisoned honey. "I'm just sorry you don't have the kind of help you need around here."

She tosses her head in my direction so we all know who she's talking about, but she doesn't have the courage to meet my eyes.

The coward.

Jake's jaw is clenched shut, and he's not saying anything. Like an actor who's forgotten his lines. I want to feed the script to him. Remind him that we've come to the part where he kicks Mommy out of the house.

Unfortunately, Patricia's not nearly so tongue-tied. "You know, back when you and Abby were little, I had to learn how to do everything myself. Your father wasn't around to help."

"That's because my father is an arrogant jerk who'd be better off …"

"Easy, easy." Patricia's eyes are wide as if she's surprised by Jake's outburst. As if she didn't know what kind of reaction to expect after mentioning his dad. "All I'm saying is if you want your home to run smoothly, you find a woman who knows how to take care of the children and who doesn't run off whenever she gets it in her head."

I'm not about to risk the chance that Jake will forget how to stand up for me. Now my hands are in fists, too. "I told Jake exactly where I was going," I declare. Of course, what I told him was a lie, and I'm sure everyone here knows it by now, but how dare she accuse me like that to my face?

Patricia opens her mouth to respond, but I'm not about to give her the smallest inch of leeway.

"And you know what? While you were sleeping, Jake was out here watching Natalie, and he was doing a perfectly fine job." He was probably glued to his smartphone, but I don't care. Patricia's got to learn her place, or so help me she won't be alive to welcome in the New Year. "So he ran into a problem with the Yankauer. Know what? They warned us about that in the NICU. Said it happens to everybody no matter how careful they are. So I don't see where you get off telling him the he doesn't know how to take care of his own daughter, or that I'm some sort of irresponsible, flighty mother who ..."

"It's all right, dear." Patricia's smile reminds me of the snake in that Disney cartoon who can hypnotize other animals on command. "Nobody's mad at you. Nobody expects you to ..."

"To what? Take care of my own child? Let me tell you something. You're absolutely right. You don't expect me to do anything for her. Do you know why? Because you're an old, lonely dog with two failed marriages and you think that taking care of a sick little girl is going to give you some sort of edge over the rest of us. Time for a wakeup call. We didn't ask you here. We don't want you here. And the sooner you get out of my house, the sooner I ..."

"Tiff," Jake snaps, and I realize he's been trying to get my attention for a while now. He grabs me by the elbow and pinches me. Hard. "What are you doing?" he hisses. His breath is hot on my ear.

Patricia gives her head a regal tilt. "No, you don't have to say anything." She's addressing Jake still. I'm not even worth her energy. "You've made your choices, and I've done what I can to try to shelter you from the consequences, but it's obviously time for me to move on." She sniffs. Her speech might be more effective if she weren't so congested. "Let me go get my bags. I'm sure I can find some sort of hotel to spend the night while I make arrangements to fly home."

Jake's on his feet, blocking her from her room. "Now wait a minute."

I stare at my daughter. I'd almost forgotten I was still holding her.

"No," Patricia insists. I know how this dance will go. Jake will beg her not to take off. She'll argue. They'll tango like this for five or six rounds until she lets out a melodramatic sigh and agrees to stay, but only because she's worried about what will happen to Natalie if she leaves her alone with the likes of Jake and me.

It's all so preordained I don't pay much attention. My husband's whines and his mother's harsh counters become background noise as I study my daughter. I was so scared when I saw that ambulance in front of the house. I've got to talk to Jake tonight, let him know I canceled the DNR. But right now, my fingers soak in the softness of Natalie's cheek. Does she feel warm? She's awake but just barely. Just enough to let me study the color of her pupils. Chocolate skin and almond eyes.

So stinking gorgeous.

It's a shame that Jake's about to convince his mom to stay. I'm sure by tonight, I'll be ready to let him know how I feel. But for now, I want to enjoy my daughter. I nestle my cheek against hers. She does feel a little hot. Jake probably turned the thermostat up while I was out. I swear that man has no concept of how much we spend on utilities. I don't even want to see what the heating bill will rack up to this month.

"The only way I would even consider staying here is if that hussy apologizes to me."

I smile, thankful Patricia's back is to me. The woman is even more delusional than I first gave her credit for if she thinks she'll get a sorry out of me.

"Don't call her that," Jake pleads. Like a stinking knight in shining armor, ready to defend his lady's honor.

"I didn't call her anything. I just said that I need an apology if she expects me to be her babysitter and her housemaid and her cook and her nursing staff ..."

They're talking about me, but this isn't my argument. They've forgotten that I'm Natalie's mom. That I could take her and leave any time I choose.

"We appreciate everything you do for us." It's a good thing Jake doesn't work a union job. He'd get eaten alive at the negotiation table. "We both appreciate you," he lies. "You've been amazing. I get three home-cooked meals a day, my daughter's getting the best of care ..."

I roll my eyes. I know Jake so well that this kissing-up act of his hardly bothers me at all. It's like getting mad at a seven-week-old puppy who pees in the entryway and acts all proud because at least she missed the carpet.

I rub my nose softly against Natalie's. *One day*, I think to myself. One day she might smile at me. One day I might hear her laugh. I'll even be excited once she learns to cry. Will she ever know? Will her little heart ever find a way to understand how much I adore her?

"... if that's what you really want." I only catch the last half of what Patricia says, but I gather by her tone and by Jake's relieved expression that she's decided to stick around until after Christmas.

Whoopetty stinking do.

Then again, I already knew that's what the outcome would be. I'll have to suffer Patricia's stony silence for another few days, and then we'll slip back into our comfortably spiteful coexistence.

Merry Christmas and bah humbug.

I think that the bulk of the argument's over, but apparently Her Royal Highness won't accept Jake's surrender without a little more show of force.

"I'm not asking for much. You of all people should know that. I'd just like to know that my efforts are appreciated."

"We're really thankful for everything you've done for us. Both of us are." Jake throws me an imploring glance. It's cute that he thinks highly enough of me to assume I'll jump in. I keep my gaze turned toward our daughter and pretend not to hear.

"Oh, I know I'm appreciated by you." Patricia draws out that last word, and I'm sure she's turned around to glare at me, but I'm not about to join in and pay homage to the queen. Stinking dictator is more like it. This is between her and her son. He's the one begging her to stay. If it were me, it would have been good riddance ten minutes ago.

Heck, if it had been me, she would have been out the door before her first weekend.

Fish and company ...

Natalie's asleep again. So much for our little bonding moment. That's ok, though. I need to remember what Grandma Lucy said. I need to remember that we have years and years ahead of us to snuggle and hug and kiss and love each other.

It will be years, right? Isn't that what the old woman promised?

No more than ten feet away from me, Patricia's reciting my faults one by one, and Jake's standing there taking it all like the henpecked mama's boy he is. I wonder if they have any idea how little respect I hold for either of them at this moment.

"If that's what she thinks, then I'm better off going."

Great. Now she's threatening to leave again. I wish that woman would make up her stinking mind instead of wrangling her son through all these hoops. It's psychological abuse, that's what it is.

"I mean, if she thinks that I've got nothing better to do with my time than suction the snot out of a little retarded baby ..."

The hair on the back of my neck jumps straight up, but Jake reacts faster than I do.

"What did you call her?" I can feel the heat from his anger all the way over here.

Patricia shifts her weight from one foot to the other. "I only meant that ..." Her eyes dart around the room. She can't even face her son.

"Don't you ever use that word in my home. Don't even think that word in my home."

I'm glad Natalie's asleep now. Glad she doesn't hear the fury dripping from her daddy's voice.

"It's just an expression ..."

"It's not just an anything." Jake stares down at his mom who seems to have shrunk half a foot. His voice trembles when he talks, like it's taking superhero strength to keep from vaporizing her with his wrath. "That little girl is my daughter. I thought you understood that. I thought that's why you were here. I thought you loved her ..." He struggles to regain control of his voice. "I thought you cared about her as much as I do," he adds a little more quietly.

"You know I care about her." I've never heard Patricia use

this tone of voice before. Like she's actually scared. The reigning queen might not get her way after all. Is it a Christmas miracle in the making?

"We both know what a good girl she is," she stammers. "I only said that because ..."

"Get out." He's speaking so low I can hardly hear him. The words escape like a hiss between his clenched teeth.

Patricia straightens her spine. "What did you just say to me?"

"Get out of my home." He stomps ahead and throws the front door open.

"What about my things?" she asks. Her voice has a small crack in it, but I can't tell if that's from her cold or her emotions.

He pulls the keys out of his pocket. "Take the car to the hotel on Main Street. I think they have a shuttle to the airport. Leave the keys at the front desk. I'll get it later."

She puts her hand on the doorframe like she's going to stop her son from slamming it on her face. "Let me get my bag and you can drive me there. We can talk about it while ..."

He points to the porch. "Go. Now. I'll drop your stuff off later on."

"But, son ..."

He shakes his head. "You have no idea what you just did, do you?"

"I was only trying ..."

He clears his throat. "Get out. And don't expect to come back."

CHAPTER 54

It's like the moment in the *Wizard of Oz* when the Munchkins come out one by one to make sure the wicked witch really is dead. They don't break into joyful singing right away. There's that first minute of eerie silence, the fear that maybe they were wrong. Maybe a creature that evil and horrid will defy death, resurrect herself, and rain fiery torment on them for the rest of eternity.

Jake's still standing behind the door. He's stunned, like how a man who beats his girlfriend in a drunken rage probably feels when he wakes up sober and remembers what he's done.

I haven't moved from the couch, partly because I don't want to wake up Natalie and partly because I don't know what to expect from Jake now. I'm sure in his mind he'll find a way to make this all my fault. I'm sure he'll regret kicking out his mom and blame everything on me.

Except that's not what he does.

He catches my gaze. I lift my eyebrow to him, and he laughs. It starts like a little chuckle. He's got this annoying habit of giggling when he's nervous, and that's what this is like at first. But soon it turns into an all-out laughing fit, and I join in too. It's like we're watching *Saturday Night Live* reruns and we're both completely baked so everything's that much funnier.

"Did you hear what she said?" he asks.

"Did you see how she looked?" I answer, and we're going at it again. My abs will be sore in the morning. I just know it.

And then the laughing stops. I wonder if this is the moment when regret will kick in. I brace myself for the accusations I'm sure are coming. He lifts Natalie out of my arms and carefully straps her in her bouncy chair. He takes my hand in his and sits next to me on the couch. Except his eyes aren't angry.

He's kissing me before I have time to catch my breath. I lean backward on the couch.

"I can't believe she's finally gone," he whispers, and I'm so ready for him it doesn't bother me that he's talking about his mom while we're making out.

"What's gotten into you?" I ask him as he kisses my neck. My skin tingles with expectation. Hunger.

His hand runs up my leg. "You have no idea how long I've been waiting for this." His lips are hot, his kiss probing and deep.

Maybe it'll be a good Christmas after all.

CHAPTER 55

We made ourselves Ramen noodles for dinner and threw out our last batch of leftover brown rice. We put Natalie to bed early and are cuddling on the couch watching a movie.

"Your hair smells so good," he whispers.

"Blame it on that long shower we took." For once, I'm not worried about the utility bill.

We're not paying attention to the movie. It's pretty dumb anyway. All that happens in the whole two hours is a woman gets laid off and travels Europe trying to find herself. It's just nice having something besides a cooking show on for a change.

"I have to pick up the car tonight," Jake says. I still can't believe the way he got his mother out the door. I keep worrying he'll change his mind. Run down to the hotel, throw himself on his knees, and beg Patricia to come back. It's like this is too perfect to last. Too many good things happening in one day. Grandma Lucy telling me my daughter will live. Jake manning up and kicking his mom out of the house. Blame it on my tendency to self-sabotage if you will, but I'm fighting the uneasy feeling that something terrible has to happen soon to balance out all the good.

"How are you going to get to the hotel?" I ask.

"It's not far. I'll ride my bike."

"What about her things?" I remember the oversized suitcase Patricia showed up with the day she arrived on our porch. I should have known at that point what an ominous sign all that baggage was.

Jake frowns. "Guess I'll have to walk."

I don't want him to go out. It will be dark before long. I want to stay here in our little toasty trailer and enjoy each other's company. The funny thing is this feels more like our wedding night than the Ronald McDonald house ever did.

Jake pauses the movie. "We can finish this when I get back. I don't want it to get too late."

I surprise myself by saying, "Well, why don't we come with you?"

"You and the baby?"

"Why not?" Natalie will sleep right through it anyway, and the temperature's been in the forties all day. "I'll put her in that front pack," I tell Jake. "I can zip her up in my parka so she doesn't get cold."

He frowns. "You sure you want to?"

I shrug. "Beats sitting around here."

He stands up. "Ok. I'll pack the suitcase while you get Natalie ready. Just make sure to bundle her up real well."

It's cute the way he worries about his daughter. I tell him I'll be extra careful and watch him walk down the hall, right past the spot where he told his mom off and slammed the door in her face. I told you that man surprises me sometimes.

It takes me a few minutes to dig the front pack out from under my bed. A friend of mine from Winter Grove gave it to me when she found out I was pregnant. I haven't tried it on yet. I don't even know how to wear it. Everything gets tangled up before I can figure out where my arms are supposed to go.

It takes me about a dozen tries, but I finally get it on over my hoodie and walk into Patricia's room. I'm going to have to get used to calling it the nursery again. Jake's zipping up his mom's oversized travel bag, and I reach down to pick up our baby.

"Uh-oh."

My body tenses.

"What is it?"

I'm trembling. Didn't I tell you I had a premonition that something like this was about to happen?

I can't find my voice.

"What's wrong?" Jake is standing beside me, and we're both staring at our daughter. "What?"

I reach out, praying that I'm wrong. I touch her forehead. "Feel this," I tell Jake, hoping to heaven that it's just me.

Jake's frown is enough to tell me I'm not mistaken.

Our daughter is burning up with fever.

PART THREE:

Natalie

CHAPTER 56

I've never been a big fan of the whole Christmas-miracle motif. Goes back all the way to a foster family who kicked me out of their home the day before Christmas Eve so they could give my bedroom to the cousins coming in from out of state. And here I am complaining about how my husband's got a chip or two on his shoulder.

Jake and I are staring at each other. It's like we're stuck here. Time's frozen, but just for the two of us.

I knew something like this would happen. Didn't I tell you everything was too perfect to last?

Jake pulls out his cell phone. I swear he's about to call his mom, and I'm not going to argue with him. If Patricia were here, she'd know what to do. That woman is as torturous as a hill full of fire ants, but she's efficient. She knows how to take charge, a skill which Jake never learned and I've apparently forgotten in my panic.

But he doesn't dial his mom. He's staring at his blank screen. "What do we do?" he asks.

"Call Dr. Bell," I tell him. Where's my phone? I swear I had it with me a minute ago. Is it on the couch?

"I don't have her number," Jake whines. Of course he doesn't. I'm the one who arranges all the appointments. I'm the one who takes Natalie to the pediatrician's. Why would Jake bother storing her number in his phone? It's not like he does anything with that stupid thing besides play Candy Zapper. I'd despise it less if it were at least a game designed for adults.

No, I can't do this. I don't have time to hate my husband right now. All that can come later.

"Call my cell," I tell him, but he's still stuck on the fact that he doesn't have the pediatrician's number in his contacts. "Just call me," I snap at him.

Ok, I hear it ringing. There it is. I must have taken it out of my hoodie when I was putting on the front pack. Seconds later I'm talking with the after-hours call center.

"I need to speak with Dr. Bell," I tell the woman. Her voice sounds young enough she could still be in high school. Let's hope she's got more medical expertise than a teenager.

"Can I get the name and birthdate of the patient?" she asks. So polite. Like she's got all the time in the world before her shift ends and she clocks out to go home and watch *Elf* with her parents.

"This is for Natalie Franklin. She's a patient of Dr. Bell's and has a really extensive medical history." I grab the thermometer from the bathroom drawer and shove it under my daughter's armpit.

"And what's Natalie's date of birth, please?" She's got a voice like Barbie. High-pitched and shrill.

I want to throw the phone against the wall. I can't think straight. Who cares what her birthday is? My daughter might be dying, and I need to talk to her doctor.

"She's four months old." Why can't I remember her stinking birthday?

"Four months exactly?" Barbie asks.

Why can't I ever figure out what time of year it is? "I just need to talk to Dr. Bell." Jake is staring over my shoulder at the thermometer. Doesn't he know he's in the way? "What's her birthday?" I ask him.

"I beg your pardon?" Barbie replies.

"Not you." I hit Jake's shoulder to get his attention. "What's her birthday?"

He's looking at me funny, but I don't know if that's because he can't believe I've forgotten or he can't believe I expect him to know. With Jake, I can see it going either way.

"August 21," he says, and I probably give Barbie a blown eardrum by yelling the date into my phone.

"This year?" she asks.

It's too stupid of a question to even answer. "How long until I can speak with Dr. Bell?"

"The way it works is I'll get a little more information from you and have a nurse call you back. If she has any questions or concerns, she'll contact your son's pediatrician for you."

"It's a girl," I tell her but don't know why I bother. It's not like that matters.

The thermometer lets out a weak beep. Jake snatches it before I can. Barbie is asking me something stupid, something about Dr. Bell's clinic, but I'm not listening.

I grab the thermometer out of Jake's hand. "Listen," I interrupt. "I need to talk to Janice Bell from Orchard Grove Family Medicine about my daughter right away. She's on an apnea monitor, a feeding tube, and needs a suction machine because she can't swallow. She's on seizure meds and is one step above vegetative, and her temperature's all the way up to 104.7."

CHAPTER 57

I've never ridden in an ambulance before. If Jake hadn't given his mom the car, we could have taken Natalie in ourselves, but when we explained to the triage nurse it would take at least twenty minutes before we could get on the road, she told us to call 911 instead of waiting around. The paramedics arrived just a few minutes ago. The same man with the blondish beard is still the captain on the crew, and now that we're en route to the county hospital, he's trying to get my mind off my daughter's raging fever.

"Your family must have clipped out the two-for-one coupon from the paper."

I can't understand his words. Why is he talking to me about coupons?

I hate Jake right now. Hate him for not being here in the ambulance with us. For some reason, he in all his gifted intelligence decided to get the car from Patricia's hotel and meet us at the hospital. As if Patricia and her stinking baggage couldn't wait.

At least Orchard Grove's a small town. Natalie and I will arrive at County in a few minutes.

One of the EMTs gives me a sympathetic smile. "I thought you'd be relieved to know your daughter's pediatrician is the on-call doctor tonight."

I don't even grasp what that means. I just wonder if Jake's going to meet us there like he said or if this was his way of bailing out on our daughter and me for good.

The captain's trying to ask me questions about Natalie's history, but I'm so nauseated I can't answer. I don't know if it's the fast ride or what, but I swear I'm going to throw up. My daughter looks so tiny in here. The paramedics have her buckled in her car seat, which they've strapped to the stretcher. So much empty space. She only takes up one-sixth of the gurney. Maybe less. So much room to grow. God, do you see how little she is? Do you see how tiny? You can't take her from me.

You said so yourself, remember?

A sermon that Sandy's husband once preached is whizzing through my brain. He was talking about how God used prophets to deliver his messages in ancient times, but now that we have the Bible, the Old and New Testaments, there's no need for prophecies anymore. I didn't think I was paying that much attention, but now his words haunt me like I'm in some low-budget horror movie. *No such thing as prophecy... Only valid in Bible times* ... So why did my heart speed up when I first heard Grandma Lucy pray? Why did my spirit feel so secure when she said my daughter would live, as if she was giving me a direct promise from the Lord?

That was a promise, wasn't it? Or was it what I wanted to believe? Another sermon, this one about people who only listen to what their itching ears want to hear, plays through my mind. With all of Carl's preaching I've got downloaded in my brain, it's a shock I'm not some missionary or other kind of saint.

We slow to a stop, and my very first, very bumpy ambulance ride is over. I'm back on autopilot now, scarcely functioning as the paramedics open the back doors and lower Natalie's stretcher to the ground. I follow them, lugging that massive suction machine slung over my shoulder even though the hospital room will have one built in by the bedside.

I follow my daughter and her troop of first responders down blurry hallways that are far too bright. My brain doesn't turn back on until I see a familiar face looking at me with so much compassion I feel like either hitting the liquor store and getting completely wasted or sitting down and treating myself to a long, hard cry.

"I'm so sorry to hear she's sick. How long has she had the fever?" Dr. Bell asks. I could hug her for being here for me and my baby.

"I don't know. I thought she felt a little warm this afternoon, but nothing like this …" I'm going to start bawling. It's stupid of me. There are lots of other things to get worked up over besides a fever, but it's everything compounded. Jake and Patricia and that Grandma Lucy lady and now Natalie. I've never felt somebody that hot. My fingers have this strange, creepy sting to them where they touched her forehead.

"Is she still congested?" Dr. Bell asks. She's not wasting a single second. She's conducting this interview while the ambulance crew wheels my daughter into one of the rooms. "Has she been around anyone else who's been sick lately?" She's asking me so many questions I can only answer one out of every two or three.

"Her grandma has a cold or something."

Dr. Bell frowns. "Any fever?"

"Not until just now. That's why I called the ambulance."

"No, I mean does her grandma have a fever?"

"I don't think so." I don't want to think about Patricia right now. I swear, if that woman is the one who got my daughter sick …

"How high did you say her temp was?"

"104.7." I hate the way the words feel slipping out of my mouth. Like I'm defiled. Unclean. What kind of mother lets her daughter get this sick?

"And that was on a home thermometer? We better retake it here."

"Got a new reading on the way over," Captain Blond Beard's says. "104.5."

Dr. Bell's not smiling. She's not giving me a hug, telling me my daughter's going to be just fine.

I need to get myself to a bathroom because I swear I'm about to puke.

We've stopped. We're in a room now, and there's at least one nurse in here for every EMT. All this for a fever?

Dr. Bell slips the ear tips of her stethoscope in place. I never would have guessed a face that pretty and youthful could appear so strained. Is she angry at me? Does she think I did this on purpose?

Something's beeping behind me. I turn. Man, I hate those stupid monitors. The numbers are flashing and the buzzers yelling at us all as if we didn't know. As if we couldn't see for ourselves.

My daughter's blood is only 84% oxygenated. The number drops to 82% after a few more beeps.

Dr. Bell turns to a nurse. "Get her on two liters of O2."

I wonder if I'm the only one who can hear the desperation in her voice.

CHAPTER 58

An hour and a half. The flight team from Seattle is going to be here in an hour and a half.

Assuming Natalie makes it that long.

Pneumonia. That's what Dr. Bell's thinking. That or RSV, the baby-killing virus. But that doesn't make sense, because Natalie's been getting shots against it every month since she was born.

So it's pneumonia? Or maybe something else. Dr. Bell wanted to get an X-ray done at County, but the flight team told her to hold off until they reached Seattle. Something about their equipment being more accurate.

So it's back to the city for us. Aren't we lucky? It's like we won the prize at the Christmas bazaar. Oh, and did I tell you the other good news? Jake hasn't shown up yet. Natalie and I arrived at the ER almost an hour ago, and he still hasn't come. Hasn't called either.

I'm so angry I didn't even text to demand what's going on.

If he wants this to be goodbye, I'm not about to get down on my knees and beg him to stay. What is it they say in that *Home Alone* movie? *Merry Christmas, you filthy animal.* He and Patricia can spend the holiday together in that stupid trailer. It would serve both of them right. They were made for each other. I'll ask Jake to mail me my things at the Ronald McDonald house.

Never look back, right? Might as well tattoo it onto my forehead.

"How are you doing?" Dr. Bell pokes her head into my room.

I fold my hands inside the pocket of my hoodie. "Better now that she's getting the extra oxygen."

"No, I mean how are you?"

I sometimes wish Dr. Bell weren't so kind to me. It makes me feel that much guiltier knowing what I've done to my daughter. Knowing what she'd think of me if I told her the truth.

I shrug and try to cough up a little bit of a laugh. "Not bad. I'm getting sort of used to this." I'm about to make a stupid joke about the medevac company giving out frequent flyer points, but the words stick in my throat.

Dr. Bell tells me to call if I need anything, and she slips out of the room gracefully. I glance down at her feet, half expecting to see pink ballet slippers.

I'm a mess. The only reason I haven't completely fallen apart is because I need to function to make that medevac flight with my daughter.

I should call Sandy. I really should. I haven't posted anything online yet. I'm too tired to bring the phone out of my pocket. Too exhausted from wondering when Jake will show up, wondering why he hasn't called yet.

Deep inside, I already know. He's not ready for the

responsibilities of having a daughter. Especially not one as fragile as Natalie. Heck, I'm not even ready for this, but I don't have any choice. So here I am. Maybe I shouldn't be too hard on Jake. If I could have left by now, don't you think I would?

At least we had a good evening together. One good evening out of our whole whirlwind marriage. I just wish Washington had more lenient annulment laws. I looked into it a month or two ago. Since neither of us were drunk or anything like that when we signed the papers, we'd have to go through an actual divorce. No quick and easy dissolution like you'd find in some states.

I shouldn't have ever left Massachusetts. What do Natalie and I have out here?

Each other. That's it.

I just hope to God it's enough.

CHAPTER 59

"I'm sorry, Mom. This will all be done in another few seconds."

The flight nurse from Seattle is here, and he's apologizing because he has to dig around with the needle before he can get my daughter's veins to cooperate. Natalie doesn't need any IV meds right now. They just want to have the port ready in case she needs treatment on the way to Seattle.

Everything's gone smoothly so far. Natalie's oxygen levels are hovering in the low nineties, with an occasional bounce to 88 or 89. Dr. Bell put her on one of those nebulizer machines earlier. Reminded me of that foster brother I used to tease so mercilessly for his asthma. I'm surprised I still remember Eliot Jamison. Wish I could look him up. Maybe it'd be good karma if I apologized to him.

Natalie looks ok to me, not blue or anything like that. And the flight nurse is taking his time. That's got to be a good sign. No rushing around like she'll die if we don't get her to Seattle in the next half hour. I'm trying to tell myself everything's going to be ok. They'll take her to the Children's Hospital, monitor her for a day or two, and send her home.

We could be back in Orchard Grove by Christmas.

Or not. I've already decided that if Jake doesn't call me or at least text me to ask how everything's going, I have no reason to return. Natalie and I can stay in Seattle. Find a place to live there. I'm so sick of medevacs already. Today's the last time I'm going through something like this.

The flight nurse gets the IV port in place and tapes it to Natalie's skin. "I'm sorry."

I don't know if he's apologizing to me or my daughter.

Dr. Bell is at my side now, rubbing my shoulder. "Looks like they're just about ready."

I force myself to return her smile. "Thanks so much." I hold her gaze for a moment. I hope she understands I'm grateful for so much more than her taking care of my daughter.

Small laugh lines soften around her eyes. She looks tired. I pray she doesn't hate me for putting her through an ordeal like this. And right before Christmas, too.

"I hope everything goes well for you in Seattle," she says.

I want to tell her merry Christmas, but I hate to admit I might be spending the holidays at the Ronald McDonald house like some kind of pathetic charity case, so I don't say anything and end up looking like an idiot instead.

"I'm going to give you my cell number," Dr. Bell tells me, grabbing a birth control pamphlet from the counter. "Let me know how she's doing, ok?"

I bite my lip so I don't make an even bigger fool of myself

and start blubbering. She really cares about my daughter. How did we get to be so lucky?

I take the paper she's holding out and nod my head. She understands I can't talk right now. I'm sure she does. I know we'd be good friends if we'd met somewhere else, an exercise class or something. When you're with her, you want to open up and be vulnerable, but it's not like she demands anything from you. This whole ordeal she hasn't even asked about Jake. Isn't she the least bit curious where Natalie's father is at a time like this?

I sure am.

A nurse enters the room, looking straight at me instead of any of the other workers. "Your husband's here."

He's panting when he comes into the room, like he's just run ten flights of stairs even though County's small enough that everything's on one level. "There you are." There's relief in his voice, so much so that I don't rip into him right away for ditching us like that.

"I'm sorry I didn't call," he pants. "I left in such a rush I forgot my phone at home."

It's a reasonable excuse. Besides, I'm too sick with worry right now to stay angry at him. "Did you get the car?" I still can't figure out why he's so late or why he's as winded as Eliot Jamison in the first stages of an asthma attack.

Jake shakes his head. "I went to the wrong hotel."

"The wrong hotel?" It's not like Orchard Grove has more than one to choose from.

He shrugs. "I got there, asked the guy at the front desk to let my mom know I was there, and he said she hadn't checked in. Said he hadn't had any new guests all evening."

That's so like Patricia. She gets my kid sick enough to land us another all-expense-paid flight to Seattle, and then she ditches town, leaving us stranded and carless.

Mother of the Year, right?

I don't care that Jake's late. Not anymore. But I do care about that witch stealing the Pontiac. Who does she think she is?

"What are you going to do?" I ask him.

"I'm sure it's just a misunderstanding. She probably went to one of the hotels off the highway or something."

I call her a name I may regret tomorrow, but right now I'm not worried about etiquette. Jake bristles at my outburst but doesn't get mad at me. "How's Natalie?"

I don't know if he's asking because he's anxious about her or because he wants to change the subject. "They're getting ready to fly her back to Seattle."

His eyes widen. "Seattle?"

I shrug. What was he expecting? County's not the kind of place that can handle a sick kid like her. It was dumb to bring her back here in the first place. If she and I had stayed in Seattle, she'd already be getting all the x-rays and medicine she needs.

"We're leaving in just a few minutes."

"I'll come with you," he says.

"They only have room for one of us." He already knows that.

269

This is the exact same scenario we went through when Natalie was born.

"Then I'll make the drive tonight and meet you there."

It's cute the way he wants to rush in and be involved, but he's not thinking at all.

"What are you going to drive?"

Jake doesn't have an answer for me.

A member of the flight crew enters the room. "We're ready."

I look at Jake, and he looks at me. This might be goodbye, but I'm not certain. Right now, I need to get Natalie to Seattle. All these questions about Jake and our relationship will have to wait until later.

"Call me as soon as you get there," he tells me.

"Ok."

We are as awkward as two strangers who just got set up on a blind date. I feel like we should hug or something, but everyone is watching. Waiting. Natalie's got to get on that jet.

"Bye," is all I say.

"Yeah. Bye." Jake's voice follows me out of the hospital room like a soulless echo.

CHAPTER 60

I haven't slept in nearly twenty-four hours. It was almost three in the morning by the time Natalie got situated at the Seattle Children's Hospital. The rooms are bigger than when she was in the NICU. We're in the pediatric intensive care floor now. Moving up in the world, aren't we? I hate the fact that I'm spending the week before Christmas in the hospital, but something feels right about the entire thing. Like maybe my brain knew we'd be here all along. Or maybe I'm just a glutton for punishment.

God knows I deserve this and so much worse. But does he have to take it out on my daughter?

I think I dozed for a little bit around four. I remember waking up as a technician came in with a giant rolling machine. "Just getting some x-rays on your daughter," he told me, and I zoned right out again after that.

Now that it's morning, I'm not even sure I'll book a room at the Ronald McDonald house. They've got a couch chair here that's plenty big enough for me to sleep in. Sure, it's kind of loud with monitors beeping and nurses coming in every few hours to change Natalie's meds or check her stats, but it's not like I'd manage any better in a room by myself.

271

As soon as I answer a few questions from the day-shift worker coming on duty, I go to the nursing station and request a meal card. I'm one of those veteran parents, I guess, the kind who know the ropes already. Know how to get things done. Five minutes later, I'm on my way to the hospital cafeteria. It's like time held still between now and when Natalie was discharged from the NICU last fall. All that's changed is the hospital decorations. There's paper Christmas ornaments taped to the walls and a big fancy tree by the main entrance. The music's different, too. Julie Andrews and Frank Sinatra instead of that dumb piano stuff. I'm sure I'll be sick of this soundtrack in another day or two, but right now it's a welcomed change from that idiotic elevator music I listened to during our first stay here.

The cafeteria's not quite as crowded as I expected. I must have missed the big surge of night workers coming off duty and the day shift arriving in time to pick up their bagels and coffee. I grab a cinnamon roll and stand in line to get a cappuccino. If there ever was a day for caffeine, this was it.

I'm already anxious about abandoning Natalie in her room. It's not like it was when she was in the NICU. I could leave her there for hours at a time and not worry about it. But something's changed. She's my daughter now. It sounds stupid, because she was my daughter even in the NICU, but it feels different since I'm the one who took care of her for the past two months.

I haven't called Jake yet. I don't know why I'm avoiding him. I sent him a text to let him know when we got into Seattle, but I haven't responded to his half a dozen questions. Maybe I'm just tired. Or maybe I'm starting to pull away because I know.

Jake's never going to leave Orchard Grove, and Natalie's too sick to be that far away from the city. Some things just weren't meant to be, I guess.

Once I get my caffeine for the day, I stand behind a doctor who's paying for a fruit salad and side of cottage cheese. Maybe I'll feel better if I start eating healthier. It might give me more energy, I don't know. I'm focusing so hard on his cantaloupe and honeydew I don't even notice him turn around to stare at me.

"I'm sorry, do we know each other?" he asks.

I squint my eyes. There's something vaguely familiar. Was he one of Natalie's specialists from the NICU, maybe?

He's sticking out his hand. "Dr. Jamison."

I'm sure my eyes are about to bug out of their sockets. "Wait a minute. Are you from Massachusetts?" But I see his nametag now and already know.

I'm laughing and pumping his hand like he's just offered me a million bucks. "Eliot Jamison. It's me. Tiffany Franklin. We went to school together, remember?"

Before I know it, he's offering me an awkward hug and telling the cashier to put my coffee and cinnamon roll on his tab. "Tiff," he says, and I'm glad he remembers that's what I've always gone by. "I knew I recognized you. What are the chances?" He hands me my cappuccino. "I have a few minutes before I need to start making my rounds. Care to take a seat with me?"

I want to stay. Man, I want to stay. I don't care that it's Eliot Jamison, the kid I pestered to death because of his inhaler. It's nice to have someone — anyone — who seems genuinely happy to see me.

"I can't." I hate myself as soon as I say the words. Hate the way Eliot's eyes immediately cloud over with disappointment. "My daughter's here in the PICU. I really have to get back."

He's looking at me like it literally hurts him to know I have a child that sick. For once, I don't mind having someone feel a little sorry for me.

He sets down his fruit and pulls a business card out of his wallet. "Listen, if you ever want someone to talk to about ..."

I glance at the card. *Eliot Jamison, Oncology Resident.* "It's not cancer." I want to add *thank God* but figure that might not be the best move. I don't want to offend him or any of his patients, and I certainly don't want to jinx my daughter. After all the x-rays and procedures she's gone through these past four months, it'll be a miracle if she doesn't end up needing an oncologist at some point in her future. "She had a brain bleed when she was born ..." I realize I'm about to give Eliot an entire rundown of her medical history, but I don't want to bore him to death or act like I'm out for a free consultation. "It's a long story, and I know you've got to be busy." Aren't medical residents notoriously overworked?

He's all smiles. I feel awful that I used to tease him so horribly. "We're in room 205 in the PICU," I tell him. "Stop by any time."

Once Natalie and I get out of here, I'm going to be sick of people looking at me with so much sympathy, but right now, I want to hug Eliot for how kind his eyes are. He promises to come by and visit soon. I actually believe him, and we part ways.

I get a text from Jake as I take the elevator back up to the peds floor. *How's she doing?*

I tell Jake what the night nurse told me before she clocked out, which wasn't much, and return to my room. Natalie hasn't woken up yet. She's got an oxygen cannula taped to her cheeks. She looks a little ashen, but her oxygen levels are mid-nineties today. Maybe she's already getting better.

I count down the days until Christmas, hoping to God we're out of here by then.

CHAPTER 61

"Smelly Elly? I seriously can't believe you forgot about that."

I'm back at the cafeteria having lunch with Eliot, aka Dr. Jamison, the oncology resident. I decided it was time to come clean and apologize for how mean I was to him when we were kids, except he doesn't remember half of it.

"Ok," I laugh. "What about the time I hid your inhaler in a tampon box? You can't have forgotten that one."

Eliot's smiling at me, but his eyes are soft. Maybe it's the white coat and official nametag, but he looks like he could be ten years older than I am. "Actually, there's a lot about those days I don't remember."

I bite my lip. Of course. It should be the golden rule of foster brats. Don't bring up the past. What was I thinking?

"I'm sorry," I mumble. When he called up to Natalie's room to invite me to lunch, it had sounded like such a good idea. Now I'm not so sure.

"Hey, don't apologize. If what you did to me was really that bad, there's no way I could have forgotten it so easily, right?"

We both know this is a lie, but I pretend to agree with him.

"So, tell me about your daughter," he says. "Her name's

Natalie, right?"

It's ironic, really. Here I am wanting to talk about the past to forget all the pain that's going on now, and he's the exact opposite. Is there any safe ground between us?

I give him the sixty-second summary of Natalie's condition. Tell him the doctors think she got a lung infection from breathing in so much of her drool.

"Poor little thing," he says.

I still can't believe he's already a doctor. If I remember right, he was only three or four years older than me. Of course, he's a genius. Probably graduated early and all that. But still, he's already got his MD? Meanwhile, what do I have to show for myself? A sick baby, a marriage license that may or may not be valid come summer, and a trailer in the middle of nowhere that I doubt I'll ever see again and isn't even in my name.

I pull out my phone to show him a picture of Natalie.

"She's a cutie," he says as he takes my cell, and I want to kiss him for being so kind.

"Yeah, she is," I agree.

My phone beeps from an incoming text, and he hands it back to me. "Oh, this must be for you."

Mom's at the Omak hotel. Having a buddy drop me off there this afternoon.

"Everything ok?" Eliot asks.

"Yeah, it's just …" I find my cheeks warming up and I don't know why. "It's Natalie's dad. He's trying to find a way to get here from central Washington. Kind of crazy."

I shouldn't be embarrassed, but I am. Eliot Jamison, my asthmatic foster brother from a dozen lifetimes ago, now probably makes enough money in a single day to get a private flight from Orchard Grove to Seattle. Ok, so maybe not that much yet, but once he's out of his residency he sure will. Meanwhile, my husband's stuck four hours away because his car's a piece of trash and won't make it over the North Cascades without burning the engine.

There's karma for you right there.

Eliot and I make some small talk while we finish our lunch. I find out he went to Yale on a full scholarship for his undergrad, got accepted into some posh med school in New York City right after that, and has been doing this oncology residency for about six months now. He doesn't mention a wife or a family, and I don't ask. When we're done eating, we promise to connect again soon even though I wouldn't be surprised if I never hear from him again.

I get back on the elevator to the peds floor, and I find myself wondering if Eliot Jamison's is the one soul in this world who's as lonely and lost as mine.

CHAPTER 62

I call Jake after the sun sets. It's the first time we've talked since Natalie and I flew into Seattle last night.

"Hey." I hate the way my voice sounds so tired. I hate that I'm not even trying to make my husband feel like I'm happy to be on the phone with him.

"What's going on?" His voice is funny. Like I called him right in the middle of something important. Like he wasn't expecting to hear from me.

"I just thought I'd give you a ring."

"Yeah? How's it going?" He's distracted. What could he possibly be doing? Is he playing that stupid candy game and trying to have a conversation with me at the same time?

"It's pretty good," I tell him. "They've got her oxygen levels to stay in the nineties most of the day. They've been giving her steroids. I think it's helping."

"Steroids? Isn't that bad?"

I roll my eyes, certain he's thinking about athletes and bodybuilders and sports scandals. "Not that kind. These are different. They put them in through the nebulizer. It's supposed to be good for her lungs."

279

"Put it in the nebu-what?" I hear dishes clatter in the background.

"What's going on over there?" I seriously doubt that Jake is emptying the dishwasher when he's got the trailer completely to himself. I'd be surprised if he runs a single load this whole week, especially after he's been trained to think that his mother …

His mother? Nobody could be that stupid. Not even my husband.

"It's nothing," he says. "Just dropped a plate, that's all." He lowers his voice. Like he's got something to hide. Like he's trying to keep somebody from listening in.

"Your mom's not over there, is she?" No. I refuse to believe my husband, the man I agreed to marry, the man whose child is the most important thing in my world, could be that big of an idiot.

"What? No, she just …"

"Jake, what happened to the serving bowl? The big white one I use for the rice?" Patricia's voice on the other line is as obvious as that zit on Jake's chin from his online profile pic. I could laugh if I wasn't so disgusted.

"Listen." He's whispering. I can just picture him crouching low and trying to sneak down the hall so he can have a private conversation in the bedroom. "She's really sorry about what she said. She came and apologized. She's old-school, you know. Back when we were kids, that word meant something else …"

"I've got to go."

"Please, don't be mad at me. If you're not comfortable with

this, I'll ask her to leave before you get back. I just …"

I hang up before I can hear any more of his pathetic excuses. It's not that I'm surprised he invited Frankenmother back to the trailer. It's not that I even blame him. You can't expect that boy to stand up to his mom twice in the same calendar year.

I didn't hang up on Jake because I was mad at him. I hung up because my daughter is acting weird. I've already pushed the alert button. Why is it taking the nurse so long to get here?

Half a minute later, she bustles through the door. "Everything ok?" It's a stupid question. Why would I have called her if everything was ok?

"She's doing something funny." I'm standing over Natalie's crib, watching her pump her legs like she's trying to ride a bicycle and lie on her back at the same time. Her head's moving rhythmically from one side to the other. I would have never guessed she had that much muscle strength.

The nurse is shining a flashlight into my daughter's eyes. "She's never done anything like this before?"

"No. I've never seen her move her legs at all."

"I'm going to call the doctor in."

"What's going on?"

"Looks like she's having a seizure."

CHAPTER 63

Natalie's got at least twenty wires taped to her little head. It's all color-coded. Reds and greens and yellows. Like in those stupid action movies where the hero doesn't know if he's supposed to cut the blue wire or the red one. Except have you noticed it's never the same color from one film to the next?

There's some tech in here, a cute guy in his twenties or early thirties. He's really talkative, but not in a flirty way. More like the "I'm a dude but I'd make a great BFF and you'd never have to worry about me hitting on you" sort of way. I like him. He puts my mind at ease.

"How old's your little sweetie?" he asks.

"Four months." I hate saying it because she still looks like a newborn. A very out of it newborn who just spent half an hour pedaling her legs in the air like she was watching an aerobics video from the eighties.

"She's adorable." He's gushing, but he's not overdoing it. I get the feeling that he's being sincere.

"Thanks."

"Is she part Asian?"

"Yeah." I answer even though I don't want to think about Jake right now.

"I thought so. You can really see it in her eyes."

"Uh-huh."

He plugs some of the wires into his portable machine. "Well, I'm just about done hooking her up."

"Then what happens?"

"We watch. The EEG'll print out a scan of her brain waves, and that will give the neurologist an idea of what's going on in there."

I don't want to deal with the same neurologist I met in the NICU, but if I don't have any choice, I guess it's better than nothing. We're here to figure out what's wrong with Natalie, right?

We don't say much once Natalie gets hooked up. The tech makes small talk every now and then, but I'm so exhausted I end up being pretty bad at conversation. I don't know how long the test goes because I'm back on hospital mode where my biological clock completely shuts down and I have no concept of minutes or hours. I'm surprised when he unhooks my daughter and starts peeling off the tape stuck to her scalp.

"That's all?"

"Yup."

I eye the chart on the screen. "What does it say?"

"I have to send it to the neurologist to look at. I'm sure he'll be here soon to talk to you."

Be here soon. Great. I know enough hospital-speak by now to realize the guy must have found a problem but isn't allowed to tell me himself. I don't know why I'm surprised. I shouldn't have let that Grandma Lucy lady get my hopes up. She's nothing but an old bat who doesn't know anything about me or my child. Was I so desperate I clung to the wild promises of a perfect stranger who doesn't have a hint of medical training?

The tech leaves. Part of me wishes he would have stayed. I feel like an unwanted stray puppy, willing to shower all my love on the first person to show me the slightest hint of attention. I hate that I'm so pathetic right now. You know what I need? My foster mom. Sandy's perfect in situations like this. That's why she does so much foster care in the first place. She was made to nurture unwanted, needy creatures. Some people like that work at animal shelters. Others take in foster brats.

Sometimes I wonder if I'm special in Sandy's mind. If I stand out more than some of the other placements she had. I was there for four whole years. That's got to count for something. But on the other hand, she's been doing this for decades now. I wouldn't be surprised if she's had a couple hundred kids in and out her door. There's no way she can remember all of them.

Man, I need to stop this line of thinking. If Sandy didn't care about me, she wouldn't have flown out to Seattle when Natalie was little. She came because I needed her. Why couldn't Natalie have been born in Boston? Why did I ever leave home?

There's a huge man blocking the entryway. "Mrs. Franklin?" he asks. I wonder if he's the neurologist.

"Come in."

He's so tall, I didn't see the petite woman standing behind him at first. Her black hair goes down past her waist, and I doubt she's five feet tall even in those two-inch heels. She's all smiles as she stretches her hand out to me. "Hi. I'm Riza Lopez, one of the chaplains here. This is Dr. Fletcher. Mind if we sit down?"

CHAPTER 64

I don't want to know what a chaplain is doing in my daughter's hospital room. Is this standard procedure? Do they just go around from room to room checking up on people? And why the bodyguard dude?

She looks nice enough. Filipina if I had to guess. Probably weighs half of what I did when I was full-term with Natalie, but her smile is genuine. It's the doctor I don't trust. Dr. Fletcher is six-foot-six if he's an inch. He's the size of a football player, and his hands are so big he could rest my baby in one palm. He's got rich, dark skin that makes my hodgepodge complexion pale in comparison. I study the two of them. They look so mismatched, and for a second I wonder if that's what Jake and I look like to others when they see us.

Riza sinks into the swivel chair the doctors use and crosses one ankle over the other. "We're here to talk to you about your daughter."

I start to wonder if the only criterion you need to meet to become a hospital chaplain is the keen ability to state the obvious. I glance at Dr. Fletcher, who is standing behind her like a looming volcano about to erupt. He clasps his massive hands behind his back, obviously waiting for Riza to take the lead.

She looks at Natalie in her crib. "How's she doing?"

Natalie still has sharpie marks on her head where the tech prepped her for the EEG reading. "All right." She's not moving her feet around anymore. Whatever seizure or weird activity was going on earlier, it's over now, thank God.

"I guess she had a pretty high fever." Riza still hasn't told me a single thing I don't know.

I nod, wondering how long this interview's going to take. I haven't had dinner yet, even though it's almost eight.

Riza frowns and looks at a note. "So, it looks like she's having a hard time keeping her oxygen levels up."

I nod again, glad that I'm not getting billed for this visit or consultation or whatever this meeting is. Maybe Dr. Fletcher has something helpful to add. "Did you get results yet for the EEG?" I ask.

He leans over, and he and Riza both pout at her little notebook. "EEG?" she repeats.

"Yeah. There was someone in here just a little bit ago. Hooked her up to the EEG?" I wonder if I've gotten my acronyms wrong. It certainly wouldn't be the first time. "You know, brain scan stuff. Is that why you're here?"

Their eyes widen as if I've just enlightened them with the secrets of the universe. "No," Dr. Fletcher answers. "I'm not the doctor assigned to your daughter's case. I'm here because ... well, this is more of a visit to see how you're doing."

Something in my stomach clenches shut. What if he's not a

medical doctor at all? What if he's a social worker or something, here with CPS? What if they know about what I did in Spokane when I went to the women's clinic there? What if they're about to arrest me for attempted murder? What if they're going to steal my daughter from me until I can prove to some court that I'm fit to parent her? What if Patricia …

"There's nothing to worry about." Riza's taken the conversational reins one more time, and her partner morphs into the background as easily as anyone that large can blend in anywhere. "We're here because the last time your daughter was at Children's, you and your partner signed a DNR form stating that you didn't want her placed on a ventilator." She leans forward in her chair. She must be real into the whole active-listening thing. It's like she's the poster child for open communication. "We're just here to check if those are still your current wishes as far as your daughter's future is concerned."

I'm usually pretty good at reading a variety of different folks, but I'm having a hard time figuring these two out. Does Riza want to intimidate me into redacting the DNR the hospital has on file? Is that why she brought the gigantic doctor here as some kind of heavyweight backup? Or is it the other way around? Does she know that I talked to Natalie's pediatrician and canceled the DNR? Is she trying to change my mind? I figure the doctor must be here to intimidate me into doing whatever Riza thinks I should. The problem is I don't know what her angle is. Not yet.

"We're not trying to get you upset," Riza begins, "but this is a sensitive subject, and we just want to make sure there's a plan in place now so you don't have to make a major decision like this in the middle of an emergency." She says the last word apologetically, as if she's terrified of reminding me my daughter could stop breathing any minute.

Trust me, woman, I'm not that fragile. I already know.

I glance at Dr. Fletcher. He's big enough to play that guy Bear in the *Armageddon* movie, and I'm beginning to doubt he's a medical doctor at all. So what is he, then? A psychologist? Some shrink here to tell me what decisions I'm supposed to make for my baby's future?

I'll pass, thank you very much.

"What have your daughter's doctors said so far about her condition since she's been here?" he asks.

"Not a lot," I answer. "She's doing better. Her O2 levels are mostly in the nineties now. She's been on steroids." I'm trying to prove to them my daughter is ok. This isn't a conversation I need to have right now. Natalie's the most stable she's been in twenty-four hours, and she's only going to get better. Whether I do or don't cancel the DNR shouldn't make any difference here, because she's not going to need the ventilator one way or the other.

"Tell me about her neuro-development," Riza prompts. "You said she recently had an EEG?"

I nod and glance at my daughter. She looks so peaceful now. If it weren't for the oxygen cannula taped to her face and the sharpie marks all over her head, you might not know anything was wrong with her.

"The nurse was a little worried when she started pumping her legs. It only lasted a few minutes."

Riza glances at Dr. Fletcher. *I wonder why I feel like I've just betrayed my daughter.*

"Well, we certainly hope you get back a good report from the neurologist." *She's back to smiling again. Smiling like a cobra before it strikes.* "And we don't anticipate it coming down to drastic measures, but have you decided if you'd like the hospital to keep the DNR we have on file or make changes to it?"

I still get the feeling there's a certain answer I'm expected to give, that if I make a mistake I'll fail some sort of test. "I talked with her pediatrician this week," I begin tentatively. *Neither one of them looks upset when I offer this information, so I venture out a little further.* "At this point, what I told her was we'd like to cancel the DNR and just see what happens."

"And did you make that change in writing?" Riza asks.

"No. She said she'd make a note in the file. Was I supposed to do anything else?"

Riza shakes her head, and Dr. Reynold's stoic face appears a bit softer than it was a minute ago. *Maybe I gave them the answer they wanted to hear after all.*

Riza taps her pen against her folder. "You did absolutely perfectly. And are you still in favor of cancelling the DNR? Would you be willing to sign a form for us so we have that on file?"

I feel like something's missing. This is a conversation about whether I'm going to let my daughter die or not. Is three minutes as long as it really takes? Is it as simple as signing a piece of paper or not signing?

"I guess."

Dr. Fletcher must detect the hesitation in my voice. "If you need more time ..." he begins before I cut him off.

"No, I'll sign. I really don't expect her to need anything like this anyway ..."

"Of course not," the two of them both affirm with vigorous head shaking all around.

"So I guess I'm ready." I still can't figure out why I feel so uncertain. This isn't like me. I'm the one who wanted to cancel the DNR in the first place. This was my plan a week ago before I even knew Natalie and I would end up in Seattle again.

"And your partner?" Riza asks. "Have you had this discussion with him?"

"Oh, yeah." It's so easy to lie. "He agrees, too. We want to give Natalie a chance to mature a little bit, you know, see how she progresses." The words sound so morbid coming out of my mouth. Like going to the dog pound and saying, *I'll take this one. If it doesn't work out, I can always bring him back, right?* And everybody knows but nobody's willing to talk about what happens to the unlucky pup who gets returned.

Riza pulls a piece of paper out of some fancy folder she's carrying, I scribble my name, and it's as simple as that. I still don't know who Dr. Fletcher is or why the chaplain thought to bring him along, but there's a lot about hospital politics I'll never fully understand.

Riza stands up. I still can't tell if she's disappointed in me or not. Her Goliath of a partner follows her out the door without another word, and I wonder if I've just made the biggest mistake of my life. My daughter is officially off the DNR list at Children's. It's a good thing. I know it is.

So why do I feel like I just signed my daughter's death sentence instead of the other way around?

CHAPTER 65

"Hello?" I don't want to talk to Jake, but this is the third time he's called me since Natalie's EEG. I can't go on ignoring him forever.

"It's me." He always starts his phone conversations the same way. As if my caller ID was suddenly broken and I didn't have a clue who I might be talking to. "How's she doing?"

I guess I should be grateful he's so concerned about our daughter. But asking how I'm doing would be a nice change every so often.

"She's all right." I don't have the energy to tell him everything about the seizure or whatever that was. I'm not sure why the neuro guy hasn't come yet to give me his report. Do they just expect me to wait all night while they take their sweet time?

"How are her oxygen levels?"

I glance at the monitor. "Ninety-one right now. They've been doing pretty good most of the day."

"She still getting those steroids?" There's worry in his voice. I should have never mentioned the nebulizer drugs.

"Yeah, they're what's making her so much better."

I can tell he's unconvinced even though all he says is, "That's good. How much longer do they think she'll be there?"

"No clue." Does he expect me to read minds all of a sudden? Have a crystal ball to tell me the future? "You know how it is. They keep you in the dark until the last minute."

He doesn't respond right away. Am I being too negative? I can hardly remember when we talked last. Hadn't we been fighting about something?

That's right. His mom.

I don't say anything either. It's his problem if he called me just to listen to a bunch of dead space.

I hear a buzzer in the background. "You at work?" I ask.

"Yeah."

Figures. He waited to call me until he was out of the house. Out of Patricia's earshot. I swear, that boy's going to spend the rest of his life either hiding from Mommy or obeying her every single whim.

Silence again. Remind me what I ever saw in him?

"Listen, I'm umm ..."

I roll my eyes, ready to endure the apology he's about to spew out.

"I'm really sorry my mom was so ... Well, I know you're probably still upset and all ..."

I don't bother telling him I'd forgotten all about Patricia until just a few seconds ago.

"Anyway, sorry."

What are you supposed to say to that? The best I can do is something like, "Yeah, ok."

His voice grows hopeful. "So, umm, listen. I was thinking that if you're gonna be there a while, if you think it's gonna be more than a day or two, I might come on over. If, you know, if that's all right with you."

"She's you're daughter, too." What does he think? That I'm going to forbid him from coming? That I'm a tyrant who needs to give him permission before he can visit his own child?

"What about work?"

"Yeah, well, I've been thinking. Maybe, you know ..." He's hemming and hawing so pathetically I want to shake him by the shoulders. "Maybe we should try to find a place in the city. You know, just look around a little bit."

I can't believe he's actually talking about leaving the trailer. About leaving Orchard Grove. Am I in that *Family Man* Christmas movie? Am I Nicholas Cage being given a chance to imagine my life in some other dimension?

"How are you going to get out here?" I don't want him to get too far ahead of himself. One thing at a time. He can't seriously be planning to drive the Pontiac ...

"You know, I was thinking ..." His voice is so nervous I know what he's going to say before he says it. The gist of it, at least. "My mom's planning to fly out to visit Abby over Christmas, and the tickets are a lot cheaper out of Seattle, so ..."

I roll my eyes, waiting him to get to the actual point.

"So, I think what we're hoping to do is my mom can rent a car, we'll drive to Seattle together, and I'll drop her off at the airport and come see you two."

"Yeah, fine."

"Fine?"

I roll my eyes. Is he seriously about to nag me to death for not having more enthusiasm in my voice? Does he have any idea what I've lived through the past twenty-four hours? Does he have any idea how it feels to be woken up by a nurse who's covering you with a lead blanket so you don't get radiation poisoning while they X-ray your sick daughter's lungs? Or having to sit in a room across from some silent, WWF champion lookalike who either does or doesn't want you to sign a DNR form but won't tell you which he thinks you should do?

"Good," I correct myself without bothering to mask my annoyance. "That sounds good."

"Listen." His voice is all huffy, like he's the one gearing up for an argument now. "I know you and my mom had some issues, and she asked me to apologize to you. If this is going to constantly be some big thing ..."

"It's fine." I shouldn't interrupt. I just don't have the stomach to listen to all this whining. Not tonight. "I'm glad you found a way to come out here without having to worry about the car."

I hear him sigh on the other end of the line. "And what about the other thing? What about staying in Seattle? They have good doctors there. We can make sure Natalie gets set up ..."

"Let's talk about that once you get here," I say. Maybe it's that chaplain Riza's visit that's gotten to me. I just can't stand the thought of revolving all our future plans around a girl who may or may not be alive when I wake up Christmas morning.

"Ok." He pauses again before asking, "You sure you're not mad about anything?"

I remember how happy we were, that tiny shred of bliss we experienced right before Natalie was medevaced. Was that just yesterday? It couldn't be.

I shake my head even though he can't see me. "No, I'm not mad. Just tired."

"Long day, huh?" There's a hint of softness in his voice. He wants to end the conversation on a positive note.

Fine by me. "Yeah. You could say that."

"Well, sleep well tonight, ok? And tell my baby girl I miss her."

"I will." Maybe having Jake out here won't be so bad after all.

"Ok." He's stalling. Like he doesn't know how to end a stupid phone call. Then again, I'm not making the move to wrap things up either. "Well ..." Another pause. I swear I can picture him blushing on the other end. "Love you, ok?"

It's an annoying way to talk to your wife, but it's nice to hear nevertheless. "Love you, too." Now I'm the idiot blushing, but that's because the pediatric neurologist is standing at the door, impatient.

I end the call and watch him strut in like a juvenile court judge getting ready to deliver his verdict.

CHAPTER 66

Dr. Bhakta is one of the only specialists from Natalie's NICU days I know by both name and sight. And no, that's not because I have favorable memories of him. He's short, probably Indian judging by his accent. I'm not sure. Is Bhakta an Indian name? I wouldn't know one way or the other.

Most of the specialists I met in the NICU were all business, but Bhakta has the exact opposite problem. He's like Robin Williams in *Patch Adams*, except he's not trying to be funny on purpose. He's just a goof without even intending to be. And not in the comedian way, either, more like the clumsy-big-brother-you're-embarrassed-for way.

It was Dr. Bhakta who first taught me the difference between brain dead and vegetative. So maybe that's a hint about why I don't like him.

He's smiling now, and I don't know how much of my phone conversation with Jake he overheard. Oh, well. I should know better than to expect any degree of privacy at a place like Children's.

He reaches out his hand. "Good to see you again."

I seriously doubt he remembers me from our previous encounters, but maybe I'm wrong. I assume that since he works at a hospital as busy as this he's got a caseload in the hundreds. I'm just another face to him, and Natalie's just another chart.

"I read your daughter's EEG," he's telling me without sitting down. "The good news is she wasn't having a seizure." He's looking at my baby in her crib and not at me.

"That's good," I reply. "So what was all that she was doing with her feet?"

"That was probably a seizure."

"I thought you just said ..."

"I said she wasn't having a seizure when we ran the tests. The EEGs can't tell us what happened in the past, just what's happening at the moment. And at the moment she was hooked up to the machine, she was not having any seizure activity."

I could have told him that and saved the tech an hour's worth of work.

"So that means ..."

He still hasn't made eye contact with me. "That means your daughter probably had a seizure, most likely as a result of her fever, but her brain activity is fine now."

Again, he's not telling me anything I couldn't have assumed on my own. "What about medicine or something? Do we have to up her seizure meds?" I hate the way the meds keep her so sedated. I swear that's at least partly why she always seems so out of it, not because of the brain damage itself.

I'm relieved when Bhakta tells me he's not comfortable giving her a higher dose at this point. "Don't want to suppress her system any more than necessary, especially not while she's having these breathing problems." He glances at her monitor. "O2s are looking good?"

I'm not entirely sure if it's a question or a statement.

"Any other concerns we should discuss?" he asks.

I'm sure I could come up with a dozen if I had time to organize my thoughts, but everything's racing through my mind at once. "I guess not."

"Well, I know we talked about you signing the DNR last time she was admitted. I think you're doing the right thing."

I'm assuming he hasn't talked with Riza Lopez and her linebacker bodyguard yet, but maybe that sort of stuff is automated. Maybe it goes out to all the doctors at once when a parent signs one of those papers. But I recall how adamant he was back in Natalie's NICU days that the DNR was in her best interest given how much brain damage she'd already sustained. I get the feeling he's complimenting me for sticking to my guns and agreeing to let my child die if this illness gets bad enough.

I'm not about to correct his assumptions. What business is it of his? It doesn't matter if Natalie has a DNR on file at Children's or not because she's not going to get that sick. She's already improved quite a bit since we arrived. All this back and forth about it is a big waste of time.

"If you need anything, the nurses know how to get in touch with me."

Without waiting for a goodbye, Bhakta's gone. I feel relieved. Why would I trust my daughter's medical care to anyone who automatically assumes she's better off dead than alive?

I know canceling the DNR was the right thing to do. I really need to stop second-guessing myself now.

It's late. Who knows how many more nurses will be in and out tonight to interrupt my rest? At least Natalie is oblivious to it all. That's one blessing. I grab a blanket and cover myself up in the oversized couch chair.

If I'm lucky, I'll catch a few hours of sleep.

CHAPTER 67

"How's your daughter doing?"

I'm sitting in the cafeteria with Eliot. It's been another long day, and it's already past nine. Eliot just got off work, and we're sharing a late dinner.

"I thought she was getting better, but it looks like she's had some setbacks."

He frowns. I can't believe this put-together, handsome MD is Smelly Elly, the boy I tormented so badly back in Massachusetts. "What's going on?" he asks with more compassion in his voice than I've heard from anyone other than Dr. Bell back in Orchard Grove.

"Well, she had something like a seizure last night. It stopped by the time they got her hooked up to the EEGs, but she was doing that foot pedaling thing and stuff. The doctors think it was from the fever."

He nods. It's nice talking to someone from a medical background who isn't officially Natalie's doctor. "How's her temperature been?"

"They got it as low as 101 yesterday, but it's been climbing up since then. It's been around 103 most of the day. Not too bad, but ..." My voice trails off. Eliot's a doctor. He can fill in the blanks.

"So it's pneumonia she's got?" he asks.

"Not exactly." I try to remember the word the nurse used. "They said it's something a little different, roaming something ... adenectomy ..."

"Roving atelectasis?"

I nod, thankful I no longer have to flounder. "That's it. I don't even know what it is. I just know it's different than pneumonia."

"In a way." He goes off into some long explanation but stops when he realizes I'm completely lost. "Basically, it means her lung function is compromised."

"Yeah. I got that part."

He sighs. "You've been through so much. I'm sure you're ready for a break by now."

I don't tell him what I'm really thinking. That I won't get a break from taking care of Natalie until she's dead. This is my life from now on. I can see it so clearly, for as long as she lives. Hospital stays. Ambulance rides. Medevac jets. Freaking out over every single fever, every single drop in O2. Could I use a break? God knows I need one. But since that's not going to happen as long as my child's still breathing, I guess I'm resigned to this kind of existence. Some women are soccer moms. Others have kids with special needs.

"Tell me something about yourself," I say. It's kind of late to be having dinner, but here we are, me with my burger and fries and Eliot with his huge no-cheese Caesar salad.

Eliot's always had a nice smile. Soft eyes. I think that might be why I was so hard on him when we were kids. He took everything to heart, which made him such an easy victim. He refuses to let me apologize to him anymore, but I still feel bad for what I put him through. "What do you want to know?"

I grin. "Any girls?" My smile vanishes when I watch the pain darken his entire countenance. *Good one, Tiff.* "Or, you know, pets or anything?" I add.

He shakes his head slowly. "I was engaged a few years ago. You might remember her, actually. Amy Matthews? She was a grade behind me in school."

The name means nothing to me, but I see how vulnerable he looks and wish to God I hadn't brought this up. "I'm not sure if I knew her."

"You'd remember her if you did. She was ..." He's staring at his half-eaten salad. Why did I open my big mouth? "She was studying to teach kindergarten when she ..." He takes a sip of his bottled water. "She came down with ovarian cancer. Had spread too far by the time they caught it."

I should have known. There was something quiet, something sad about Eliot I noticed from the moment we bumped into each other in that cafeteria line. I thought it had to do with all the drama he went through as a foster kid. How could I have been so blind? I need to take lessons from Sandy or something. She's always so kind and comforting, and here I am sticking my foot in my mouth five minutes into our conversation. "I'm so sorry."

"Don't be." He's smiling again, but it's like I can feel the heaviness weighing down on his shoulders.

I don't know what I'm supposed to do next. Am I supposed to ask him what happened? Ask if she ever recovered, even though the answer's already pretty obvious? I can't just change the subject. How rude would that be?

"So did she ... I mean, is she ..." My face is hot from self-loathing.

"She passed away. Three years ago Christmas Day."

"Christmas Day?" *What were you thinking, God?* Eliot's not the type of guy to deserve any of this.

"Yeah." He lets out a sad chuckle. "She wanted to make it to New Year's Eve. Wanted to watch the ball drop ..."

"Is that why you went into oncology?"

My question seems to surprise him, like he was so lost in his memories he'd forgotten what we were talking about.

"Oncology?" he repeats, like he's testing the word out for the first time. "Yeah, you could say that. Before she died, she wanted me to promise her I'd keep up with my studies. Wanted me to help others like her."

I can't imagine how hard it would be work your butt off at a job where you're dealing with folks sick and dying from the same disease that killed your fiancée. Why did I ever bring up such a depressing subject?

"I think another reason I went into the field is because I saw how much of her life was stripped away at the end. The chemo. Everything like that. I found myself asking if it was really worth it. She was in so much pain. And all that did was extend her suffering a few more months." He sighs. "There's so many things wrong with today's medical field. I just wonder ..."

His voice trails off. I've lost my appetite.

"She loved kids," he's saying, and I'm smart enough to let him talk and let go of whatever's on his chest. "That's why she chose kindergarten. She'd just gotten her first classroom of her own when she got diagnosed. Had to quit. Doctors told her she couldn't be around all those germs. Sometimes I wonder ..." He takes a noisy gulp from his glass jar full of lemon-infused water. "I know it was the right call. Medically, I mean. But sometimes I think if she'd been able to stay in the classroom, she might have stayed healthier. Or at least happier. Had more to live for, you know?"

"She had you," I remind him even though it sounds cheesy.

Eliot doesn't respond. Something beeps in his pocket. He pulls out a pager. "I've got to go."

"Everything ok?"

"Yeah, just a patient I've been ..." He mumbles the rest of his sentence and snatches up his tray. "Nice talking with you."

"You, too." I can tell he's in a hurry, but I feel like it would be cruel to let the conversation end like this. I grab his wrist. Gently. Just enough to get his attention. "I'm really sorry."

He smiles. His eyes are so kind and deep I could get lost in them for weeks. "Thank you," he says. As I watch him leave, I wonder how many of Natalie's doctors and nurses have horribly tragic stories like his in their pasts. And I wonder if I'll be stuck here at Children's long enough to learn each and every one.

CHAPTER 68

"Did you press your button?" Tonight's nurse is middle-aged. Somewhat cross. Her hot pink scrubs are two or three sizes too small. That woman is trying way too hard.

"Yeah. She's acting a little strange."

It's not the feet pedaling this time. There's something else going on. Hot Pink leans over my baby's crib, and I catch a strong whiff of Listerine. She's not a smoker, is she? There's no way a hospital like Children's would allow a peds nurse to take regular cigarette breaks. I'm just being paranoid.

"It's her legs," I say. "She's been bending them like that for the past five minutes or so."

Hot Pink glances at the monitor. Natalie's oxygen levels are around 86. Not great, but not terrible. I've seen worse.

"Let me check her temperature."

I move out of the way so the nurse can do her thing. She frowns at the thermometer. 103.9. It's creeping up again.

"Is she going to be ok?" I ask.

"We'll have to wait and see."

It's not the encouraging sort of response I was hoping for.

By midnight, I've got two nurses standing over Natalie's

bedside. There's Hot Pink and now the charge nurse, a skinny twenty-something who's far too perky for this hour of the night.

"I think we better call the doctor in," says Skinny as she flits from one side of Natalie's crib to the other.

"What's going on?" I ask. It's a simple question, really. One someone should have answered nearly an hour ago.

Skinny is all smiles and all movement. "I'll have the doctor come in and have a little chat with you." She reaches out and turns up my daughter's oxygen flow before flitting out the room.

Hot Pink doesn't move. I think just watching the bouncy charge nurse has left us both exhausted.

I should text Jake. He might still be awake, and even if he isn't, he'd want to know what's going on. The problem is I don't know what's going on. Natalie's legs are pulling towards her each time she lets out her breath, but it's not that weird seizure thing she was doing earlier. Her color's gray, and her O2 levels have dropped another three points since I first pushed that red call button.

Something's wrong. I just don't know what.

The nurse leads the doctor in. It's not Bhakta or any of the other specialists, just the PICU doc. They change them by the week. Something like seven days straight living and sleeping at the hospital, then four weeks off. I don't know. Sounds kind of cush if you ask me.

This week, Natalie's doctor is short, bald, and remarkably nondescript. I could pass him in the cafeteria tomorrow morning and forget I ever met him.

"What's going on?" he asks sleepily. He's not grumpy, but you can tell his brain still hasn't decided if it's time to fully engage or not.

Skinny chatters away like she's just downed two quad shot caramel macchiatos. It's a little more techno-babble than I'm used to, but I understand that the tugging in my daughter's legs has got everyone concerned.

"What's her O2 at?" the doctor asks as he checks the dial himself.

More medical-speak, and then he tells Skinny to give Natalie a steroid treatment early and leaves. He completely ignores Hot Pink and me.

"So what's going on?" I ask.

Hot Pink's not making attempts to be anyone's BFF tonight. "It's her lungs. She's working too hard."

"What does that mean?" *Too hard?* What is she trying to say?

Hot Pink isn't meeting my eyes. I can smell the Listerine on her breath from here, but right now I don't care if she smokes cigarettes or shoots heroine in the staff bathroom. I just want her to tell me what she knows. Will my daughter be ok? Do we need to give her new medicine?

"It means that if your daughter continues having problems breathing like this, she'll probably have to go back on the ventilator."

CHAPTER 69

It's like I'm on one of those stupid pirate ship rides at a cheap carnival, and I'm ready to get off. I can't take this incessant back and forth, back and forth a minute longer. One second my daughter's fine. She's improving. Her fever's down. The next minute some middle-aged chain-smoking nurse who's nearly bursting out of her scrubs is telling me it's time to think about the ventilator again.

I'm holding Natalie. The charge nurse, Miss Skinny, said if I keep her against my chest and focus on taking deep breaths myself, it can help. Don't ask me how. The problem's in my daughter's lungs, not mine. This is New Age bunk if you ask me, but I'm not about to leave my daughter alone in that oversized crib. Not when she's this sick.

Now that she's against me, I can feel how hard her little body's working. She's so hot I'm in a sweat a minute after I start holding her. I can hear the rasping, wheezing sound in her lungs and can't believe I ever teased anybody, especially someone as kind and sensitive as Eliot Jamison, for having a hard time breathing. I hate to admit I was ever that cruel and heartless. It's fine if God wants to punish me, but can't he find a way to do it without destroying my daughter? Or are we all the way back to David and Bathsheba again?

The doctor's been in and out. Hot Pink and Skinny, too. And when they're not in the room, they're right across the hall at the nurses' station where they can keep an eye on Natalie's monitors and see us through the glass door. Nobody's said the word *ventilator* again since my ominous conversation with Hot Pink. I try to tell myself that she's just a floor worker. Out of everyone involved in this case, she's the one with the least seniority.

Natalie can't go back on the ventilator. Man, how much trauma can anyone expect one four-month-old baby to endure? It's bad enough she's got all these IVs and everything else. And now they want to shove a tube down her throat … I can't take it anymore. I know there's no way I'm about to sit back and let my child die, but I literally can't handle reliving what we went through in the NICU. I just can't. Doesn't God see that? What's that whole thing about *God doesn't give us any more than we can handle*? He can't expect Natalie to have to endure another round on the ventilator. I've never even been on the machine and feel like I'm suffocating just thinking about it.

All God's got to do is reach down and heal whatever infection she's developed in her lungs. That's all. He did it in Bible days all the time. What's the big deal about a repeat performance now?

I think about Eliot Jamison, about his fiancée who loved kids. Loved him. He could be a dad by now. I can just picture how comfortable and happy he'd look with little miniature Smelly

Ellies climbing on his lap and shoulders. God should have healed his girlfriend. Given them a perfect future together. Her teaching kindergarten, him bringing home the big bucks as a hot-shot doctor.

Why is life so unfair?

I hear Sandy's voice in my head, so loving. So reassuring. *Of course life's not fair. But God is good.* I can't argue with her, especially since she's currently just an echo in my mind. But if God is so good, why is my daughter bending her legs trying to force air out of her lungs? You're not supposed to have to think about your breathing unless you're a yoga addict or synchronized swimmer or someone like that. What baby should work this hard just to exhale?

I'm no medical expert, but I know my daughter can't keep this up. She's covered in sweat. Everything about her body screams exhaustion. She's expending way too much energy, and her oxygen levels keep dropping. She's in the low eighties now. I haven't seen her above 82 in almost an hour. You can't live like that forever.

We need a miracle.

The doctor's back in. He's frowning at me. Great. I know what's about to come out of his mouth even before he opens it.

"We're going to try to get this fever to break, but if things don't improve, we've got to put her back on the ventilator."

CHAPTER 70

I can't believe I'm doing this. I should hang up now. I know I should. It's after 1:30. Nobody calls anybody at this time of night.

"Hello?" Her voice is groggy. I should just tell her it's the wrong number. Apologize and hang up.

"Dr. Bell?" My throat is dry and chalky.

"Who's this?"

It's my last chance to end the call and salvage my remaining dignity. "It's Tiff Franklin. Natalie's mom."

I hear rustling in the background. Did I get her out of bed? "Is everything ok?"

"Yeah. I mean, I don't know. We're here at Children's ..." I'm fumbling over every sentence. I need to start over. "I'm sorry to bother you. I just ..." I bite my lip so my voice won't crack. "It's just that they want to put Natalie on the ventilator, and I ..."

Great. I'm calling my daughter's pediatrician in the middle of the night, and I can't get out a single word.

"How's she doing right now?"

I hear something in the background. A bathroom faucet, maybe. I can picture Dr. Bell splashing cold water on that flawless face. Why did I do this? How big of a fool am I?

"She's having a really hard time breathing. It's ..." I dig my fingernails into the skin of my forearm. Anything to get my mind off these tears that threaten to humiliate me. "It's the worst I've seen her." I keep my voice low. I'm the only one in the room with Natalie, but I already feel guilty, like I'm going behind everyone else's back. "I don't know what I should do."

"You know, at this point, I'd really need to defer to the doctors at Children's. They're the ones who are most familiar with your daughter's case. But if you're asking for my personal opinion, not my professional one ..."

"Yes," I interrupt. "That's what I want."

She sighs. "Are you having second thoughts about cancelling the DNR?"

I search her voice for signs of displeasure. Will she think I'm a monster if I choose to let my daughter die? I think about what Eliot said over dinner, how much his fiancée suffered at the end just to eke out a few more months here on earth. "I don't know," I answer.

"What are you doing?" A gruff voice breaks my illusion of Dr. Bell sitting in a quiet, serene room surrounded by white frilly curtains and flower arrangements in crystal vases.

"Hey, hon. Sorry I woke you." There's a hint of strain in her voice. Is she afraid? "It's the mother of one of my kids."

"Get back in bed."

I'm embarrassed for her. I don't know who this guy is or whether or not he speaks to her like that when he's well-rested and content, but I don't imagine it's the kind of conversation she wants someone like me to overhear.

"You need to go," I say. "I'm really sorry I bothered you. I just ... Well, thank you. For talking things through with me."

I don't know what to expect next. More yelling on other end of the line? Dr. Bell giving me an award-worthy pep talk about believing in my daughter no matter how bleak her prognosis looks?

She sighs and keeps her voice down the same way Jake and I used to hush ourselves up whenever Patricia was around. "Listen. You need to do what you think is best. No one else can tell you what that is. You're Natalie's mom. You're going to make the right decision."

I want to thank her, but I've lost my voice. By the time I find it again, she's already ended the call. And none too soon. Natalie's monitor is beeping again. Her oxygen levels have just dropped into the seventies. A minute later, the PICU doctor is in here frowning over her crib.

"Unless you tell me otherwise, it's time for us to intubate."

CHAPTER 71

I'm crying. I feel like such a baby, but I can't help it. I couldn't be in the room, not while they shove those tubes into her. My throat is raw just thinking about it.

They're giving her some kind of drug. Putting her in a coma while she's on the ventilator.

I'm in the chapel while I wait. Not the main one where they do services or anything, just a little room connected to the peds floor. It doesn't look exactly like a church. There's no crosses or anything, but they do have a piano and pews, and there's a few Bibles and a hymnal and some other religious texts on a shelf when you come in.

It's quiet in here. Of course it is. Everyone else on this floor who isn't working is asleep. I should be home with Jake, with Natalie in her room beside ours with her apnea monitor on so we'll know if she runs into any problems. None of this is right. It's not even like a bad dream. It's like an emotional hangover. That's how confused and sick I feel right now. I've got a scratch in the back of my throat, too. If I get sick, are they going to keep me from my child? And if I feel this bad from a little tickle, how's it going to be for my daughter getting the back of her throat scraped raw by these invasive tubes? I can't stand the thought of looking at her with that stuff shoved down her windpipe. I almost want to leave her here and tell the nurses to call me once she gets better.

If she gets better.

There's no guarantee, even being intubated. This might be it. She might never wake up.

I hate Grandma Lucy. That crazy lady's what got this whole thing started. If it hadn't been for her, for the way she told me with so much confidence my child would be ok, I would have never gotten this false hope, never signed those consent forms. I should have never let my guard down. This fear and disappointment and shock, it's all my fault.

My throat's burning up. It's like I can feel the scraping of that horrid plastic tube they're shoving down her windpipe …

Having a machine do all your breathing for you. Can you imagine what that's like? How claustrophobic you'd feel? What if you have to breathe faster, but the machine won't let you? What if you hyperventilate? The worst part of it is this is basically the only life she's ever known. Sure, we had those two months together in Orchard Grove. She was relatively tube-free, except of course for her feeding pump and that Yankauer attached to her suction machine. But now she's back at Children's, and she's too little to even know this isn't what her life is supposed to be. It's like those rescue animals who've been caged up their entire existence. They don't even know that things like sky or grass exist. The argument could be made that they'd be better off dead …

Better off ...

No. I can't go there. I made up my mind, and I'm not looking back.

But even so, there's no guarantee she'll recover. Will my daughter die without ever feeling the summer sun warming up her cheeks? Will the whirring sounds of her equipment and the beeps from her monitors be the only noises she knows? What about music? What about laughter?

She can't die. She can't. But how can I sit here and do nothing while that doctor puts her in a coma? Who puts their own child through torture like that? What if she never wakes up? What if she's in the coma for months? Years? It would be easier to keep her off the machine from the start than one day having to pull the plug.

Pull the plug. Is that the next major decision in my future?

If I keep her off the ventilator, I'm not actively responsible for what happens next. If she doesn't recover, it will be her lungs' fault. Not mine. But now that I've let them put her on that machine, that means one day I might have to make the decision to take her off it. I've just invited myself to become an active participant in my daughter's death.

How could you ask that of anybody?

I'm sobbing. I'm glad I'm in this room where nobody's around and nobody can hear. I'm sure other parents have come in here and cried like this. What's that depressing passage the old woman quoted? *Rachel weeping for her children and refusing to be comforted because they are no more.* I'm not the only parent who's suffered through this. Right here in this room, others have come before me. I can picture them if I want to. The husband who holds his wife in the same arms that carried their child into this hospital, only now they'll be walking out with nothing but an empty backpack. The woman who has to find a way to tell her grandchildren that their brother won't ever come home. The parents whose kid has been in a coma for a year, and the doctors have given up all hope.

Time to make the choice ...

I don't hold a monopoly on grief. I'm not the first mom who's suffered like this, and I won't be the last. And life goes on. That's what's so stinking depressing. My baby could die. She might be gone before I ever go back to her room, but tomorrow the sun will rise, folks will wake up for their morning commute, waste their money on their frilly lattes and cappuccinos, dull their senses behind their computer screens and smartphones. Life will go on without Natalie just like it went on before she arrived.

That's why I'm crying. I realize I am Rachel, the woman refusing to be comforted. Because what kind of comfort can I ever hope to find if God takes my child away from me? After all the promises I made, after how hard I tried to be a better person, after the way he got my hopes up with that stupid Grandma Lucy stunt, he could whisk my daughter off to heaven any minute, and I'm powerless to stop him.

And that's not a feeling I'd wish on anyone.

CHAPTER 72

It's Sunday morning. I can picture Sandy over on the East Coast, sitting in the front row of her husband's huge church. She's wearing one of those floral-print skirts that rustles when she walks, and her hair's in that long French braid, and she's so busy worshipping God she's not even thinking about my baby on a ventilator.

No, that's not fair. She's thinking about Natalie. I know she is. I texted her last night to tell her what was happening. The doctors got Natalie hooked up to her machine just fine. Her oxygen levels are holding steady. By the time I woke up this morning her fever was down to 102. Everyone says I made the right call.

I'm still not sure I believe them.

It's one thing if Natalie's on this ventilator for a day or two while they get her fever under control. I get that part of it. But it's totally different if we start talking about weeks or months. I mean, at some point you just have to say enough is enough, right? I know Natalie's totally knocked out, but what if that only means she can't respond? What if she can still hear and feel everything? What if she's scared? What if she thinks I've abandoned her?

I can't even hold her anymore, not while she's on all these machines. I've seriously started to wonder if it's good for me to stay here, but I don't have anywhere else to go, and of course I've got to stick around in case something changes.

Something has to change eventually, right? That's what's got me so scared. The thought that we might be here in this limbo for months. It's Christmas in a few days. Big stinking deal. And what if Easter comes and she's still on this stupid machine?

I should call Jake. I need to talk to him, but my phone's almost dead and my charger's stuck in Orchard Grove. I sent him a quick text last night. Didn't even have the heart to tell him Natalie was back on the ventilator. I just said it was something the doctor mentioned as a possibility. I've got to warm him up to the idea or he'll completely freak out. I told him to call the hospital room when he wakes up. I can't waste my phone batteries anymore.

Sunday morning. I saw something about a church service in the big chapel downstairs. Maybe I should go. There's nothing really for me to do here. But I know I won't be able to bring myself to leave. What if Natalie wakes up? What if she needs me?

My phone beeps with an incoming text. *How's she doing?*

At first I think it's Jake, but then I realize it's coming from Eliot. *Back on the ventilator*, I tell him then add *Phone's about to die. Can't really chat.*

I've got a Bible I borrowed from the peds floor chapel. I figure even if I don't make it to church, I can spend some time in here on my own. I swear I've done more praying in the past week than I have in the last three years combined.

It's hard to believe it's already Sunday. Hard to believe that a week ago I was whining at Jake for making us go to some dumb country church. If it hadn't been for Grandma Lucy, would I have let them intubate my baby? If Jake hadn't gotten the itch to make things right with God last week, would my child have died sometime overnight?

Her color's better today. Not so ashen. I always thought it'd be creepy to see a baby go blue, but really it's that sick grayish yellow that's the most frightening. Like they're already a corpse. No, I can't think like that. Natalie needs all my positive energy today. She's going to be healed. That's what Grandma Lucy said, and that's what I'm going to believe.

Any other alternatives are too horrific to fathom.

CHAPTER 73

I spent four years living with a pastor's family, but I had no idea the Old Testament was this stinking depressing. I've been flipping through some of the books named after people, you know, Isaiah and Jeremiah and all those guys. Man, if I was trying to focus on positive thinking today, I really picked the wrong material. So far, it's been about God punishing his children, calling them whores, warning them about all the plagues and devastation he's about to visit on them for their idol-worship.

And still I keep flipping from page to page. It's like when your body's so anemic you can't stop eating spinach and red meat even though the best you can do is gag them down.

Here's a passage about the day of the Lord, except it's not all trumpets and angels like Sandy's husband preaches. No, this is *a cruel day, with wrath and fierce anger — to make the land desolate and destroy the sinners within it.* See what I mean about real happy images here?

I've had enough of this. I check the clock. Is it really almost noon? I've had this book open on my lap for an hour and a half, and I still haven't received a single word of comfort.

323

I really need God to speak to me like he did last Sunday through Grandma Lucy. I need another promise like that, something I can hold onto. Heck, I'll take anything just about now as long as it's not a verse about dashing someone to pieces like pottery. Who knew the Old Testament got so dark?

I'm in Psalms now. It's Sandy's favorite book. Says she can always find encouragement there. Well, the first chapter I read ended with something like, *You've taken everything away from me, and the darkness is my closest friend.*

Thanks, Sandy. That's real comforting right there.

What am I doing wrong? Sandy and her husband are always talking about how the Bible's this living, active entity that God can use to speak to you directly. I've been searching its pages for almost two hours and haven't gotten a single message from the Lord. Don't you think he knows I'm waiting?

I pray. Somewhere in the back of my head, I remember that youth pastor with dreadlocks saying we should ask God to speak to us before we read the Bible. Maybe that's where I made my mistake.

My prayer isn't fancy or long or anything. I just ask God to tell me something about my daughter. Let me know if I did the right thing putting her back on the ventilator. If she's not going to make it, I need to be prepared. I'm so sick of false hope.

I don't feel any better after I've prayed, but I remember that same youth pastor telling me God's the same no matter how we feel.

I flip to the middle of the Bible. Psalm 118. My eyes scan the page and land on one verse as if it were highlighted in neon.

I will not die but live, and will proclaim what the Lord has done.

And there I have my answer.

CHAPTER 74

Sandy used to talk about folks having a life verse, something sort of special just for them. I don't know how much I believe her. I mean, there's billions of people in the world, and definitely not that many verses that can mean something unique, especially if you take out all the ones about who begat who and all those passages about God's wrath and punishment.

When I graduated high school, Sandy picked a verse for me. I hate to admit that I don't even remember what it was now. She said she prayed over it, and I'm sure she did. Probably spent a week's worth of morning devotions pouring over her Bible, hunting for just the right passage that would apply to me, but I don't recall being very impressed when I read it.

There's something different about this verse, though. This time, I almost feel certain the words are meant for me. Or more specifically, they're meant for my daughter. *I will not die but live.* It's too much of a coincidence that this is the very first verse I read after I asked God to tell me something about Natalie's future, right? I mean, it even lines up with what Grandma Lucy said.

For a minute, I wonder if she's online. Maybe I can find her profile page or an email address or something. I don't know what I'd say if I did, but I'm curious enough to risk the last bar of my cell phone batteries.

I find the webpage for Safe Anchorage Goat Farm right away. There's pictures of the animals, the new babies, the mamas in their milk stands. There's a map to their address on Baxter Loop and link that tells the history of the old farmhouse there.

Something in a sidebar catches my eye. It's called *Grandma Lucy's Prayers for Healing.* I click it right away. Another heavenly message?

What I read isn't really an article. It's like a scripted prayer. I guess you're supposed to pray it over the person who's sick. It's a little bit rambling, just like Grandma Lucy's speech in church last week, and it's got tons of Scripture verses peppered throughout. I'm certain she's the one who wrote it. I don't even need her name in the title to tell me that.

I feel funny reading it like this. I'm sure there's something to be said for praying off a piece of paper, but doesn't it mean more when you pray it on your own? I mean, it's the difference between a man getting down on his knee, looking you in the eye, and telling you all the reasons he wants to spend the rest of his life with you and just writing you a letter and reading it to you out loud.

I'd like to believe this prayer will work, but there's something off about it. I can't place my finger on what exactly. Maybe because Sandy's husband was so against those faith healers on

TV. *Stuff and nonsense*, he said. According to his theology, God's able to do miracles, but that doesn't mean we've got the right to run around shouting that anyone can be cured if they just believe strong enough.

Still, I'm curious enough about Grandma Lucy's healing prayer that I bookmark the tab to go back to later. I want to let it settle in first. Or maybe that's just the fear talking. Me not wanting to get my hopes up. Because if I go to battle, if I get on my knees and beg and plead with God to spare my daughter's life and she doesn't make it, I may never find the faith to trust him about anything in the future.

But isn't that the exact opposite of what those faith healers say? They say you've got to believe even when it looks the bleakest. I'm sorry. I just don't have that kind of blind allegiance. Sure, I know God might restore my daughter, but what if he doesn't? I'm not about to put all my eggs in that one, fragile basket. Maybe if I were more mature. Maybe if I were a saint like Sandy or a prayer warrior like Grandma Lucy, this faith would come easier. But I'm just Tiff, the foster brat from Massachusetts. I'm nothing special. I'm lucky if God hears half of my prayers because most of them are so selfish anyway.

I glance around the Safe Anchorage website a little more until I forget what I came here for. To see if Grandma Lucy's online so I can get in touch with her. Even if I don't necessarily believe her magic prayer is the instant cure that's going to heal my daughter, I'd like her to know we're here at Children's. I'd like her to know what's going on. Who knows? Maybe she'll pray her little enchanted words over Natalie and they'll have more effect than my own feeble attempts would.

I see the farm has a social media account, so I click on the link. At the very least, maybe I can send Grandma Lucy a message that way. I wonder if she'll even remember me.

My finger stops before I tap the next screen. My heart plummets like I'm on one of those stupid carnival rides except I've slipped out of the compartment and am free-falling to my death.

Her picture is right there smiling at me. Bright eyes, shock-white hair, spectacles sliding halfway down her nose. She's cuddling a baby goat, trying to get it to take a bottle, and she's laughing. I'm not sure I've ever felt as joyful as she looks.

Beneath the photo is the caption that literally socks me in the gut.

Please pray for Grandma Lucy, beloved friend, mentor, and prayer warrior. She's just been taken by ambulance to County Hospital, and the doctors there think her heart is failing.

It can't be.

The phone slips out of my hands and clatters on the floor.

CHAPTER 75

"So, this woman who's sick, you're saying you just met her last week?"

I don't have words for this. I can't explain how I'm feeling, but I'm going to die trying because Eliot's here. He stopped by Natalie's room on his lunch break to find me having a verifiable mental breakdown by her crib.

"She prayed for her," I sob.

He doesn't have a clue what I'm talking about, poor guy, but he makes all the right soothing noises and tries to get some more information.

"So, she was special to you because she prayed with you for your daughter?" I wouldn't be surprised if Eliot walks out of this room and never thinks about me again unless it's to wonder whatever happened to that insane woman from his past and her sick little girl.

"Grandma Lucy believed in healing." I bury my face in my hands. It's so clichéd, but I can't stand to have him look at me right now. This pain is so open, so raw. Not even my husband could handle this. "And now she's dying."

"So ..." I can hear all the questions in Eliot's voice. I know

I'm not making any sense. "So, you're sad because you'd like her to stay alive and keep praying for your daughter?"

I shake my head. He doesn't understand. I knew he wouldn't. "Grandma Lucy told me Natalie would be healed." I try to describe the conviction, the certainty that was in her voice when she made me that promise. The hope that swelled up in me, hard as I fought it at first. "But if she really could heal, if she could really pray and have someone be cured, her heart wouldn't be failing." I need to blow my nose, but there's no Kleenex anywhere within reach.

"So, you're saying if she's really a healer or whatever, she'll just go on living forever?" It's a valid question, but it makes my skin crawl. It's like Eliot's mocking me for believing Grandma Lucy's stupid prayers and prophecies in the first place.

"I don't know," I snap. I want him to leave, but I'm terrified of being alone. How's that for mixed signals?

He reaches his arm out. Touches me on the shoulder. "I know you're under a lot of stress right now. I'm sure the news about your friend's medical condition is adding to all the fear and confusion you're experiencing from your daughter's hospital stay. It's ok. You can cry as much as you need. I'm not going anywhere."

I wrap both arms around him. It's the only way I can keep from collapsing in my chair. Why can't Jake be this supportive? Why do I feel more comfort, more freedom to express my emotions with this man I scarcely know than with my own husband?

Eliot's stroking my hair. It's perfectly platonic, perfectly friend-zone boundaries, but that doesn't stop me from yanking myself away when Jake materializes in the doorway of Natalie's hospital room.

His face is set, his jaw clenched. "Who do you think you are?" he asks Eliot then glares at me accusatorily. "What the heck's going on?"

CHAPTER 76

"Hey, man." Eliot jumps away from me and stands there with his hand stretched out like he's Jake's long-lost buddy.

Jake ignores him and doesn't take his eyes off me. "What are you doing?"

His entrance has startled my tears away for now. "I didn't know you were in town," is all I can think to say.

He gives Eliot a quick once-over. "I figured that part out myself."

"Listen." Eliot takes a step forward. He's filled out since his days as a sickly asthmatic. He's a few inches taller than Jake and slightly stronger by appearances. "Tiff's had a bad day. She just found out Grandma Lucy's in the hospital ..."

"Tiff?" Jake interrupts, his steadfast eyes never losing their angry focus. "Since when have the doctors around here start calling you Tiff? And who the heck is Grandma Lucy?"

I have to rewind. Make Jake come in two minutes later. Or twenty minutes earlier. None of this is right.

"You should go," I tell Eliot. I know he's got to get back to work. Slave-driven resident and all that. He's probably already spent too much time here trying to be my grief counselor.

He raises an eyebrow. He's questioning me. Asking me if I really want him to leave. It's cute he thinks I might be afraid of Jake. "It's ok," I tell him. "Really, it is." And I know I'm right. As soon as I explain to Jake, everything will be fine.

Jake seethes over our baby's crib until Eliot leaves.

"That's a friend of mine from Massachusetts," I tell him. "We went to school together. Lived with the same foster family for a little while."

"Is that why you were so quick to come back to Seattle?" he demands.

I can't let myself get angry. Can't lose my temper. All my worries about Natalie, all my confusion at the news of Grandma Lucy being so ill, I shove them into a tiny compartment in the back of my brain. My to-deal-with-later box. Right now I've got to do damage control. It's what you'd expect when your husband sneaks up on you when you're out of town and finds you falling in the arms of some posh doctor.

"We bumped into each other a few days ago," I explain. "He just came up to check on Natalie. I was having a bad day. He was trying to make me feel better."

I know Jake's got a dozen different retorts. If I were him I'd probably have even more, but he's letting it drop for now. I'm sure this isn't the last I'll hear of Dr. Eliot Jamison, but at least for now Jake's calmed down enough we can have a civil conversation.

"What's this?" He nods toward the baby.

I bite my lip. Have I seriously not told him? "Well, I was going to call you last night, but my phone died. They put her on the ventilator a few hours ago." I've stretched the truth a little. So sue me. Right now Jake doesn't need to know all the details. He needs to know enough that he can stay calm and rational. This isn't how our first meeting back in Seattle was supposed to go.

"I thought we signed a form ..." His face is contorting, like his pity for his daughter's raging a war against his anger toward me, and right now I'm not sure which side is going to come out victorious.

"The doctor asked me. Said I needed to give him a decision right away. It happened really fast. I didn't have time to call you or anything." I'm fidgeting with my fingers. I hate when I feel like I have to pacify Jake. He's usually such a pushover. I can't stand it when I've got to take the defensive. "You're not mad about that, are you?" I frown and try to look humble.

He shakes his head. "You should have called me. That's why we signed the form together."

"I already told you there wasn't time for me to think through it or anything. Basically, the doctor said I needed to let him intubate her or she was going to die right there. I mean, her numbers were really low. She wouldn't have made it."

I'm squinting my eyes studying him. He's not mad our daughter's still alive, is he?

"Did I make the wrong decision?" There's an edge in my voice. I'm sure he must detect it, too. Must know he just walked into a verbal minefield. One false move and they'll be stumbling upon his remains from a mile away.

"No." He shakes his head again and lets out his breath. I can sense a little of the tension melt away. "No, you did the right thing. I just wish we could have talked about it first."

"I'm really sorry about that. If I'd had the time, you know I would have called. It just happened really fast."

"You said that already."

"I'm sorry." I'm offering him a hug. His muscles are tense. It's like wrapping your arms around a stinking statue or something. "The good news is her numbers are getting better. Fever's down, too."

"Ok." He's moody now. Moody I can deal with. It's when he's mad at me, when I have to prove I haven't done anything wrong, that I feel so lost.

"You all right?" I ask in my best *Mama will take care of you* voice.

"Yeah. I just need to rest. Where are the keys?"

"Keys?"

"To the Ronald McDonald house. I was up at five this morning. I've been on the road all day. I could use a nap." He stretches out his hand.

"I don't have any keys. I've been sleeping here."

He eyes the oversized chair. "Here?"

"Yeah. They've got blankets and stuff. Want me to find you a pillow?"

"No, I'll go over and talk to the people at the house. Get us a room for tonight."

"You a room," I mutter.

He whips his head around. "Huh?"

"Nothing. Sure, if you need your rest, go find a room." I give what I hope is a peace-offering smile. "I'm sure you're tired after such a busy morning."

I hope to God he doesn't sense the biting sarcasm in my remark, but he's either too tired or too stupid to notice, and he walks out the door without another word.

I slump back into the chair by Natalie's crib. It's going to be a long day.

CHAPTER 77

I manage to sneak in a nap sometime around four or five that afternoon. Jake hasn't been back since he left for the Ronald McDonald house. I wonder what's going to happen when he returns, if we'll go on like nothing's happened or if we'll get into an even messier fight. I honestly don't have the energy for either, not yet.

Another hour or two of sleep and a quad shot, then maybe I'll be ready.

The landline in the hospital room rings. I pick up, figuring it must be either Eliot or Jake.

Turns out I'm wrong.

"Tiffany?" The voice is grating. Like a fork scraping against a plate during Thanksgiving dinner.

"Patricia?" I have no clue why she's calling me. I honestly don't remember another time that his mom has used my first name. "Jake's over resting at the Ronald McDonald house."

"I know. I just got off the phone with him. I'm calling to see how Natalie's doing. I was so sorry to hear she's back on the ventilator."

I mentally rehearse every terrible interaction I've had with my mother-in-law and force myself to remain guarded no matter how much energy it expends. "Yeah, it's all right. She's doing a lot better keeping her oxygen levels up."

"Well, I'm sure it's for the best. I just wanted you to know ..."

I'm so tired and out of it that at first I think Patricia's about to apologize. No such luck.

"I enjoyed the chance to get to know you a little better over the past few weeks. Thank you so much for opening your home to me."

This is new. There's no underlying jab, at least none that I can detect, but everything still feels so off. So backwards.

"Yeah, it was good getting to know you, too." Is that how the dance works now? We lie to each other civilly until we're both blue in the face?

"I won't keep you any longer. I wanted to tell you and Jake that I made it to Abby's just fine, and I've got all kinds of pictures of Natalie to share with her. I'll be thinking of you and wishing Natalie a very speedy recovery. You hang in there. You're doing a great job."

Even after the call ends, I feel on edge. Like her kind words are just another layer of Patricia-style manipulation, but I haven't come close to mastering this level yet. It's going to take me time to mentally adjust.

But then Jake's brooding figure darkens the hospital door, and all thoughts of his mother fly out of my head.

There's no hint of a smile on his face, no trace of kindness or patience in his eyes. "Come on," he says in a voice that obviously expects an immediate reaction. "We need to talk."

CHAPTER 78

"Listen, I'm sorry I didn't call about the ventilator thing." I'm trying something new and coming straight out with an apology.

Jake doesn't respond until we exit the building. Don't ask me why he wants to walk outside in the stinking middle of winter in Seattle. I swear I'll never understand that boy.

We cross the street. I have to pump my arms to keep up with him. What's he think this is? A speed-walking competition?

"You should have let me know," he broods.

I want to remind him about my stupid cell phone battery. I want to explain how much stress I've been under, how close I came to watching my daughter die last night. Does he have any idea what that's like? If his mom hadn't taken the car to the wrong hotel and then stuck around those few extra days, I might not have had to make a decision like that on my own. He could have come to Seattle earlier. When it boils down to it, this is all Patricia's fault. From the beginning, she did nothing but jinx our relationship. I'm so glad she's gone. Out of our lives, hopefully forever.

I still can't forget how concerned she sounded on the phone, but I lived with her long enough to realize she's the master of manipulation. Not just the people around her but her own emotions as well. I'm convinced that at this moment, she thinks she and I were like long-lost BFFs the whole time she lived with us. I want to pick her out of my brain like a bad case of head lice. An hour under the bright lamp, some medicated shampoo treatments, and she's gone. Never to bother us again.

I should be so lucky.

"Your mom called," I tell him. Anything so we can get past this awkward, angry silence that's literally killing me. "She said she made it to Abby's."

"I know."

If all he wanted to do was mope, I wonder what he needs me out here for, but he takes a deep breath like he's working up his courage to say something and finally tells me, "This isn't working out."

My heart drops, but only a little. In my soul, I know he's right. I've known it all along. It goes back to that stupid women's clinic in Spokane. I should have never brought my daughter there. If it weren't for that, none of this would have happened. The hospital stays. The medevac flights. The arguments with Jake. Ok, so maybe we still would have had our fights, but it wouldn't be this bad. We've been under so much stinking stress. How is any relationship supposed to survive something like what we've gone through?

And the secrets are killing me. Jake sleeping with Charlene. Me taking our daughter to an abortion clinic. I hate to say it, but

341

part of me's relieved to hear Jake talking like this. The pretense was too much. Pretending we're a happy couple, that I have what it takes to become a perfect, doting mother.

It will be better this way. Like getting a tooth pulled, painful at first, but so much more comfortable, so much healthier after that.

I've suspected this conversation was coming, and I'm ready for it.

"You know what?" I tell him. "You're absolutely right."

CHAPTER 79

"Wait, what?" I swear he sounds just like the princess from that *Frozen* movie.

"You said it yourself. This isn't working."

He stops. Eyes me quizzically from underneath a streetlamp. "What is it that you don't think is working?"

"Any of it." I sweep my hands out to the sides. Melodramatic, maybe, but this conversation was a long time in the making, and I've got a lot of pent-up stress to get off my chest. "You. Me. Natalie. Trying to pretend we're a big happy family."

He's looking at me like I've just slaughtered his mother in front of him, and I get a horrible sinking feeling in the pit of my gut. "Wait, what were you talking about?"

"I was talking about Orchard Grove." His voice is about five levels too loud. I want to point a remote control at him and tone it down a little. "I was talking about us living so far away from Seattle." He's a shaken-up soda bottle about to explode from all that extra pressure.

"Oh." It's the most I can think of to say at the moment. We've both stopped underneath a street lamp. I can see every vein tensed in his neck. The quiver in his jaw from clenching his teeth so hard.

Oops.

"You seriously think our relationship isn't working? What, that just because we've had a few bumps in the road it's time to count our losses and move on?"

"That's what I thought you were saying." I'm too defensive. Too hot-headed right now. It's because I haven't slept. Who could expect me to have a rational conversation after what I've been through in the past twenty-four hours?

"No, that's not what I was saying. But I'm seriously concerned that it's what you were thinking."

I roll my eyes and start walking back to the hospital, hoping he'll follow me. "That's not what I was thinking. I just thought you were ..."

"What? Thought I was what?" He grabs my arm.

I yank it free. "I thought you were ..."

"An irresponsible jerk who's going to abandon his little girl when she's sick? Man, Tiff, what sort of person do you think I am?"

"I only meant ..."

"That we'd be better off split up?" he finishes for me.

"I never said that." I quicken my pace. It's cold out here, and I want to get inside.

"You didn't have to say it. Geeze. Is that what this whole four months have been to you? Some sort of experiment? Why the heck did you marry me in the first place if you didn't think that we would stick together?"

344

I whip my head around and stop dead in my tracks to face him. "Of course I thought we would. At least I hoped so. But that was before ..." I clench my jaw shut. Do I want to make this worse?

"Before what?" His shoulders are squared. His jaw set.

I should leave now. Leave and talk to him again in the morning once we've both had time to cool off.

"Before what?" he demands again. He clenches his hands into fists.

"Nothing." I can't do it. As sick as I am of all this bickering, as annoying as he gets when he falls into these broody moods, a pathetic part of me wants to hold onto him. Wants to hope we might still find a way to make this work.

It's not time to pull the plug. Not yet.

I start moving again. He grabs me by the back of my hoodie. Yanks me around to face him. "Don't walk away from me."

"Get your hands off me." I glance around. There's a few people within shouting distance. If I need to, I can make him let go. He won't dare touch me a second time.

"You know," he begins. His face is close to mine. So close I can feel the heat from his anger. I'm the one who did this to him. I should have never let things escalate like this. "I came to Seattle ready to make things right. That car my mom and I drove out here? It wasn't a rental. It was a Christmas present. She bought it for us."

I don't know what to say. I recall what I detected as that hint of kindness in Patricia's voice when she called the hospital room. If I had known ...

"I was going to sell the Pontiac. Already know a guy from work who said he'd buy it from me once he gets his tax return. You know what? I was going to use the money to get us a place in Seattle. That's where I was this afternoon. Looking for apartments close to the hospital. Care to guess why? Because I was willing to sacrifice anything for our daughter." He shakes his head. "You don't even know who I am, do you?" He's disgusted with me. I can see it in his eyes.

"Listen, I'm sorry." What else am I supposed to say? So this was some big, stinking mistake. That happens. It's where we go from here that matters.

Jake doesn't respond.

I swallow my pride and try one more time. "I had no idea you were ..."

"No idea?" he interrupts.

I grit my teeth to keep from screaming out in frustration. Will he let me get a word in?

"No idea," he repeats with a sarcastic laugh that's totally unlike him. "Yeah, I kind of figured that when you and your doctor friend were making out in our daughter's hospital room."

It's a cheap shot and a lie, and he knows it. I see the trace of shame hit his face. It's up to me now. The ball's in my court. I can placate him, explain to him one more time how Eliot's just a friend I randomly met in Seattle. I can gush over his mother's generous gift, a gift I'm sure doesn't come without a few dozen invisible strings attached, strings that are bound to tie us down for years to come if I accept it.

Or I can walk away. Take my chances. Just me and my daughter.

Whatever decision I'm going to make, it's got to be final.

"I don't even want to look at you right now," I tell him and turn back toward the hospital. Toward my daughter.

I'm four or five steps away before he calls after me. "Tiff, wait." We both know that's what he's supposed to say now. His voice isn't even all that convincing.

"Just leave me alone." I call over my shoulder, keeping my eye on the huge man walking toward us. If Jake gives me a hard time, I'll scream *rape* and get this Good Samaritan to intervene.

"Tiff, please." There's a hint of sincerity now in his tone, but it's too late. Never look back.

My life motto.

CHAPTER 80

I can't believe it's Christmas Eve. Six hours left before midnight, and I'm still stuck here at Children's.

At least Natalie's doing better. That's the good news. Her temperature is back to normal as of yesterday morning. A small Christmas miracle, maybe, or else the result of good medicine. There's talk that if she holds her stats steady for the rest of the day, the doctor might decide to extubate her before long. I'm not about to get my hopes up, but it's nice to know she's not getting any worse.

Haven't heard from Jake. Not a phone call. Not a text. He hasn't stopped by to see our daughter unless he's inherited some kind of Japanese-American ninja skills that allow him to sneak in during the five minutes it takes me each morning to heat up cold coffee from the parents' lounge.

I haven't heard from Eliot, either. Dr. Jamison, I should call him. It's just as well. He probably feels awkward about what happened with Jake. Doesn't want to make things worse. His number's stuck in my phone, the one with the dead batteries, so I couldn't get in touch with him even if I wanted to.

Which I don't.

It's been quiet around here the past few days, as I'm sure you can imagine. No calls. No visitors. It's like Natalie and I are stinking Christmas ghosts that nobody can see. Nobody wants to think about us. It's too depressing. But it hasn't been all terrible. It's given us a lot of time together. I talk to her quite a bit these days. I tell her about the people who love her, Grandma Sandy so far away in Massachusetts. The little boy Sandy and her husband adopted, who I guess is Natalie's uncle even though he's only in fourth or fifth grade. In an especially generous moment, I even told her about Grandma Patricia and how she took care of her those first few months out of the hospital.

Those aren't the only grandmas, either. We talk about Grandma Lucy quite a bit, Natalie and me, when no one else is around. Talk about the faith she had that Natalie would be healed. I don't know if Grandma Lucy's still in the hospital or if she's passed away already or what, but Natalie and I sometimes pray for her. It makes me feel weird, though, because Sandy's husband said we shouldn't pray for people who've already died, but since I don't know one way or the other, I figure God will have to understand. Besides, if Grandma Lucy's in heaven now, that means she's even closer to God so her prayers must be making that much more difference. I don't know how solid that is biblically, but it's comforting to think about.

I kept checking the Safe Anchorage website for updates on Grandma Lucy until my phone completely died on me. Apparently she was suffering from water around her heart sac or something like that. Sounded serious. I spent a lot of time on the comments, reading what people posted. Found out quite a bit about her life, actually. It's interesting stuff. Someone should really make a book or a movie about it. I guess she grew up in China. Had missionary parents there. Lived through some big war. I couldn't figure out which one, but it sounded pretty intense. After she got back to the States, she kept on having all kinds of adventures. I guess she was a sort of missionary lady for a while, even into her old age. Spent some time in the Middle East teaching English. Someone mentioned meeting her a few years ago in China, so I gather she went back there from time to time. Had all kinds of grandkids and great grandkids.

There's a place where you can sign up for regular email updates about Grandma Lucy's condition, but my battery died as I was typing in my address.

Just my luck.

Other than that, and of course everything with Jake, things are going pretty well. I mean, Natalie's getting better. Looks like my fears about her never coming off the ventilator were unnecessary. I don't know how much longer we're going to be here, but I know it won't be forever. One day, they'll take out that breathing tube. She'll be strong enough to go home …

Don't ask me where home is. I don't know. Not yet. But I'm going to figure it out. That huge doctor, the one who came in with the itty bitty chaplain to talk to me about Natalie's care? Turns out I was right and he's not a medical doctor, but he's got some crazy advanced degree in social work, and I guess one of his jobs is to help people like me get set up with services. He's been on vacation for the past two days, but he's coming back to work right after Christmas. I'm sure together we'll figure out some sort of a game plan.

I'm a little surprised at myself that I'm not thinking about Jake more. I guess there was part of me that was so certain it would end like this, I'm not too upset by it. I'm not a big sobbing mess or anything like that. It's not like this is my first breakup.

So things are all right. Whenever I get too worried about what the future will hold, like how I'll manage to support my daughter when she's too sick for me to go to work and I don't know a single soul in Seattle, I just remind myself to breathe and take things one step at a time. It reminds me of this little cross-stitched verse Sandy's got hanging up in her kitchen. I'm sure you'd recognize the passage if you read it, the one about birds and flowers and being anxious, all that stuff.

You know what? It's good advice whether you believe in God or not. *Do not worry about tomorrow.*

I'm giving myself an early Christmas present by promising to remember that one simple rule.

CHAPTER 81

The nurse pops in. It's funny how kind everyone acts on Christmas Eve. Honestly, if it were me, I think I'd be ticked if I had to work through the holiday, but I've noticed the hospital staff today are in really good moods. Compassionate, I guess is a better way of putting it. Like they feel sorry we're here over Christmas and are going out of their way to be extra nice to us. I don't really appreciate the sympathy part, but I do like the added effort.

Today's nurse is wearing candy cane scrubs and matching earrings. Kind of festive, even though she's a little too old to pull off the cute Christmas elf theme. "Guess who got a package?" she asks, and I take the large box, wondering who in the world would be sending me something. I just hope it's not Patricia. I may have read that woman wrong the whole time she lived with us — either that or she's such a master manipulator I don't even know what to think of her anymore. All I know is I don't want to be indebted to someone like her.

But the package isn't from Patricia, thank God, and I don't even have to read the return address label to recognize the flowing cursive handwriting. Man, how many years has it been, and I still know Sandy's handwriting like I've been living with her up until last week.

Tiffany Franklin. She's one of the only people I was close to who never called me Tiff. It didn't bother me, either, like it would with most people.

It takes me a minute to work my way through all the tape, but with the help of some scissors I borrow from another nurse (this one in snowflake scrubs), I get the box open.

It's a typical care package, the kind Sandy used to send me before I changed addresses and the two of us lost touch. There's some girly things, hair brushes, lip gloss. Does she think I'm ten years old? The nail polish is a deep magenta color. I might try it if I get bored.

She's included a few other things too, things that are so Sandy. A Ziploc bag full of cookies and brownies, a snowman picture colored as sparsely as possible with a note that it's from her adopted son, and a mug stuffed with at least a dozen different types of tea bags.

I miss her so much, especially around Christmastime. I can picture all the crafts up on her mantle, things her kids made decades ago that she's kept throughout the years. So many colors. There's no coordination. Not at Sandy's house. Not at Christmas. But the chaos is a theme in and of itself, and it's a happier-looking sort of décor than what you'd find in any fancy home magazine or upscale department store.

There's a letter, and I nearly give myself eye strain until I get used to reading her cursive again. She's so encouraging. There's Bible verses all over it, as well as some references she probably wants me to look up on my own. Who knows? Maybe I will.

Everything she writes, I can hear each single word in her motherly, doting voice with that Southern drawl. Man, I miss home. Remind me again why I ever left?

Dear Tiffany, I'm praying that you're out of the hospital by now with that precious daughter of yours, but if not, I want you to know that God's still on the throne and he still has a fabulous plan, both for you and your sweet little Natalie. I won't presume to know what the good Lord's doing right now, but I want to encourage you to trust him even through the heartache and stress and sadness that's come your way.

You're stronger than you know, sweetie, and that's not just because you're a smart, capable, and bright young woman (which of course we both know you are). You're powerful because the Holy Spirit lives in you. Maybe you think he's gone. Maybe you think you've wandered too far for him to ever pay much attention to you, but those are the lies the enemy wants you to believe, darling. The truth is God has never left you. He lives in you, and his love for you is just as strong as it was so many years ago when you accepted him into your heart and made a commitment to live your life for him.

I know it hasn't been easy since then, sweetheart, but I do know that there hasn't been a day that's gone by when Carl and I haven't gotten down on our knees and asked God to bless you. To show you how deeply he loves you, no matter how far you may have strayed, no matter what mistakes you may have made in your past.

The Bible says that God is gracious and compassionate, slow to anger and abounding in love. Do you know what that means, darling? It means there's absolutely nothing — and when I say nothing, I truly mean nothing — that will separate you from his love. It's right there in Romans 8, and if you're in need of some extra encouragement today, I think you'll find it in that passage. No matter what happens, precious, no matter how many trials you and your sweet baby girl Natalie have to go through, they're only meant to draw you closer to God. The choice is up to you. You can get angry. You can shake your fist at heaven and ask God why he's making you both suffer like this. Or you can curl up in his lap, rest your weary cheek against his breast, and soak in the love and comfort he has for you today.

I don't know everything that's happened since the day you professed your faith in Christ and Carl baptized you. But I do know that whatever you've done, you can't pluck yourself out of God's hand. He is the Good Shepherd, who knows the voice of his sheep and calls them by name. That means he's calling you. Tiffany. Calling you to trust him. Calling you to shake off the pain and shame of the past. To forget whatever regrets or fears or anxieties are holding you down. To cast your cares upon him because he cares so much — so much — for you. You are precious and honored in his sight. He takes great delight in you, just like you delight in your sweet little baby.

And now, my dear, I have a special prayer for that beautiful daughter of yours. My grandbaby Natalie. I don't pretend to know if God will heal her now or in heaven, but I know for a fact that her healing will come. And my prayer for her is that for however long she has on this earth, whether a few days or weeks or a

355

hundred full, rich, healthy years, my prayer for your precious Natalie is that she will always know deep in the core of her soul how much she's loved. By you, by her daddy, by Carl and me, but most of all by her heavenly Father, who's had his hand on her sweet little life from the moment she was conceived.

Nothing is an accident, darling. Nothing is out of God's control. And nothing is too painful or too tarnished that he can't redeem it. Any mistakes, any guilt, any fear — he's bigger than all of those. So trust in him, honey. He promises to never leave you or forsake you. You're his beloved daughter. Think how much you love your baby. Tired and exhausted as you are, you love that precious darling. Now imagine how much more God, your perfect heavenly Father, loves her. No matter what happens, know that he's holding her in the palm of his hand.

I love you so much, sweetie. I hope you never forget that. Carl does too, and so does your brother Woong. In fact, he's the one who helped make those gingerbread cookies and the brownies too. But be careful because the brownies have nuts, and I don't know if you're going to share with Jake or any of your friends at the hospital or anything, but I forgot to write a note to warn people with allergies.

The next several paragraphs are filled with family news. Who would be coming over for Christmas. What foods she'll prepare. I can almost smell that maple syrup glaze on the ham. The yeasty bread rolls she makes every holiday. My nose tickles with the feel of sparkling apple cider.

I don't think I've had a taste of that stuff since I left home.

Home. Not anymore. But it's the closest thing I've got right now.

There's a PS at the bottom of the page. *I don't know if this plug's the right size or anything, but we had an extra one lying around, and I thought maybe you could use it.*

I throw aside another bag of Christmas baked goods and find a charger for my phone. I can tell it's the right style before I even test it out. It's like that missionary story of the little girl who prays for a baby doll and finds one in the boxes of food aid. Who told those do-gooders to add something like that at the last minute?

I know Sandy would say it's the Holy Spirit. Right now, I'm too grateful to finally connect again with the real world that I don't think to wonder. I plug in my phone, wait an impatient ten seconds for it to get enough charge to turn back on.

I don't see any texts or missed calls from Jake. None that pop up at least. I'll look through all that later. Right now, I jump onto the Safe Anchorage website. I've got to learn what happened to Grandma Lucy. It's so slow loading up I think I might scream. I get to the main homepage with its pictures of cute baby goats and images of the lotions and soaps they make there to sell. Nothing about Grandma Lucy. Come on.

I go to the *news* tab. There it is.

No, it can't be.

There's a video right there on top of the page. *Yesterday's celebration of life service for our beloved Grandma Lucy.*

CHAPTER 82

No, they've got it all wrong. She can't have died. She believed in miraculous healings. I know she did. But she still passed away. So if her faith wasn't strong enough to fix herself, why did I put any hope in her ability to pray for my daughter?

I click on the video, morbid as it sounds. I've got to understand. Will people actually talk about that at her funeral — or her *celebration of life service* as they call it? Will they talk about the fact that she still died even though her faith was larger than a million mustard seeds?

I've got to see this. Maybe it's just because I like to torture myself. I don't know. But I want to see this service. I want to know what happened.

I want to know how God took away someone with a faith like Grandma Lucy's.

While the video thinks about loading up, I read the comments beneath.

Grandma Lucy, that was so inspiring.

I love you, Grandma Lucy! Thanks so much for sharing with us.

What's with these people? Do they think heaven's connected to wi-fi and that Grandma Lucy's really going to be spending time watching who's posting on her funeral replay?

But it gets even more ridiculous.

Praising God for your healing.

I was so excited to hear you're home! PTL!

You'd think these people were welcoming a war hero or something like that. "She can't even hear you!" I want to shout at them all.

Some of the other comments make more sense. Here's a post from a twenty-something young man who says that Grandma Lucy led him to Christ and saved him from a life of drug and alcohol abuse. There's a middle-aged woman who says Grandma Lucy kept her from committing suicide. It's a little rambling and hard to follow thanks to poor grammar and autocorrect, but I catch enough of the story to learn that Grandma Lucy once stopped a crowded bus to talk this woman down from a highway overpass and then told her how to be saved.

It's a little eerie, really. Everyone's got such powerful stories to tell. Isn't someone sad that she's gone? No matter how good of a person she was, isn't anyone allowed the space to grieve?

Enough of the video loads that I can start the service. It's the same pastor from Orchard Grove Bible, except it's not in his church. Grandma Lucy apparently touched so many lives they had to hold her funeral service in the high school gym.

The pastor greets those in attendance, and I find myself looking for his petite wisp of a wife. I know this is supposed to be a celebration of Grandma Lucy's life, but I wish the pastor looked a little more somber. He's not even wearing a suit and tie. Said that when he and Grandma Lucy were discussing the arrangements for her ceremony, she wanted people to dress in their brightest colors. She wanted her friends from different ethnic backgrounds to wear traditional clothes to represent the way heaven is filled with people from every nation, tribe, and tongue.

The pastor looks markedly American in his basketball jersey. I still can't tell if he's got more Hispanic blood or Native American. Not that it really matters. I'm just curious.

After an opening prayer that feels far too enthusiastic for an event like this, Pastor Greg talks about how Grandma Lucy handpicked all the hymns for today's service. I wonder what kind of person would be so obsessed with her own mortality they'd planned their own song arrangement.

Different strokes, I guess.

The pastor leads the singing on his guitar. I haven't heard the song before, but I'm sure it's got to be a hundred years old or more. *I Know Whom I Have Believed.* It's got a catchy enough tune, but the language is kind of clunky, which is what makes me think it must be so ancient. Everyone's singing at the top of their lungs. I don't think I've even been to a wedding whose guests are this excited.

"And now we've got something really special to share with you," the pastor says. "We weren't sure she'd be feeling strong enough, but Grandma Lucy's going to come out now and say a few words."

I'm so stunned I nearly drop my phone. The cord catches on Natalie's crib, which is the only thing that keeps it from crashing onto the floor. I know for a fact that someone like Grandma Lucy wouldn't have anything to do with a séance or anything like that. I re-read the title of the video again. *Celebration of life service for our beloved Grandma Lucy.*

Celebration of life. That's a funeral, right? Then why is she on my cell phone screen? Why is she wearing a yellow blouse with flowers the size of dinner plates and waving to everyone who's clapping and cheering as she makes her way to the stage?

The Lakers-fan pastor holds the mic for just another minute. "When the doctors told us about the water around Grandma Lucy's heart, a lot of us feared we were going to lose her. Many of us didn't feel ready yet to say goodbye. I went to talk with her at the hospital, and she said she was ready to meet her Jesus. Her only regret was that she didn't get one last chance to tell the ones she loved about the Lord. She wanted to make a video, record it one night when she felt particularly strong. It was going to be her goodbye video, but as we all know, God had other plans for our dear sister."

Cheers and shouts of *hallelujahs* interrupt him and persist for several minutes before he quiets the crowds again.

"Grandma Lucy walked out of that hospital even when the doctors expected the worst. When she got home, she joked with me and said that it was a shame the video she made couldn't be shared with the world yet. And that's how we came up with the idea for today's celebration of life service. We're still not going to watch that recording she made. We've got something even better. We've got Grandma Lucy herself, healed from what most people assumed would be her deathbed, and she's going to tell us directly what the Lord put on her spirit the other night."

This time, it's a full five minutes before the cheering stops and Grandma Lucy begins. I've got tears streaming down my cheeks, but I don't know if that's because I'm relieved to find out she's not really dead or if I'm just longing for that peace and radiance that shine out of Grandma Lucy's face. I'm biting my lip so hard it might bleed. My phone is trembling in my hand. I pray that the hospital guest wireless will give me enough bandwidth to watch the whole video without interruptions.

Grandma Lucy takes in a choppy inhale. I lean forward, forgetting to breathe myself as she begins her speech.

CHAPTER 83

"First of all, I want to apologize to those of you who think it presumptuous for me to plan my own celebration of life service. To the rest of you, I just want to thank you for being here with me today. My soul is so full. I couldn't have asked for a better life. Heartaches and all, God was there for me. I've had so much more joy and love and grace that I ever deserved. Thank you, Jesus for being the author and perfecter of my faith." She slips right into prayer without closing her eyes, and all of a sudden she's addressing us again.

"My heart's been giving me trouble lately, as of course you all know. But just like the psalmist declares, *my heart and my flesh may fail, but God is the strength of my heart and my portion forever.* He is the one who has awakened my soul and loosened my tongue, just like he did for Isaiah when the seraphim touched his lips with the fiery coals. You may believe in a God who has ceased to do miracles, but my heavenly Father still sets prisoners free and gives sight to the blind and releases those held by chains.

"Many of you today are held by chains even now. Fears. Despair. Bitterness. Unforgiveness. The chains of pride or lust or anger or selfish ambition. And that's why even when my heart is so full, even when I rejoice at the thought of being surrounded by so much love and joy today, I regret that I haven't made better use of my time here on earth. I regret I haven't prayed with more of you. Shared with more of you. Demonstrated God's love to more of you. But God has given me this chance. It may very well be my last, so I don't want to waste it.

"Jesus loves you. There is nothing that you have done, no sin you could ever commit or even conceive that would make him love you less."

My hand is shaking so hard that I can't even focus on the picture on my screen. All the guilt, the horror at the mistakes I've made, these dark secrets I've kept buried in the blackest depths of my soul for so long — they haunt me now. Stare me full in the face. Ugly. Accusing. They will not be ignored. They will not be silenced. Grandma Lucy's talking about a God of forgiveness and grace, a God who willingly forgives liars and petty thieves. Not people like me. People who contemplate murder. A mother who subjects her baby to a life of disability and pain just because …

No. She can't mean me. Guilt hooks its talons into the muscles of my neck and shoulders. I feel the icy chill. I need to turn the video off. I can't survive any more dashed hopes.

But I can't bring myself to stop the recording. Maybe I'm addicted to punishment. I don't know, but I have to hear the rest of what this woman tells me.

"Now maybe you're listening to me, and maybe you're saying to yourself, *Grandma Lucy, you don't know what I've done. You don't know how bad it really is.* Well, that much may be true, but God knows. And still he promises us in the Bible that while we were his enemies, Christ died for our trespasses. While we were lost in our transgressions, God forgave us the guilt of our sins. While we were once objects of God's wrath, we can now experience grace and abundant life in him."

My heart is racing. I've felt this way before. At that youth retreat when I was a teenager, the one where I promised God to turn my life around and serve him wholeheartedly. I feel the same way now, the same sense of excitement. The palpable energy surrounding me, some sort of cosmic Holy Spirit fire in my chest. I want to believe Grandma Lucy's words. I want to believe this forgiveness and grace can extend even to me. I want to believe that if I open my heart to this divine invitation, if I accept this heavenly love that's tugging at my soul like the strings of a master puppeteer, it will be enough. Enough to wash away the guilt of my shame, the trauma of my past, the torment of my despair. I want to believe that this grace Grandma Lucy mentions is enough to change me. For real, not just for a day and a half until Lincoln Grant gets me in the backseat of his dad's truck again. I want to believe that this time it will last. This time I won't feel like I've faked my own conversion.

But I'm so scared that I'll end up disappointed again. My faith is too immature, my soul is too weak to endure that level of cosmic disillusionment.

I have to fight it. I have to resist. This is some kind of emotional manipulation, a psychological trick meant to make me feel like I'm God's most beloved creation in the entire world. I can't give in like I did as a teen. I'm a grown woman now with a daughter to look after. A daughter who needs a mother, not some Jesus freak.

"I'm still weaker than normal." Grandma's Lucy's words are slower. I think I detect a hint of a slur, but I'm afraid to admit it even to myself.

"I'm finishing my little speech with a full heart. I've known my share of sorrows, but through them all, I can say with certainty that I know whom I have believed and am persuaded that he is able to keep that which I've committed to him against that day."

It's the same line from the hymn we just sang. The words make very little sense to me, but she speaks them with such joy and peace. I know I'll never be as faithful or confident as she is. It would be stupid of me to even try. But still, something is tugging at my spirit, urging me to take that chance. Take that leap of faith. Give God one last shot to change me.

Grandma Lucy invites us to pray with her. I bow my head and shut my eyes.

I don't know if I'm ready for this or not. There's only one way to find out.

CHAPTER 84

I don't know what I was expecting when I bowed my head with Grandma Lucy. I still can't believe I did it, followed a prayer by some woman who's preaching at her own end-of-life ceremony. First, she prayed with anyone who wanted to become a Christian for the first time. It's all the stuff I remember from Sandy's church. You know, *I admit I'm a sinner, please forgive me, come into my heart, I make you Lord of my life.* And I remember enough from her husband's preaching to figure I'm set because I prayed that one a long time ago, and everyone there told me you've only got to do it once. But I do it again, just to be sure. It can't hurt, right?

Next, Grandma Lucy looks straight at the camera and I swear she's watching me with some third eye or something. She says, "Now, I know there are some of you who have been Christians for years. You know that Jesus died to take the punishment for your sins, you believe he was raised back to life through the power of the Holy Spirit, and you've asked him to forgive your sins and prepare a place for you in heaven. But deep in your heart, you realize something is still missing, only you can't figure out how to find it."

I'm bending down over my phone so that my face is as close as I can get to the screen without making Grandma Lucy's image blurry. I'm not trembling anymore, at least not outwardly. All those physical symptoms, they're now confined to one spot in the center of my chest. I'm no longer nervous. I wouldn't even say I'm afraid. It's more like dread, this emotion I'm feeling. But when you call it an emotion, that makes it sound like it's coming from somewhere within me, except it's not. It's this Presence. This conviction. This certainty that I know I didn't conjure up on my own. And I'm terrified. I don't think there's a word strong enough to express this sort of fear.

I'm no longer afraid that God's mad at me. I'm afraid that whatever it is Grandma Lucy's going to ask me to do to get right with him is going to be too hard. I'll be too stubborn. I won't have the strength to follow through, even though something in me knows — just like I knew that Jake and I wouldn't be able to make it together for the long haul — something in me knows that if I don't respond to this tugging at my spirit, I may never get another chance like this for as long as I live.

Now you can understand when I say there's not a single expression in human language that can describe this level of terror.

Help me, God. I'm not sure what I'm asking him to do. I just know that without his strength, I'm going to be too weak to take this step of faith, whatever it is. I'm so exhausted by this bleak, dismal existence I've been leading. If you were to take all the moments in the past twelve months where I've been truly happy,

I don't think it would even total half an hour. Not a single hour out of the entire year. I know enough about Christianity to realize that it's not all about me being happy, but I also know enough about myself to understand that if something doesn't change, if I don't find some sort of higher purpose, some outside source of joy that's not tied to my emotions or my circumstances, I might not be here in another twelve months when next Christmas rolls around.

That's why I'm bending so attentively over my phone. That's why when Grandma Lucy begins what she calls her *prayer of repentance and renewal*, I'm soaking in every single word like I'm a sponge that's been sitting out in the desert heat for months. I take each phrase, each individual word, and make it my own. I wrap it up as a prayer that I toss up to heaven, hoping against all my uncertainties and fears that, as weak and sinful as I am, it will still be enough.

I beg God to free me from guilt and shame. I invite him to fill me with the Holy Spirit until I'm overflowing. I ask him to give me victory over sin and doubt. And I surrender my future, uncertain as it is, and I surrender my daughter's future to the God who has promised that those who put their hope in him will never be put to shame.

Right after Grandma Lucy says *amen*, my phone pauses to hunt for more bandwidth. There's a soft tapping on my door. I glance up like a third-grader who's been caught cheating off her neighbor's test.

"Hey," Jake says. His voice is so soft, I can hardly hear it over the pounding of my own pulse. I hardly feel human at the moment. What just happened to me? What did I just do?

He steps into the room tentatively. Glances at our daughter in her crib, his look full of compassion and pain.

"Sorry to bother you." He doesn't meet my eyes. Or maybe it's me that's keeping my gaze so low.

He pulls up the doctor's swivel chair. "Do you have a minute? I came by to talk to you about something."

CHAPTER 85

For a second, I think Jake's here to apologize. That's the look he's got on his face, that sort of humble expression. A little timid. But he doesn't come right out and say he's sorry, and I'm glad he doesn't because I honestly couldn't tell you right now what that boy has to feel bad about. Of course, some of that's my mental fog. It's like everything in that Grandma Lucy video was so intense, my brain cells have shut down one by one until all I've got are the basic functions left.

Jake looks me right in the eyes. I can hardly keep my heart from jumping out my throat. I seriously wonder if I'm going to gag on it. I'm not nervous about Jake being here. I'm just so confused and emotional after that whole prayer thing. It couldn't have been worse timing for him to stop by.

Unless he came while I was wrapped up in the arms of a doctor I hardly know. But I don't want to think about that right now.

Jake clears his throat. I can tell he's about to die of embarrassment, and he says, "I talked with your friend. That doctor guy."

Ok, now I'm nervous. I didn't think he'd come to confront me about Eliot. I try to offer some sort of apology, but he cuts me short.

"Hear me out first. I got his name off his badge, called around until I figured out where he worked. Stopped by to talk to him."

I'm surprised my eyes haven't bugged out of my head by now. Jake actually confronted Eliot at his office?

"He said exactly what you did, that you guys knew each other back in Massachusetts, that you were having a real hard day, and that he was just there as a friend trying to comfort you."

My face burns as I recall the soft feel of the skin on Eliot's smooth jawline. I can't think about that now. Instead, I look at Jake and nod.

"Anyway, he apologized, said he should have acted more professional. He's a decent guy."

I'm not sure if I'm supposed to agree with Jake or not. Is this a trap?

He's staring off past my shoulder. What is he looking at? There's nothing over there but a wall. "We got to talking. I told him we were thinking of moving to Seattle so Natalie could be closer to the hospital."

My heart still doesn't know if it's supposed to keep racing or stop entirely. Is this how Grandma Lucy felt when her health was failing at County Hospital?

Jake clears his throat again. It sounds gross. I hope it's not a new habit he's developing. "So, Dr. Jamison said he knows a guy. This radiologist he works with. Says he's got a home just three blocks from the Ronald McDonald House. I guess he lives in some ritzy suburb but keeps a little apartment local for when he works late. Anyway, he's on vacation for the next two months. Poor guy's off to some tropical island. But that means his apartment's totally empty, and he's looking for someone to stay there and water his plants. Keep an eye on things." He clears his throat once more, quieter this time. "Rent free."

I feel like I'm supposed to react a certain way. Half of my brain is telling me to jump up and down and scream like those singers who make fools of themselves on those TV talent shows. The other half of my brain is completely paralyzed while it tries to figure out why Jake looks so depressed. It's like having someone tell you that there's a million-dollar settlement check coming for you in the mail, but by the expression on his face you'd think he was saying your grandma just died.

"That would be cool," I offer tentatively.

"Yeah." Jake licks his lips. I still can't figure out what's so interesting about that wall he's been staring at.

"So ..." I begin, hoping he'll catch on and give me a little more information.

He pries his eyes away from the off-colored white and lets them glance over me for just a second. "So, I was wondering if ..." He clears his throat again. This is going to be hard to get used to. "I wanted to talk to you about ..." He glances again at Natalie in her crib. I swear he looks like he's got a hundred nurses injecting him at once. "If Natalie gets released, I mean when she's well enough to leave here, I wanted to know if you think we should stay there." He swallows so hard I can see his Adam's apple bob up and down. "You know. The three of us."

His eyes stop their nervous darting and meet mine. I see fear and hopefulness and something else, too. Something I could probably name if my mind hadn't just gone completely blank.

"Sure." It's not the appropriate response, but it's the best I can conjure up. This time I'm the one to clear my throat, and I try again. "Yeah. That sounds like a pretty good plan."

CHAPTER 86

Christmas Day. Who would have thought there would be anything good about spending a major holiday like this in the hospital?

Jake stayed with me in Natalie's room until late last night. We went and borrowed *The Muppets Christmas Carol* from the peds floor library. Man, someone should have warned me about that scene where the young and handsome Scrooge breaks up with his girlfriend. I sobbed like someone had just drowned my puppy, I swear it was that bad.

It's funny because last Christmas Jake and I hadn't even started officially dating yet, but we got together with a few other people from work and all watched *Die Hard* together. *Die Hard.* I mean, I guess you could call it a Christmas movie if you really wanted to, but it's not the kind of flick you could borrow from the little old ladies who volunteer on the pediatric floor. Now Jake and I are a year older, but our taste in entertainment is on the same level as a seven-year-old's.

Oh, well. The movie was cute, and even though that one song made me blubber like an idiot, I felt happy when the whole thing was over. Maybe there really are things to be thankful for.

Like tiny little puppets that reenact Christmas stories and make you laugh.

Jake went back to the Ronald McDonald house just before midnight. He's actually been staying there the whole time. He never went back to Orchard Grove after our fight. I feel kind of lousy that I didn't try to get in touch with him sooner, but that would have been hard without a phone charger.

I slept pretty well last night. I must have, because I didn't even wake up when someone sneaked in and left about a dozen wrapped presents by Natalie's crib. We haven't opened them yet. Jake said we'll do that with her after they take her off the ventilator, which might even happen this afternoon if she keeps on holding her vitals steady.

Christmas miracles, right?

So now we're just waiting around, staring at all these unopened packages. At three, some volunteers at the Ronald McDonald house are doing a Christmas carol sing-along. It's not something I'd ever dream of doing in my right mind, but Jake kind of wants to go, and I'm curious enough to at least give it a shot. If I can force myself to leave Natalie for that long. I'm still not sure, but we have a few hours before we have to decide.

I want to talk to Jake about that radiologist's apartment, but I feel awkward bringing it up. I don't want him to think any more about Eliot Jamison than he has to. But it would be nice to get some details. Like, does *rent free* really and literally mean rent free? Are we still going to have to pay for utilities and things? I know at one point Jake mentioned looking for jobs here in Seattle, but I don't know how serious he was about that either. If we can make it until his friend pays him for the Pontiac, that can hold us over for a while. If we've got room and board covered, we've got our food stamps. And since the hospital would be close enough to walk to, we'd manage just fine, I think.

I can't believe I don't have to go back to that stupid trailer.

Jake and I have been watching Christmas movies all morning. Now we're on *Home Alone*. I swear it's been fifteen years since I saw it last. Before long, we'll have to go get ourselves some food, and I imagine that could get a little depressing. I mean, who wants to eat Christmas dinner in a hospital cafeteria? But right now, the whole day has a happy, lazy feel to it. Part of me is tempted to stop the movie and tell Jake about what happened last night, about that Grandma Lucy video, but I need more time to sort through my own thoughts and feelings before I'm ready to share them with anybody else.

I've still got it though, that little excited flutter in my heart. I feel, I don't know ... I feel human. Like I haven't been myself for the past several years, but I'm finally waking up. Coming out of my coma, if you will. Seeing the world as it really is for the first time in a very long while.

Maybe it sounds cheesy. It probably does, but I don't care. I haven't felt this way since I was a teenager, since I was living with Sandy and still trying my best to live a good, Christian life even if I did mess up every so often. Except now I'm more mature. I've learned more. Gotten more experience, experience that makes me not want to take this feeling for granted again.

I'm sure life's going to have its ups and downs. I mean, my little girl still has a breathing tube shoved down her throat, so how could it not? But there's a lightness in my spirit now. I don't dread each minute of each day. I'm looking forward to what's to come with new expectations. New eyes. With hope.

It might not be a huge change, in your opinion, but it's a start.

CHAPTER 87

I ended up not going to the Christmas singalong. It sounded like it might be fun if you could get over how campy it'd be. I just couldn't bring myself to leave Natalie for that long. Jake understood. He's been here all day too. I guess it's a good thing we both stuck around because the respiratory therapist and the PICU doc came in just a few minutes ago.

They're going to extubate our daughter.

I know I said I was nervous when Jake stopped by yesterday, but that was nothing compared to this. I mean, everyone says Natalie should do just fine off the ventilator. She's been holding her sats really well, and we haven't seen even a hint of fever in days. Besides, if something does go wrong when they take the tube out, they can always put it right back in. Not that I hope that would happen. I'm just saying that logically, I know my daughter's not in any real danger.

But still, I'm so nervous I'm dizzy. I mean, the room is literally spinning around me. I'm holding Jake's arm. He probably thinks I'm being romantic, but I seriously have to cling to him just to keep from falling. I can't watch when the tube comes out. Even when I turn away, I feel my own throat closing up just at the thought of what my daughter is experiencing.

And then I hear it.

At first, I think someone's let a cat into the hospital room. I have no clue why. I mean, I've heard of therapy dogs, but who in their right mind would ever think of trying to train a therapy cat?

Except it's not a cat. It's my daughter who's making that sound. I make myself a promise that I will never, ever complain about listening to my daughter cry.

It takes the nurses and tech another minute or two before they've got Natalie completely free and untangled, and that whole time she's letting out this faint little bleating protest, no louder than a newborn kitten.

It's the most beautiful sound I've ever heard.

I glance over at Jake, my heart swelling. He doesn't look at me. I don't think he even notices me standing next to him, doesn't realize he has a tear streaming down his cheek. He looks perfectly awestruck, as if our daughter just recited the Greek alphabet or something like that.

"Do you want to hold her?" the nurse asks. At first, I'm so focused on Jake I think she must be talking to him, except she's looking straight at me.

"Um, is it safe? She's ..."

"She's doing great." The nurse tilts her head toward the monitor. My daughter's breathing on her own, and her oxygen levels are at a safe and stable 95%. The nurse holds my crying baby out to me. What can I do but take her in my arms?

Jake wraps me in a half hug. I'm so overwhelmed I have to sit down. Thankfully, there's a chair to lower myself into. I don't know if it was waiting for me all along or if Jake or one of the nurses positioned it there right in time.

Jake sinks down next to me. He's on his knees, his forehead pressed against our daughter's, his tears leaking down his cheeks. She lets out one more feeble wail and then stops. My heart's too full from the sound of her first cries that I don't believe what I'm seeing.

"Look at that," Jake breathes in amazement. "Look what she's doing."

I bite my lip. It can't be true. It's too much all at once. Too much happiness. Too much joy. Too much, too fast. It's more than I can bear.

Jake nudges me with his elbow, apparently dissatisfied with my lack of response. "Don't you see it?"

I squeeze my eyes shut for a moment. I'm so scared when I open them again, it will all be gone. Except it's not. My daughter is still here, awake and fully alert in my arms. I'm sure it's my imagination, but I almost think there's a hint of a smile on her face. And she's staring right at me with those big almond eyes.

Chocolate skin and almond eyes.

So. Stinking. Gorgeous.

A NOTE FROM THE AUTHOR

I hope you enjoyed Tiff's story. *Beauty from Ashes* is actually a major revamp of the very first novel I ever completed but never published. I began it one night when my son Silas was about nine months old and in the hospital after a birth event similar to baby Natalie's.

I usually take this space to thank everyone who helped me get my book published, but this time I want to start by thanking God for saving my son, who we were told would be no more than a vegetable if he survived at all. (Spoiler alert: Silas is now a healthy, happy, and intelligent almost ten-year-old boy who astounds me with his humor, positive outlook, photographic memory, musical genius, and so much more.) You can read Silas's full story in my memoir, *A Boy Named Silas*. I feel like this acknowledgement section would not be complete if I didn't thank God for bringing all the doctors, therapists, and specialists into our son's life who helped him on his miraculous road to recovery.

Grandma Lucy first appears in my novel *Turbulence*, one of

the books in my Kennedy Stern Christian suspense series. It's been a neat challenge and change of pace for me to write Christian women's fiction after focusing for so long on suspense. I have to admit what when I first started writing novels, this is far closer to what I envisioned for myself.

God, you've carried me through so many things in my life and in the writing of this book. Thank you for *not* answering my prayers years ago when I wanted to publish that first NICU novel I wrote, but thank you also for allowing Tiff, Jake, and Natalie's story to finally come out in *Beauty from Ashes.*

My husband is my biggest encouragement. Amy and Elizabeth are life-saving editors (or if not life-saving, at least they save me a lot of embarrassment). A big thank you to Cathy as well for her good eye and for my friends (real and virtual) who prayed for me while I worked on this story.

I'm grateful for the chance to work with Victoria Cooper for the first time on the cover for *Beauty from Ashes,* and I think she did a great job. It's the first time a cover has literally taken my breath away. Thanks also to my OB nurse friend Tara for answering a few medical questions.

If you're interested in more novels, the Orchard Grove Christian women's fiction books show God at work in the lives of everyday couples going through common (or not so common) struggles. My hope is to offer encouragement to readers who sometimes need a reminder that God is a God who is loving and powerful enough to "bind up the brokenhearted, to proclaim freedom for the captives and release from darkness for the prisoners, to proclaim the year of the Lord's favor and the day of vengeance of our God, to comfort all who mourn, and provide for those who grieve in Zion — to bestow on them a crown of beauty instead of ashes, the oil of joy instead of mourning, and a garment of praise instead of a spirit of despair" (Isaiah 61:1-3).

Whatever joys or trials you face today, may God's comfort and love be close to your heart, and may your joy be full in him.

DISCUSSION QUESTIONS

For group discussion or personal reflection

1. Have you ever known a family with a baby in the NICU?

2. Do you know any mothers-in-law like Patricia?

3. What do you think of Tiff's relationship with Jake?

4. If you were Tiff, would you have signed the DNR?

5. Have you ever known anyone like Grandma Lucy?

6. Was there any part of the story that inspired or encouraged you?

7. What's the oddest thing that's happened at a church service you've been to?

8. Has God ever used someone else to speak directly to you?

9. God promises to work all things together for good. When have you seen him do this in your own life?

10. What are your thoughts on miraculous healing?

11. If you could offer Tiff some encouragement in the hospital, what would you say to her?

12. Is Tiff right to feel guilty for Natalie's condition?

13. Who is someone that's encouraged you during a hard time?

14. If you are a parent, have you ever had to call 911 for your child? What's the sickest or most injured they've ever been?

15. If you have biological children, how long was the labor? Did everything go all right during the delivery? Who was with you?

16. If you're married, how long did it take you to decide to get engaged? What was the most difficult season in your marriage? What was the biggest change you went through after becoming parents (if you have children)?

Books by Alana Terry

Kennedy Stern Christian Suspense Series

Unplanned

Paralyzed

Policed

Straightened

Turbulence

Infected

Abridged

Whispers of Refuge (Christian suspense set in North Korea)

The Beloved Daughter

Slave Again

Torn Asunder

Flower Swallow

See a full list at www.alanaterry.com

25820995R00233

Printed in Poland
by Amazon Fulfillment
Poland Sp. z o.o., Wrocław